DEADLY VALOR

CRIMSON POINT SERIES

KAYLEA CROSS

Copyright © 2021 Kaylea Cross

∽

Cover Art: Sweet 'N Spicy Designs
Developmental edits: Deborah Nemeth
Line Edits: Joan Nichols
Digital Formatting: LK Campbell

∽

This book is a work of fiction. The names, characters, places, and incidents are products of the writer's imagination or have been used fictitiously and are not to be construed as real. Any resemblance to persons, living or dead, actual events, locales or organizations is entirely coincidental.

All rights reserved. With the exception of quotes used in reviews, this book may not be reproduced or used in whole or in part by any means existing without written permission from the author.

ISBN: 9798470788733

She's been targeted by a killer.

Widow Danae Sutherland moved to Crimson Point a month ago with her teenage son to begin a new chapter in their lives. Adjusting to small town life is a big change for them both, but it's been especially hard on her son, and the holidays are making it even harder. When a sexy stranger moves into the cottage next door, she's not prepared for the undeniable attraction between them. He's only in town for a couple weeks, so getting involved will only lead to heartbreak. That doesn't stop her from falling for him. And when danger strikes, she has no choice but to put her life in his hands.

He's the only man who can save her.

Former Marine Ryder Locke has come to the Oregon Coast to spend the holidays with his cousin Molly and her family. It's his chance to face his demons head on before returning to his job as a bodyguard for one of Hollywood's brightest stars. The last thing he expects is to fall for the single mom next door, and for danger to blow up around her. When the threat closes in and her life hangs in the balance, Ryder must risk everything to save her from the man who wants her dead.

AUTHOR'S NOTE

Welcome back to Crimson Point! This story picks up just a month after the end of ***Broken Bonds***, and I'm excited to link this well-loved cast with my **Kill Devil Hills** crew. Get ready to meet some new characters, and enjoy the ride!

Kaylea

ONE

"Ladies and gentlemen, welcome to Portland."

Ryder stared out the window at the wet, green landscape and rolled his head and shoulders to stretch his tight muscles as the plane taxied to the gate. After enduring three flights and two layovers, he was more than ready to get his ass in a car and hit the road. Local time here in Portland was 15:25, and he still had a four-hour drive down to the coast ahead of him.

This trip was either going to make him or break him. And he couldn't afford to break.

As soon as the plane parked at the gate, he turned his phone back on. Immediately text messages began popping up. His mom, checking to see he'd made it okay. And one from his cousin, Molly, an ER nurse living in Crimson Point, whom he'd come to spend Christmas with.

Sorry, got called in to work a night shift last minute. Jase is meeting you at the cottage instead. Wish we could have had you stay with us, but we'll make the best of it. See you tomorrow! xo

Since a long-term tenant currently occupied their downstairs suite, Molly and her husband had arranged for him to stay in a rental the company Jase worked for had recently renovated. Ryder didn't mind. It gave him more privacy and was only a short drive from Jase and Molly's place.

He typed back a response.

Looking forward to it! Can't wait to see you guys.

It had been way too long since they'd spent time together. He felt bad about that, because he and Molly had been really close growing up.

Shrugging on the backpack he'd brought as a carryon, he filed out into the terminal with the other passengers. He wasn't hungry, but he deliberately looked away from the bars he passed and kept going. This was all part of the test, and so far, he was passing with flying colors. He'd even avoided the temptation to order alcohol from the drink cart every time it had come by on the flights.

After getting his bag at the luggage carousel, he went to get his rental vehicle and began the drive down to Crimson Point. It was dark out, light rain falling on the windshield, slicking the road and making it hard to see with the glare of the headlights coming at him.

His phone rang twenty minutes into the trip. His best friend, Chase, calling from L.A. "Wow, miss me already?" he joked as he drove south on the I-5.

"So much," Chase answered, his Outer Banks accent stronger than Ryder's. "Where y'at now?"

"Just south of the airport, about to get on the highway out to the coast. What are you two lovebirds up to? Or should I not ask?" Chase had just gotten engaged to Becca Sandoza, a famous actor, and they were taking a few weeks to themselves out of public view, holed up in an ocean-front villa they'd rented.

"Just had a couple's massage, took a soak in the hot tub, and now we're about to watch a movie I picked out."

He smirked. Chase getting a couple's massage? "Y'all make me sick."

Chase laughed. "We make ourselves sick sometimes. So? How's the other thing going?"

The drinking. Or not drinking. "So far, so good."

"Awesome."

Yeah. Trying to tame his demons with booze was a bad habit he'd developed over the past couple months, and it needed to stop. This trip was the perfect chance to reset before returning to L.A.

"Any word about the stunts for the new movie yet?" In a few weeks they'd all be heading to Australia for at least three months. Becca was the leading lady; Chase was one of the stunt performers. And as Becca's personal bodyguard, Ryder would be going with them.

"Just got the script last night. It's awesome," his friend said, voice laced with excitement. "There's an epic underwater sequence I'm looking forward to doin'. Sure you wouldn't rather join me on crew, rather than watch Becca all the time?"

"I'm sure." The little bit of stunt work he'd done with Chase had been fun, but he couldn't see himself doing it full time. Chase was the adrenaline junkie, not him. "Becca's a lot better looking than you anyway."

He ended the call feeling a bit wistful. With Chase and Becca having a private, romantic getaway, they hadn't needed —or wanted—him around. While he completely understood, it underscored something he'd been subconsciously feeling ever since coming home from his last tour with the Corps.

In so many ways it felt like he didn't fit in anywhere now.

With his best friend crazy in love and getting married next year, it made Ryder feel even more alone. All he had at the moment was his job, though if it weren't for working with Becca and still getting to hang with Chase, his heart wouldn't really be in it.

By the time he reached the turnoff for Crimson Point hours later, he was looking forward to a hot shower and crawling into bed. With fewer lights around and the area more sparsely populated, the darkness seemed to envelop everything, the moon completely hidden behind a thick wall of cloud.

Reaching the end of the access road, he turned right onto Front Street, just able to make out the waves rolling onto the beach to his left. The town was cute, and the citizens had gone all out with the holiday decorations.

Tall, old-fashioned streetlamps were done up like candy canes with strings of red and white lights for the season, more lights strung between them in the shape of messages like Happy Holidays. A heavy layer of fog was rolling in along the beach. The rain had stopped, leaving the road wet, the multicolored lights of the town glistening on the damp surface.

With Christmas just a few days away, the town was busy for a Thursday night, both sides of the street lined with vehicles, people out for dinner or doing some shopping. All the little shops and businesses along the waterfront were all lit up with colorful strands of lights, with decorated wreaths hanging in the windows, and one place had a pair of tall nutcrackers standing guard on either side of its front doorway.

At the end of the main strip, he turned right at the T in the road and began the climb up the hill away from the water. Given how heavily wooded the area was, the GPS was no help. He managed to find Honeysuckle Lane on his own and turned left off it, immediately spotting the gray craftsman-style cottage set back from the road amongst some tall cedars surrounding the lot.

A big silver pickup was parked out front. When he pulled into the driveway, the front door of the cottage opened to reveal a man wearing a brown, WWII-era bomber jacket, and holding a toddler on his hip.

His cousin's husband, and their little girl.

Ryder climbed out of the rental vehicle, glad to stretch his legs. "Hey, man."

"Hey. You made good time." On the top step Jase shook his hand and clapped him on the shoulder with a grin, aqua eyes glinting under the porch light. "How was the drive?"

The little girl was staring at him warily from wide, dark eyes. "Good," he answered, giving her a smile that got him nowhere. "Thanks for finding me a place."

"No problem. We thought you'd probably appreciate some privacy, peace and quiet while you're here."

He definitely appreciated that. "And you're Savannah-banana," he said to the little girl clinging to Jase's neck. He'd talked to her via video chat a couple times, but apparently that didn't matter.

"Say hi to Uncle Ryder," Jase told her.

Savannah buried her face in her dad's neck, then peeked at Ryder with deep brown eyes. Carter's eyes. Molly's first husband, and Jase's best friend. He'd died right after Molly had gotten pregnant.

"Hi, sweetheart." He was careful not to crowd her, didn't reach for or try to touch her. "You can play shy now, but by the time I leave, we'll be best pals."

"I don't doubt it. Come on inside." Jase stepped back out of the way to let Ryder pass.

The inside of the cottage was cozy and tidy, with new

furnishings and appliances. It also smelled like fresh paint. "Nice place."

"It's our most recent rental we just finished up. Was supposed to be one of our easiest and quickest projects, until we started the plumbing and electrical upgrades and realized we had to rip everything out and redo it all from scratch."

"Never fails with renos," he said, glancing toward the master bedroom door left open at the end of the hall.

"Don't I know it. Moll stocked the fridge and pantry for you this morning, and the last renters left some things too. Go ahead and eat whatever you want. There's a grocery store and other little food shops in town, and there's a supermarket about a mile north of town if you need it." He shifted Savannah on his hip, the toddler now squirming and fussing. "Need anything else before I go get this little girl home to bed?"

"No, I'm good." He leaned down slightly to put himself at eye level with Savannah, who froze, and gave her a grin. "See you tomorrow, cutie."

She merely stared at him as if she was convinced he was a criminal or something. Jase ruffled her curls with a chuckle. "Don't worry, she'll warm up to you in no time once she's had her beauty sleep. And then you'll be sorry."

"Thanks for meeting me, man."

"No problem. The town sheriff, Noah, and his wife Poppy live just two doors down around the corner on Honeysuckle. You'll probably meet them in the next day or two. Moll will call you once she has some sleep tomorrow, probably around noon or so. If you need anything before that, just gimme a shout," Jase finished as he stepped outside onto the porch.

"Sounds good. See you tomorrow."

He locked the door behind Jase and let out a sigh, drinking up the quiet. Once Jase's truck pulled away, the only sound was the wind swirling in the trees outside, and the distant, muted roar of the ocean in the distance.

Perfect.

On his way to the bedroom, he stopped to check out the fridge. As usual Molly had thought of everything, setting him up with enough food to last several days. Not that he planned on cooking much while he was here.

The cupboards were stocked with peanut butter, tea, coffee and pasta. And the pantry...

He stopped, fingers still on the light switch, as his gaze locked on the glint of bottles lined up neatly on a shelf at the back. Some were vinegars and oils. But his eyes shot past them right to the one with the distinctive square, black label with white font.

His new nemesis, Jack. The crutch he'd been using to help get him through the nights when his demons wouldn't let him rest.

There were other kinds of booze as well. Vodka and a couple bottles of wine. But that Jack drew him. His mouth watered, and the sudden, intense craving took him off guard. He had to stem the impulse to reach for it.

You should pour it out. All of them. Right now.

He shut the pantry door and made himself walk away, shocked by how much he'd been tempted to uncap that bottle and take a pull. He was stronger than the craving. Strong enough to leave that bottle untouched, to use this trip to shed old habits and get his head on straight.

He'd been a warrior his whole adult life. This was his new battle, and there could only be one winner.

Him, or the bottle.

DANAE PAUSED in front of her son's bedroom door and knocked twice. There was no answer, but she could hear Finn talking animatedly to someone in the background. Lost in gaming land.

Withholding an impatient sigh, she opened the door to find Finn at his desk on his computer, headset on while he gamed with someone. She wrinkled her nose at the heavy smell of teenage body oil infusing the air, and mentally shook her head.

The room looked like a vampire lair. The blinds shut tight to block out even the merest hint of light that might otherwise have seeped in from outside. Various empty glasses and cups cluttered every flat surface, and junk food wrappers overflowed from the trash bin next to his desk.

Pick your battles, mama. Nagging him to clean up or air out his room always ended in an argument. Sometimes it seemed like their entire relationship was an endless cycle of nagging and arguing.

When he continued to ignore her, she sighed and motioned with her hand to get his attention. Finn gave her the body language equivalent of an eye roll and reluctantly pulled his headset down around his neck, where the hair he refused to cut now reached the collar of his hoodie. "Yeah?"

"I have to head into the clinic for a bit. Not sure when I'll be back, but I'll grab us something for dinner on the way home. Feel like anything in particular?"

"Nah, I won't be here anyway. Going out with friends in a bit."

She frowned. They'd only been here a few weeks, and he hadn't mentioned making any friends yet. She was glad he was at least making an effort to be social and fit in. The move hadn't been easy for him. "How are you getting there?"

"Bus."

That was a first. She'd never been able to get him to take the bus back in Seattle. "Okay, but be home by ten. You have work in the morning."

"I *know*, Mom." This time he did roll his eyes, and pulled his headset back up, dismissing her as he turned his attention back to his computer.

A pang of hurt hit her, even as she scolded herself and shut the door behind her. He was a teenager. Apparently, this whole pulling away thing was normal. Healthy, even. Finn's way of distancing himself from her, to gain more independence and a strong sense of self-identity in preparation for striking out on his own in a few years.

Except right now the thought of all that just made her want to cry.

She walked back down the hall of the little bungalow they were renting, swallowing the lump in her throat. The glow of the multicolored lights on the Christmas tree in the living room made her pause, a moment of wistfulness taking hold.

Being a single parent was so much harder than she'd expected. One of the things she missed most about her late husband was the absence of the other half of their united front they'd always used with Finn. She was trying her best to keep a happy face on, but it was so damn hard, and Christmas made it all worse.

Finn still resented her for dragging him here from their former life in Seattle, to take a better job with better pay and benefits, and to give them a change of scenery. To get them away from the painful reminders of loss everywhere they looked back home.

Pulling on her coat, she paused in the foyer to leave a twenty-dollar bill on the little table for Finn, along with a note.

Have fun and keep your phone on. Love, Mom

He'd probably roll his eyes again, but it made her feel better. Nobody had warned her how hard it was to watch your baby pull away. Until three years ago he'd been crazy attached to her. Then tragedy had struck, and nothing had been the same since. For either of them.

Outside the air was cool and damp, the wind sighing in the tops of the tall evergreen trees. She climbed into her purple MINI, Professor Plum, and backed out of the driveway. As she turned the corner, she spotted Jase out in front of the rental cottage, setting Savannah into her car seat in the backseat of his truck. An SUV was parked beside it.

She pipped her horn lightly and got a friendly wave in return. The lights in the cottage were all on, signaling someone was staying there.

Whoever it was, she hoped they were friendly. Given the state of her life at the moment, the last thing she wanted was another source of tension or conflict.

TWO

Finn stepped off the bus two towns north of Crimson Point to find his friend waiting for him on the sidewalk across the street from the movie theater.

Paul grinned at him, phone in hand. "Hey, glad you could make it."

Finn nodded and shoved his hands into the pockets of his Seahawks hoodie as he fell in step with him. "Are we seeing the movie?" The new Becca Sandoza action flick looked really good.

"Nah. Meeting up with some other guys from school instead. They invited us to hang with them."

He brushed aside the flicker of disappointment. "Cool." Much as he hated it here, this was his life now whether he liked it or not, so he should at least try to make some new friends.

They talked about the latest video game they'd been playing online together on the way to the meeting spot. A group of teenage kids stood outside the entrance, smoking. Finn recognized one of them, a senior from school who seemed popular.

He was surprised when the guy nodded at them in greeting. "Paul. Who's your friend?"

"Finn. He's new. Just moved to Crimson Point a few weeks ago."

"Yeah? Perfect." He stuck out a hand. "Grant. Good to meet you."

"Same." Finn shook with him, pumped that a popular senior would pay him any attention at all. Feeling out of place, he stood back while the others—four guys, including Paul—talked and smoked. Glancing around, he caught sight of someone else from school standing in line at the theater doors, and his pulse jumped.

Carly. A girl from his English class that he'd noticed right away on his first day. She was pretty, with big blue eyes and blond hair pulled up in her usual cute ponytail. He caught her eye and smiled, lifted a hand to say hello. She smiled back, then glanced past him, and her smile faded a bit.

She motioned him over. Finn started toward her without even realizing he'd moved. She'd been nice to him from day one. It was safe to say he'd developed a crush on her.

"What are you doing here tonight?" she asked when he got close. "Don't you live down in Crimson Point?"

Unfortunately. "Paul invited me out." He nodded over his shoulder at the others. "What movie are you seeing?"

"The new Becca Sandoza flick."

"Oh, yeah, I heard it's good."

Her eyes shifted past him again for a moment, then came back to him. "You're not hanging out with Grant and his crew, are you?" she said, her voice just above a whisper.

"Yeah, why?"

Worry filled her eyes. "You're new here, so you wouldn't know, but...those guys are bad news. You should stay away from them."

Finn frowned, a little concerned now himself, then shrugged it off. Paul was a good guy, and obviously liked Grant. Maybe Carly had just been listening to rumors floating around school. Besides, Finn wanted her to think he was big and tough and could take care of himself. "They're all right."

She didn't look convinced. "Just be careful."

"I will."

They talked for another minute, then Paul called out to him. "Yo, Finn. You comin', or what?"

He didn't want to. He'd much rather stay here and see the movie with Carly, maybe hang out with her for a while after before he had to catch the bus home. But he was too nervous to ask for her phone number. "Guess I'd better get going. See you in January. Have a good Christmas."

Her smile was so gorgeous and genuine it made his heart thud. "You too."

He followed Paul and the others to an SUV parked around the back, still thinking about Carly. She was so nice to him and smiled at him a lot. Plus, she'd seemed concerned about him just now. Did that mean she *liked* him liked him? Because he would love that to be true and his life would suck so much less than it currently did.

Grant got behind the wheel. Finn stopped, suddenly uncertain as the others all piled into the back of the new, expensive-looking vehicle. Grant shot him an irritated look. "Get in, sophomore."

Not wanting to look like a loser, even though he wanted to turn around, rush back and ask Carly if he could sit with her during the movie, he caved and got in the back anyway. The very back.

There wasn't enough room for them all in the seats, so the older guys shoved both him and Paul into the trunk area. The two of them huddled there while Grant fired up the engine, and bass immediately began pulsing through the interior, so loud it made the windows vibrate.

Finn watched Paul, who was listening intently to the conversations going on in the back seat, trying to stay included. About fights they'd been in recently, and shit they'd done.

For the first time he wondered if Carly was right, and was starting to wish he hadn't come out tonight at all. He stayed silent as Grant drove them across town, to a wealthy neighborhood and parked out front of a big, expensive-looking house with a silver Audi sedan in the driveway.

"Everybody out," Grant announced.

The others jumped out and followed him to the side door. Finn hung back with Paul, wondering what the hell they were doing with these older guys who seemed to love fighting. But Grant waved them inside impatiently and Paul hurried forward, so Finn followed him into the mudroom.

"Who wants a beer?" Grant asked, heading for the kitchen.

A chorus of eager voices answered, and thirty seconds later, Finn found himself holding a cold can of beer. He opened it and took a sip, just so he wouldn't look lame. He'd had alcohol before back home with his friends, but this felt different, and the beer was disgustingly bitter on his tongue.

The guys all gathered around the TV in the living room and started playing a video game. Finn relaxed a bit and took a seat on a chair off to the side of the room, but with everyone pretty much ignoring him now, he secretly couldn't wait to get out of here and go home again.

A few minutes later, a man appeared in the doorway. Big, with wide shoulders and a hard look to him. He scanned the room, his gaze halting on Finn, and something in Finn's stomach grabbed. "Who're you?" he demanded with a suspicious look.

"That's Finn," Grant answered without looking up from the TV, his thumbs busy on his controller. "New guy in town."

"Yeah? And how old is Finn?"

Grant glanced at him. "Yeah, how old are you?"

"Fifteen," he answered, trying to push aside the buzz of nerves. Nothing about this felt right. He'd have given anything to be home playing online right now instead of here.

The man studied him for a long moment, then folded his arms across his broad, sculpted chest. "You looking for a job, by any chance?"

"Already have one."

A smirk twisted his mouth. "For minimum wage?" He said it like he thought it was a joke.

"Yes. And tips."

The man's expression turned sardonic. "Well, good for you. But if you're ever interested in making more than chump change for bus fare and Starbucks, let me know."

The others snickered, shooting him amused looks like they thought he was stupid. Finn lowered his gaze, his fingers tightening around his beer. He wanted to leave but wasn't sure how to get out of this situation without causing more of a problem for himself.

Instead of leaving, the man walked over and nudged one of the guys off the couch to take his spot in the game. He downed beer after beer, and from the snippets of conversation between him and Grant as they played the video game, Finn guessed the guy was either Grant's dad or stepdad.

Before long, the coffee table was cluttered with empties. The dad/stepdad was clearly drunk as he tossed the local newspaper from the table onto the floor. Finn glanced down at it. The front-page story was about a girl he recognized from school. A senior, he thought. He'd seen her around the hallways in between classes, and in the cafeteria at lunch.

Local Teen Still Missing, the headline read.

"Still missing, huh?" Grant mused as he picked up another beer.

"Yeah, how 'bout that?" the man said.

"She's a fuck-up," one of the other guys said. "Probably just ran away again."

The man and Grant shared a look, and the man chuckled. "Yeah, probably. Guess we won't be seeing her around these parts again anytime soon."

"Nope," Grant agreed.

Something about the underlying message in their words made Finn's stomach hurt. He glanced at Paul beside him, who was oblivious, focused on the game happening on TV.

Finn nudged him, then got up and went into the kitchen. He glanced behind them to make sure they were alone and no one had followed them, then frowned at Paul. "What are we doing here?" he whispered.

Paul blinked at him. "Hanging out."

"We shouldn't be here. They're all ignoring us anyway."

His buddy glanced toward the living room, looking uncertain. "You wanna go?"

Finn opened his mouth to say yes, but then Grant strode into the kitchen. "You guys want another beer?"

"No, I'm good," Finn said, trying to figure out a way to leave while still letting him save face. "I should take off. Gotta work in the morning."

Grant stared at him a moment, amusement gleaming in his eyes. "I'll drive you home. Gotta stop to make down that way anyhow."

"Uh, I—"

"I'll go with you guys," Paul said, locking them both in.

The other guys filed into the kitchen. Along with the dad/stepdad.

The man leaned against the doorframe, watching Finn. "Remember what I said about that job. If you change your mind, let Grant know. You too, Paul. I could use a couple more good workers."

Not a chance in hell. "I will. Thanks."

He put on his shoes and went outside, relieved to be leaving. He and Paul once again climbed into the back of Grant's SUV, while the others piled into the seats. The whole vehicle shook with the loud music as Grant peeled away from the house, the others laughing. And Finn suddenly had a feeling he knew where Grant had gotten the money to pay for his ride.

They drove south for a while, then stopped outside a store at a strip mall in the town directly north of Crimson Point. Grant got out and sauntered up the walkway toward the front door.

Another man stepped out to meet him. They spoke for a few moments, then the man handed something over that Grant quickly tucked inside the front pouch of his hoodie before walking back to the SUV.

Finn mentally groaned. Great. Drugs.

Grant got in, passed around something to his buddies in the back, and moments later the entire vehicle reeked of weed. Someone from the backseat turned and offered the joint to him and Paul.

Finn waved it off. Weed was legal in Oregon, but all of them were underage.

Anxiety built with every mile they got closer to Crimson Point. The interior of the SUV reeked, and his mom would freak if she smelled it on him. He was cutting it close to his curfew. She hadn't texted yet, but they both had a family locator app on their phones, so she could see exactly where he was.

"Finn, dude, how do we get to your place?" Grant called out over the music.

Seeing no way around it, he gave Grant directions, itching to get home and put this night behind him. It took another twenty minutes to reach Crimson Point, and the whole time Finn prayed they wouldn't get pulled over, and that Sheriff Buchanan didn't see them when they turned up their street.

Finally, Grant made the turn onto Finn's street. "Honeysuckle Lane? Are you fucking serious?" he said, laughing. The others joined in, except for Paul, who gave him a sheepish smile.

Finn ignored them all, focused on his house. His mom's MINI was parked in the driveway. All the lights were off except the Christmas tree, glowing cheerfully in the front window. But she definitely wouldn't be asleep yet. Not with him still out, and a few minutes past curfew.

Grant stopped on the street and popped the back hatch for him. "See you around, Finny-boy."

"Yeah. Night," he muttered, climbing out and shutting the hatch, unable to get out fast enough. Grant drove off before Finn had even reached the door, music pulsing in the otherwise silent neighborhood.

Hand on the doorknob, Finn paused, to sniff the front of his hoodie, wincing at the smell of weed. Probably smelled like he'd bathed in it. Damn.

He locked the door behind him, then made a beeline for the guest bathroom next to his room to shower the smell off him. He was only a step away from his destination when his mom suddenly appeared in her doorway, dressed in her robe, a lamp illuminating her annoyed expression and folded arms.

"It's after ten," she said, an edge to her tone.

He hoped he was far enough away that she couldn't get a whiff of him. "Yeah, sorry. I couldn't get home sooner. Caught a ride back instead of taking the bus, and the guy driving took the long way here."

She scanned him from head to foot and back again, her posture relaxing. "Have fun?"

Not at all. And he didn't feel like talking about it. "Yeah, it was okay. Anyway, I'm beat. Gonna have a shower and go to bed."

He caught the flash of disappointment in her eyes before she masked it, then she nodded and put on a smile. "Okay. Have a good sleep. Love you."

"Love you too," he muttered, and hurried to the bathroom.

He stripped and got in the shower, planning to bury his clothes in the depths of his closet to hide the smell until he could wash them tomorrow after his shift without his mom noticing. But as he scrubbed himself, a tingle of unease started in the pit of his stomach as he realized something.

It made him uneasy as hell that Grant and the others now knew where he lived.

THREE

Ryder locked the cottage door behind him and paused on the front porch to zip up his thin running jacket. The morning was fresh and cool, with a layer of mist clinging to the ground and settling in puddles in the hollows. He breathed in deeply, catching the scent of cedar and the underlying tang of the ocean carried on the gusty breeze.

He'd made it to day three of being dry and felt pretty damn good about it. Last night he'd fallen asleep almost as soon as he'd crawled into bed, except he had been woken twice by nightmares. By sheer force of will he'd avoided the temptation to grab that bottle from the pantry, but he was all too aware of its presence, waiting there.

He'd decided against pouring it out. That bottle was a test, and he wasn't going to fail it. He'd allowed what had happened overseas to eat away at him until he was only a shadow of the man he'd been before, but no more. Either he found the strength to face and deal with it now, or he was looking at a lifetime of misery.

A run was exactly what he needed. His job required him to stay in top condition, and not only that, increasing his exercise was part of his plan to deal with his demons, instead of drinking them away.

He started out at an easy rhythm, the soles of his running shoes tapping against the surface of the road. The neighborhood was quiet, the houses set far apart and back from the roads, nestled between areas of forest. His breath fogged the air, his blood pumping with each stride.

He re-traced his route from the drive in last night in reverse, winding his way back down the hill as the scent and sound of the ocean became stronger. At the bottom twenty minutes later, he reached the far northern end of Front Street, the town's main drag.

It was busier this morning, all the little businesses open for shoppers. He passed several restaurants and specialty stores, a few gift shops and a museum. Partway down the street, his eye caught on a sign down the street on the opposite side.

Whale's Tale was painted on a wooden oval sign out front, the script painted above a humpback fluke. The nutcrackers he'd noticed last night stood guard on either side of the brightly painted, yellow front door trimmed with garland glittering with white lights and shiny, multicolored baubles.

The incredible smell coming out of the place drifted to him from two blocks away, making his mouth water. Roasted coffee and something sweet and buttery.

He'd already given up booze. He wasn't passing up freshly baked goodies too.

Slowing as he got closer, he crossed the street at a walk, allowing him a minute to cool down and catch his breath. Through the large windows at the front of the cafe he could see the bistro-style tables set up inside, the lineup at the counter and the pastry display cases on either side of the cash register. There was another room at the back, stacked with bookcases.

When he walked in, he spotted a pretty blond woman behind the counter wearing an apron, and a tall teenage boy busy working the espresso machine behind her. Ryder got in line to wait his turn, and more people quickly came in behind him. A young family who looked like they were dressed for a day outside, and an elderly man behind them.

The blonde behind the counter gave him a friendly smile when he reached the front of the line. "You must be Ryder. I've seen a picture of you at Molly's," she added when he gave her a startled look, then stuck out a hand. "I'm Poppy, Noah's wife. Molly's told me all about you."

He shook it, careful of his grip pressure. "Nice to meet you finally."

"Molly's really excited you're in town. How's your first day in Crimson Point so far?"

"Good, but I have a feeling something from that pastry case will make it fantastic. What do you recommend?"

"A latte and a frosted cinnamon roll, or maybe a blueberry streusel muffin. Honestly, you can't go wrong. Everything's made from scratch each morning."

Sure smelled good. "I'll go with your first suggestion."

She called out the drink order to the teen, then went to the pastry case to pick out a cinnamon roll. "This is one of your neighbors, by the way. Finn." She nodded at the boy. "He and his mom live in the house between our place and your cottage."

The kid glanced back at him and gave him a polite smile. Ryder nodded at him and pulled out his wallet, but Poppy waved his money away. "Nope, this one's on me," she whispered.

"I appreciate that, but—"

"No buts. You're Molly's cousin and came all the way from North Carolina to visit us." She shooed him toward a table. "Go sit down and I'll bring it over when it's ready."

Ryder stuck a ten in the tip jar and found himself a table with two chairs over at the side window. Molly had told him how friendly everyone was around here, and it was definitely noticeable. He liked the vibe of the town so far, and scanned the café as he waited.

"Wow, you guys are busy in here," he said when she brought over his cinnamon roll and drink a minute later.

"Never a dull moment," Poppy said with a good-natured laugh.

He scooted his chair over as she lowered herself into the one opposite him, leaving the teenager to deal with the other customers. "So, you run this place?"

"Own it, run it, practically live in it," she said with a smile, sipping on her own coffee that smelled like cinnamon. "You seen Molly yet?"

"She got called into work last night, so she's home sleeping right now. I'll see them this afternoon."

"Great. You'll meet Noah soon too, and probably the rest of our little circle within a couple days. We're a close-knit bunch," she added, a twinkle in her warm brown eyes.

He'd spent all of five minutes in her presence, and he already liked her. He was good at reading people, and between his gut and what Molly had told him, Poppy was the real deal. "This cinnamon bun is crazy good," he told her, taking another bite.

She beamed at him. "Thanks. Personally, I think it's the cream cheese icing. Oh, look, it's Danae. Great timing." She waved at someone near the door, motioning at them to come over.

Ryder turned to glance over his shoulder and stilled. The

dark-haired woman standing just inside the door smiled and raised her hand in greeting, then wove her way over to them.

For the life of him, he couldn't seem to look away. She was tall and trim, around his age, maybe late-thirties or early forties, and her eyes were the most incredible ice blue, made all the more startling with the contrast of her dark brown hair and eyebrows.

"Saw the lineup and thought I'd better get my butt over here to snag a cinnamon bun before they were all gone," she said with a killer smile that revealed a dimple in her right cheek, her curious gaze flicking from Poppy to him.

"Good idea. This is Ryder, by the way, Molly's cousin. He's staying in the cottage around the corner from you. Ryder, this is Danae. Finn's mom."

"Oh!" Her eyes lit up and she held out a hand. "Hi, neighbor."

He shook it, for some reason feeling a little tongue-tied. "Hi."

"And how's my favorite Whale's Tale employee doing?" Danae asked Poppy, hitching the strap of her purse up higher on her shoulder.

"He's doing fantastic, just like I knew he would."

"Good. Glad to hear it." She met Ryder's gaze once more, eyes twinkling. "I like to come in and spy on him from time to time while he's at work. Privilege of being his mother."

"I'd do exactly the same thing," Poppy said, rising. "Have a seat and I'll have him bring your order over. You want your usual?"

"Yes, please." Danae stopped and raised her eyebrows at him. "You mind?"

"Not at all," he said, a little surprised, but pulled his chair in so she could get by him. She was wearing a lab coat over her sweater and jeans. "Just come from work?"

"Yeah, the vet clinic's just down and across the street. I work for Sierra. Noah's sister. You met her yet?"

"No."

"You will soon enough. So, you're here to spend Christmas with Molly?"

And to get his shit together. "Yeah, I'm here until New Year's Eve." He found himself glancing at her left hand and noticed her ring finger was bare. Single mom?

"You'll love it here. My son and I just moved down from Seattle about a month ago, and it's a great place. Not that he's very happy with me about the move," she added, glancing toward the counter.

Okay, definitely a single mom. A hot one. Divorced?

It used to be easy for him to talk to women. Now he felt rusty. Clumsy. Her kid seemed like a sure way to keep the conversation going. "How old is he?"

"Fifteen, but pretty sure he feels more like twenty-one." Her tone was dry.

"That sounds about right." He'd been the same way at that age. Full of hormones and attitude.

He glanced behind him. The lineup was long enough that her son wasn't going to be able to come over with her order anytime soon, and Ryder had suddenly run out of things to say. What the hell? "I'm gonna grab a refill."

"Sure," she said and sat back in her seat, her long legs stretched out before her.

He couldn't help picturing them bare, or his gaze roving up the length of them, all the way up to the secret flesh between the juncture of her thighs.

He shook the thought away and stood in line, ordered another latte and offered to take Danae's order over. Finn stopped in the act of sliding the order across the counter to him, his eyes fixed on the tat on the back of Ryder's left forearm. "You a Marine?" he asked in surprise.

"Former. Just got out this year." It still sounded weird.

He gave Ryder a proud smile. "My dad was a Marine."

Was? "Yeah?"

Finn nodded, then Poppy called out another order to him.

Given the lineup, the poor kid was gonna be swamped for the next while. "I'll take this over to your mom for you," Ryder offered. "Looks like you've got your hands full."

"Thanks."

With a nod he headed back to the table, intrigued by the woman waiting there. "He said to say hi."

"No, he didn't," she said with a laugh. "But thanks for saying so."

He grinned and reached for his running jacket, draped on the back of the chair.

"You heading out already?"

"Yeah, need to get back and cleaned up before I go over to Moll's." And the trip back was all uphill, so it would take him longer.

She stood, gathering the to-go cup and box. "Want a lift? I'm heading home to grab something anyway."

He'd planned to run back but spending more time with her sounded a lot more appealing than an uphill run. "That'd be great."

"Follow me." She waved at Finn, blew him a kiss that made him shake his head—but points to him for not rolling his eyes—and headed for the door, her long legs eating up the distance.

She had to be five-eleven, maybe even right at six feet. It felt strange that she could practically look him in the eye without heels on, but in a good way.

Outside, she crossed the two-lane street and turned left,

heading toward the vet clinic a half-block down. "This is me," she said, using her keyfob to unlock a purple MINI Cooper parallel parked at the curb out front.

She got behind the wheel while Ryder folded himself into the front passenger seat, adjusting his legs to keep his knees from hitting the dash. Her car was tidy, and it smelled subtly of perfume.

"I'll resist the urge to pip the horn at Finn when we go by," she said, turning on the ignition. "I've already embarrassed him enough for one day. Probably."

Even if Finn was embarrassed, at least he knew his mom cared. "Yeah, go easy on the embarrassment," he said as she pulled a tight U-turn and headed north up Front Street.

"I will. Not that I see him much these days."

"What made you move to Crimson Point?"

"For a change of scenery, and hoping to make a fresh start. I came through here once with my husband years ago and thought it was adorable. He died three years ago, and it's been tough, but especially on Finn. Mostly he avoids me now, staying holed up in his room playing video games online with his friends back in Seattle." She was quiet a moment. "Pretty sure he resents me for dragging him here."

That was rough. Had her husband died in combat? "Sounds like he's being a pretty normal teenage boy."

She grunted. "Maybe, but it's new to me, and not my favorite stage. Anyway, what about you? Where are you from? You've got an accent like Molly's, but stronger. North Carolina?"

"That's right. Our moms are sisters, and they pretty much raised Moll and me together."

She glanced at him. "Was your mom a single mom?"

"Yeah. And I'm pretty sure she didn't love my teen years either," he said with a wry grin.

Her lips curved, making that dimple reappear.

"Oh, good thing you took the ride back instead of running," she said as she turned the corner onto the street where the cottage was. "Molly's already here."

A red SUV was parked in the driveway. Danae pulled in behind it. "Thanks for the lift," he said.

"Anytime." Those gorgeous, pale eyes sparkled with the smile she gave him. "See you around, neighbor."

He sure hoped so. He wouldn't mind seeing a lot more of her during his visit.

She pipped the horn at him as she drove away. Before he could reach for the door handle, it opened to reveal Molly standing there with huge grin on her face and Savannah balanced on one hip.

"Well, look who's already making friends with the neighbors." She reached out her free arm for him.

Ryder pulled her into a hug. "Good to see you. And you too again, little miss," he told Savannah, who shrank from him and buried her face in her mama's neck.

"Don't mind her. She'll warm up to you quick enough." She stepped back, allowing him inside, and eyed him critically, either in nurse or concerned cousin mode. "You've lost weight."

Of course *she* would notice. "Maybe a little."

Her eyes searched his. "You gonna tell me what's going on with you?"

Nope. "I'm good." He hooked a thumb over his shoulder, pointing down the hall. "Just gonna grab a shower and change, then we can go."

Savannah squirmed, pushing to be let down. Molly set her on her feet, and Savannah immediately took off, toddling around the room, examining everything she could see.

"She looks like Carter," he said.

"I know. I'm glad I still have at least this part of him." Her smile as she watched her daughter was full of maternal love and pride.

It suited her. "You seem happy."

She met his eyes, hazel gaze warm. "I am. Happiest I've ever been." Her smile faded. "But something tells me you're not."

Her words triggered a sharp hitch in his chest, the weight of guilt suddenly pressing on his lungs. "I'm okay, Moll," he said and strode for the bathroom, glad to escape her scrutiny.

They both knew he wasn't.

Either he figured out how to defeat his demons, or they would destroy him.

FOUR

By the time she'd managed to string the newly purchased strands of lights along the edge of the lower gutter, Danae's fingers were numb and stiff from the cold. It would be dark out in another hour, and if she didn't want to risk serious injury, she needed to be off the ladder by then.

She glanced to her left when a vehicle turned down their street in the approaching twilight. The SUV slowed in front of her driveway, and the passenger window lowered. "Need a hand?" a male voice called out.

She ducked down a bit, smiled when she saw it was her temporary neighbor. Her insanely attractive, sexy, *temporary* neighbor. "Why, does it look like I need one?"

Rather than answer, he parked and got out, and even though she prided herself on being practical and responsible, her heart rate spiked as he strode toward her. Six-feet-plus of built, gorgeous man coming her way. Dusky brown skin, black hair cropped close to his head, and a short, neatly trimmed goatee framing his mouth and chin.

Gripping both sides of the ladder in a move that emphasized the breadth of his chest and shoulders, he peered up at her, his dark brown eyes filled with a mix of amusement and concern. "Have you done this before?"

"That obvious, huh?"

"Kinda, yeah."

"Terry always did it, and I haven't bothered putting any up since he died. I wasn't going to this year either, but today I got home and thought, screw it, we need more holiday spirit around here." Just one more thing she missed about him. And his cooking. And a million other little things.

"Where's Finn?"

"Inside. I brought him home from work half an hour ago and he went straight to his room." It was like living with a financially dependent roommate she was responsible for. She had to pay for everything, and yet he wanted nothing to do with her.

Ryder motioned with one hand. "Come down from there. Finn and I'll finish up."

"Really, it's okay. You don't have to do that—I can probably finish up without killing myself."

"I want to. Well, mostly I want you off this ladder."

She chuckled. "Wow, I must really look awkward up here. And as for my son, good luck trying to pry him away from his video game to help out."

He nodded once and gestured again. "Just come on down."

A little embarrassed that he was so worried and thought she was inept, she slowly climbed down the ladder. He stepped back only when she reached the ground, giving her room.

"See? Still in one piece," she said, turning toward him. "I really don't want to put you to any trouble—" She let out a squeak of alarm when her foot caught on a coiled-up extension cord and she started to topple backward.

Strong, hard arms banded around her back, drawing her to an equally hard chest. Danae flattened her hands on the front of his jacket, a velvet fist hitting her in her stomach at the feel of him, the knee-melting power in his muscles.

Whoa.

Her head swam for a moment, pulse skipping, his spicy, evergreen scent filling her nose. His face was close to hers, his gaze holding hers with an unnerving, magnetic force.

Before she could remove her hands and step back, he bent his head and leaned down, his warm breath caressing her neck, and inhaled. Like he was breathing her in.

The primal action caused a shocking burst of heat to explode in her belly, making goosebumps break out across her body. Tightening her nipples and making her incredibly aware of their positioning.

Unsettled, she pushed at his chest gently. He raised his head and released her, leaving her feeling strangely abandoned.

She cleared her throat, avoiding his gaze. Okay, she might be out of practice when it came to men, but she definitely hadn't imagined that. Him breathing in her scent as if he hadn't been able to help himself. "Thanks," she murmured, suddenly flushed and warm all over.

"No problem." He stepped back, giving her space, and it was immediately easier to breathe. "Can I go in and talk to Finn?"

"Sure. Just through there and down the hall to the first shut door." She gestured to the open garage.

As Ryder walked away, she couldn't help sweeping her gaze over the back of him, tall and strong and way more appealing than was good for her. It was the first time since Terry died that she'd been attracted to a man, yet the intensity of her reaction to him startled her.

Not that it would come to anything, she reminded herself, grabbing another bin of lights to drag onto the front lawn. He was only in town until New Year's, and then she'd never see him again.

IT WASN'T HARD for Ryder to find Finn's room. As Danae had said, it was the only door shut along the hallway, and he could hear Finn's excited, animated voice coming from inside it.

He knocked sharply twice and waited. "Finn?" he said when there was no answer.

A rattling noise. "Yeah?"

He opened the door, almost staggering back a step because of the teenage funk hanging heavy in the air. It was like Finn hadn't opened the door or a window since he'd moved in. "Hey."

Finn stared at him a second in astonishment, then whipped off his headset, his long bangs falling over his face. "Hey."

"What are you playing?"

"Call of Duty." He pushed a hand through his hair, face full of confusion.

"Nice. Listen, I was just driving by and saw your mom on a ladder out front, trying to hang the Christmas lights. Watching her almost gave me a heart attack, so I made her come down and said I'd do it for her. Mind giving me a hand finishing up?"

Finn tipped the mic on his headset toward his lips. "Gotta go. Back later," he blurted, put the headset on his desk and hurried toward him.

Good kid. "Ever put up lights before?" he asked as Finn followed him down the hall.

"No. I used to help my dad a bit, but that was a few years ago, and mostly I just stood by the ladder and held the lights coiled up on my arm."

High time he learned and started helping his mom out more. "Grab your jacket and some gloves. We might be a while."

In the garage Danae had pulled out various tubs and containers holding outside decorations and lights. "Want to put up anything else, or just the lights?" he asked as Finn tugged on gloves.

Finn glanced in the bins, surprise filling his face, then a hint of a smile, as if the items were sentimental to him. "Yeah, maybe a few of these. If you don't mind."

"Not at all." He noted the basketball hoop and the sports equipment stacked in the far corner. "You play sports?"

Finn followed his gaze. "Used to, before we moved. Basketball and baseball. You?"

"Same. And football." He picked up a big container and started carrying it into the front yard.

"How long were you in the Marine Corps?" Finn asked, following with another bin as they stepped onto the lawn.

"Long time. Joined up after I graduated from high school, and just got out a few months ago."

"How come you left?"

"It was time."

Thankfully, he was saved from answering more questions about his time in the Corps by Danae coming around the corner. She stopped, her eyebrows hiking up when she saw Finn carrying a bin. "Wow, hi. You're going to help put these up?"

"Yeah," he muttered.

"Here, let me help," she offered, reaching for one end of the container Ryder held.

"I got it." He shifted his grip, eyeing her. She had on a thin coat, and no gloves or hat. Her cheeks and the end of her nose were bright pink, and so were her fingers. "It's cold out. You go on in and warm up, we'll handle all this."

She looked from him to Finn and back uncertainly. "You sure?"

"Positive."

A smile broke over her face, full of gratitude. "Okay, but only if you'll stay for dinner."

He glanced at Finn for permission and got a nod of assent with the hint of a grin. "Sounds good."

Danae went inside. Ryder adjusted the angle of the ladder and climbed up to check on the installed section of lights. She'd clipped them to the edge of the gutter fine, but the placement of the plug end nearest the edge of the house was awkward, making it hard to hide the bright orange extension cord she'd used.

He undid everything and moved it all, directing Finn on the ground to shift the cord around and use a different outlet. Together they strung the lights across the sides and front of the bungalow, but there were more strands left over when they finished. "Want to put more up anywhere?"

"Around the front windows," Finn said. "And then we need to wind some really close together around the tree trunks. That's what Dad always did."

Ryder felt for the kid. While his own father hadn't been a part of his life since his parents divorced when Ryder was still in elementary school, Finn's clearly had, and it must have been really tough on him and his mom when they lost him. Then to be ripped away from his home and friends around Thanksgiving and made to start over in a small town during the holidays... Not easy.

He'd braced himself for Finn to be sullen and maybe even

a pill about helping, and was pleasantly surprised to find the opposite. With everything he did, Finn was right there helping, even seeming keen on putting everything up. Ryder asked him about his interests while they worked, about school and any friends he'd made so far.

"There's one guy, Paul. We hang out together a bit. But my best friends are back in Seattle."

"That who you play online with?"

"Mostly, yeah. You play CoD?"

"Been known to play the odd campaign from time to time," he answered, reaching up to connect two strands of lights together at the corner of the large, left-hand picture window at the front of the house. "Got any other hobbies?"

"Not really anymore. You?"

"I like to be out on the water, love to hike, and I still like hitting the range."

"You mean golfing, or shooting?"

He grinned. "Shooting."

"I'd love to do that, but my mom won't let me go yet."

Ryder would have offered to take him, but that was overstepping when he barely knew Finn and Danae. He could see her moving around in the kitchen on the opposite side of the house, her back to him, the strings of her apron tied right above her heart-shaped ass framed in those snug, dark jeans as she bent over and—

"Wanna play some CoD after dinner?"

He jerked his gaze down to Finn. While he might not have a ton of experience with kids, he recognized that the offer spoke volumes, and there was no mistaking the quiet yearning in the kid's eyes. "Sure, I'd like that."

A grin flashed on Finn's lips as the kid turned away.

After they finished outlining the windows, they strung more extension cords across the lawn and got to work winding lights around the three thick cedar trunks. "What now?" Ryder asked when they finished, rubbing his gloved hands together. It was dark now, the multicolored strands of lights glowing brightly on the trees and the front of the house.

"These," Finn answered, digging some pre-lit lawn ornaments from one of the trunks. Two snowmen, a deer, and a Mickey. "Mickey goes on the front doorstep."

Ryder acted as assistant this time, letting Finn place everything as he wanted it. The Mickey seemed particularly important to him, weather-beaten and faded though he was. "This guy looks like he's seen his fair share of Christmases already."

"He was my dad's. Bought him the year he and my mom started dating." Finn knelt to plug Mickey into the extension cord they'd tucked around the foundation and up the edge of the front steps. "Oh, damn."

One strand of lights around Mickey's head were burned out. "Got a toolbox?"

Finn looked over at him. "You think you can fix it?"

"I'll give it my best."

Finn hurried to grab the tools. Ryder unwound the burned-out strand, then showed him how to check the wires and bulbs. It was an old series strand, and they didn't have any replacement bulbs to fit.

The dejected look on the kid's face was too much. "Saw a hardware store in town earlier," Ryder said. "Think it's still open?"

Finn's expression brightened. "Yeah, they're open until six. We can make it if we hurry."

"Then let's get going."

Thirty minutes later they were back with a new strand of lights to match the others as closely as possible. Finn had come to life on the drive there, especially when Ryder let him play a playlist from his phone. Finn had laughed and joked around all the way there and back.

Ryder was doubly glad he'd come home in time to find Danae up on that ladder. And the big smile on Finn's face when Mickey once again lit up in all his glory was all the thanks Ryder needed.

They packed everything else away in the garage and tidied up. "What do you do now? For work?" Finn asked him, stacking the bins back in the far corner.

"Did a little stunt work for a bit in Hollywood. Now I'm a professional bodyguard."

Finn stopped and spun to look at him, then laughed as if Ryder had been joking. "Whatever."

He raised an eyebrow.

Finn's eyes widened. "You're serious?" He cocked his head, looking skeptical. "What kind of people do you protect?"

"CEOs, celebrities."

"Anyone I know?"

"Maybe."

Finn was clearly hanging on his every word. "Who?"

Ryder decided there was no harm in telling him. "Becca Sandoza."

"Bullshit."

He grinned. "No, for real. I did a stunt sequence with my buddy in her latest movie. Big motorbike chase. Just came out a couple weeks ago."

Finn's eyes narrowed. "No way."

Chuckling, Ryder took out his phone and called her on video chat, watching Finn's expression shift from deadpan to uncertain when she appeared on the screen.

"Hey, we were just talking about you," Becca answered. "How are things on the Oregon Coast?"

"So far, so good. Listen, I'm with someone I want to introduce you to. This is Finn, one of my neighbors. We were just putting up some Christmas lights for his mom. Say hi." He turned the phone around so the screen faced Finn, and the look on the kid's face when he saw Becca staring back at him was absolutely priceless.

"Hi, Finn. I'm Becca."

Finn's cheeks flushed an even deeper red than the cold had managed. He opened his mouth, seemed to have a brain short out. "Um, hi."

"You guys just put up some lights, huh? Can I see them?"

"Uh, yeah," he blurted, grinning at Ryder as he walked out of the garage to show her their work.

He came back a couple minutes later to hand the phone back, smiling from ear to ear. "Okay, that was insane. Like, *insane*. How did you meet her? She said to say goodbye, by the way. And someone named Chase did too."

Ryder slipped it back into his pocket. "That's my best friend. Did the motorbike scene with him. Fellow Marine. Can I trust you to keep a secret?"

Finn's eyes lit up. "Yeah, of course."

Ryder believed him. "They're engaged now. But don't tell anyone, because they haven't announced it officially."

"I won't." Finn shook his head, laughed like he still couldn't believe it. "Can I tell my mom though?"

"Yeah, that's okay."

As if she'd been conjured, Danae opened the door to the garage, smiled at them. "You two done yet? Dinner's ready."

"Good, I'm starving," Finn said, then shot Ryder a frown. "If Chase is your best friend, doesn't that make guarding Becca a conflict of interest for you?"

He hid a grin. The kid didn't miss much. "Let's just call it a…gray area," he said, ruffling Finn's hair on the way into the warmth of the house.

In that moment he realized he felt lighter inside, the constant weight in his chest easing. It was the lightest he'd felt since making the painful decision to leave his beloved Corps behind.

FIVE

What a difference a day made.

This morning the thought of struggling through the holidays had made Danae feel tired and down. Now, sitting at the table in the cozy nook off the kitchen with Finn and Ryder, she felt full to bursting with Christmas spirit for the first time in three long years.

It thrilled her to see Finn so animated. It was as if, in the space of the past two hours, Ryder had magically injected her son with all the life he'd been lacking since his father died. She couldn't remember the last time she'd seen him so engaged with anyone—outside of his video games. Something about Ryder had resonated with Finn, and...

Her son wasn't the only one drawn to him.

Throughout the meal, her gaze kept getting pulled back to him, watching him as he talked to Finn or laughed at something her son said. He had a deep, booming laugh that was contagious, and his smile, the white of his teeth against his brown skin and black goatee, was mesmerizing. She loved his accent. The slower cadence of his speech compared to hers and Finn's, the *y'alls* and other Southernisms he probably didn't even notice.

She thought about that brief but startling embrace by the ladder earlier. The way her body had suddenly come to life when he'd lowered his face to her neck and inhaled.

She lowered her eyes to her plate, berating herself. *Stop reading anything into it. It's not like anything's gonna happen between you.*

After dinner Finn jumped up to clear the table. Danae's eyebrows shot up and she aimed a surprised look at Ryder. "I'll help you," he told Finn, a half-smile on his face as he carried plates and serving dishes to the sink. My, my, he had nice manners too. Someone had taught him well.

"What's for dessert?" Finn asked her, busy rinsing the dishes to go into the dishwasher.

Ah, there was the kid she knew. "Chocolate pots de crème. Poppy gave me the recipe. Ryder, do you want one?"

His gaze slid to her, and the impact of it made something flutter deep in her lower abdomen. "I'd love one."

Okay, she hadn't flirted with anyone since Terry died and she was woefully out of practice, but there was no denying the attraction humming between them. Even she remembered what that felt like.

After dessert—which was shockingly good considering how easy and fast it had been to make using a blender—she did her own clean-up of the kitchen while Ryder went to play a video game with Finn in the living room. She smiled at the sound of them laughing and trash talking.

It did her heart good to see her son having a good time for a change, and she appreciated that Ryder seemed genuinely interested in spending time with him. Finn missed his dad, missed having a male figure in his life. Noah, Beckett, Jase and Mac were awesome, but she could already tell there was something special about Ryder.

"And that's how it's done," Ryder said, his deep voice carrying into the kitchen.

"I'm totally gonna use that move with the guys tonight," Finn gushed.

She looked up from the table where she was sipping a mug of apple-cinnamon tea when they appeared in the kitchen doorway a moment later. "Have fun?"

"It was *awesome*," Finn said.

"He's pretty good. But I can still show him a thing or two." Ryder's eyes gleamed with humor. "Anyway, I'm gonna head out. Thanks for dinner."

"Yeah, later," Finn said, bumping fists with Ryder before heading down the hall for his room.

Ryder turned the opposite way and she followed, catching his tempting scent on the air. She wouldn't mind burying her nose in his neck and breathing him in. "Thank you *so* much for everything today," she said as she walked him to the door.

"It was nothing."

"It meant a lot to us," she insisted. "Both me and Finn. I haven't seen him this happy and not moody in forever."

One side of his mouth lifted. "I was like that too at his age. Don't worry, it'll pass. He'll be himself again eventually."

"Hope so. I miss him." Even more now that she was alone.

She smiled at Ryder, careful to keep her distance from him when they reached the door. She felt strangely nervous all of a sudden, a little uncertain. "Well, thanks again. And you're welcome anytime you feel like popping over. We'll have you over for dinner again before you leave, for sure."

"I'd like that." He paused, then his dark gaze moved over her face like a caress before it dropped to her lips.

Her heart stuttered, the urge to step into him and lift her face to his so strong she had to force herself to stand still and wrap her arms around herself to keep from reaching for him.

His dark eyes lifted to hers once more, and held, the invisible connection pulsing in the space between them.

Danae held her breath, staring back at him.

The edge of his mouth tipped up in the hint of a grin, then he reached out a hand, his long fingers sweeping a lock of hair back from her cheek. "See you around, neighbor," he murmured, his voice as gentle as the caress of his fingertips.

Shutting the door behind him, Danae leaned a hand against it for a moment, closing her eyes. Wow. The man had charisma in spades.

She caught herself before she could spin a useless fantasy about him and shook her head at herself. Better that nothing happened between them. She was a single mom trying to raise a teenage son and make a new life for them both. She wasn't interested in involving a man in their life, especially not for a fling that would just bring more heartache when it ended.

There had been no one since Terry, and she wasn't getting involved with someone who was only here for another week, no matter how attracted she was to him.

She pulled herself from the door, surprised when she turned around to find Finn standing in the hallway by his door. "You two seemed to hit it off."

Finn nodded, his face glowing with enthusiasm. "Did you know Ryder was a Marine? He just got out a little while ago. Since then, he's been a stuntman in Hollywood, and now he's a bodyguard—for Becca Sandoza."

"What? Get out." Molly had never said anything about that.

"No, swear to God. He called her up when we were in the garage and introduced us. It was her," he said excitedly. "I'm not allowed to tell anyone else except you, but she's engaged to Ryder's best friend. He was a Marine too and does stunts in movies. That's how he met Becca."

"Well, wow," she said, impressed. How come Ryder hadn't told her any of that? And ooh, yeah, she could totally see him as a bodyguard, all intense and protective. *Yumm...*

"I know, right? And he played baseball, basketball and football, too. Can we have him over again soon? He's awesome."

A sudden lump formed in her throat. She loved seeing Finn so excited and happy, but... "Buddy, you know he's only staying for the holidays, right?"

He shrugged, smile fading. "That's okay. I just wanna hang with him more while he's here." He paused, pulled out his phone and glanced at it. He texted something and started to turn away, his attention diverted.

"That it? You're in your room for the night?" She said it teasingly, mostly to draw attention to him basically cutting her off mid-conversation and walking away.

"Yeah, I've gotta head out," he said, barely glancing at her, busy texting away. "I'm meeting Paul in a bit."

He started to edge past her, but she grabbed his wrist. "Hey," she said, and waited until he looked at her. It was still strange to look up at him. Wasn't so long ago that she could tuck him under her arm or pull him onto her lap for a cuddle. Wasn't so long ago that he'd been attached to her, wanting to hang out and do things together.

"Yeah?" he asked, phone in hand, thumb poised over the keypad.

She bit back what she wanted to say. It wasn't his fault she was lonely. It wasn't his job to keep her company or fill the void. He was young and had his own life to live, and friends were an important part of that.

So she hid it all with a smile, telling herself to toughen up. "Where will you be?"

"Paul's place. I'll be back by eleven."

"Nice try. Ten. Have fun. Love you." Before he could escape, she wrapped her arms around his slender waist and hugged him.

He returned it with one arm, then let go. "Love you too. See ya."

"See ya."

After he was gone, she stood there in the foyer. The sudden silence surrounded her, heavy and oppressive, loneliness creeping toward her like a thick fog.

Unbidden, she thought about the sexy man next door who she was insanely curious about. And how she'd love to get to know him better.

SIX

"Get that guy!" Paul ordered, thumbs working like mad on the controller.

Finn toggled his character's rifle left toward the enemy soldier and opened fire. Blood spurted, and the man fell. "Got him."

"Good, now get your ass over here and back me up."

They'd been playing at Paul's place for close to an hour now. Or maybe two, Finn wasn't sure. It was impossible to keep track of time when you were this deep into a game.

Neither one of them moved when the doorbell rang. Then rang again a few seconds later. And yet again, repeatedly this time.

"Who the hell could that be?" Paul muttered in annoyance, glancing toward the front door at the end of the hall.

Obnoxious, impatient pounding came next.

"Jeez, calm down," Paul said, reluctantly putting down his controller and striding for the door.

Finn kept playing, paying hardly any attention to his friend, until other voices registered from the foyer. One more distinct than the others.

Grant.

He glanced at the living room doorway just as rapid treads approached. Grant appeared there a moment later, eyeing him. "Get up, loser," he said with a grin. "We're going for a ride."

The last thing Finn felt like doing was hanging out with Grant, much less going for another ride to deliver more drugs. He looked at Paul, who hung back in the hallway, hands in his pockets, an uncertain expression on his face.

Finn got the message. Paul would go along with whatever he did.

"I'm good," he said to Grant, two other guys now standing on either side of him. "Paul and I are in the middle of a game."

Grant rolled his eyes, strode over to the console and turned it off. "Now come *on*, dude."

Clenching his jaw to hold back an angry retort, Finn glanced at Paul. His friend shrugged, apparently resigned to spending the rest of the night with these guys instead of hanging out here, as originally planned.

Finn wanted no part of it. "You guys go ahead. I'm gonna head home. Gotta work in the morning."

"Uh-uh, you're comin' with us," Grant said, grabbing Finn's arm and towing him down the hall.

Short of yanking away and starting an argument that wouldn't end well for him, Finn tamped down his irritation and didn't resist, shrugging into his jacket on the way to Grant's SUV. Sooner he did what they wanted, the sooner it'd be over. And after tonight he seriously had to rethink hanging out with Paul.

At least he got an actual seat in the back with a seatbelt this time, but he still couldn't shake the unease coiling in his gut as Grant headed across town to the coastal highway and turned south. "Where we going?" he finally asked, already kicking himself for not sticking to his guns about going home.

"Got a little errand to take care of," Grant answered evasively.

They stopped at the same apartment complex as before. Grant parked at the curb where a guy in his late twenties or early thirties stood waiting for them on the sidewalk in a black winter coat. Finn said nothing, watching everything in silence as the front passenger rolled down his window.

The guy in the black coat leaned in, scanning them all. "Who're they?" he asked, staring at him and Paul.

"Guys from school. They're all right," Grant answered. "What've you got for me?"

The guy held Finn's gaze for a long, unnerving moment, then passed a padded envelope over to Grant. "I'll text you the drop address. Get moving. This guy won't wait around if you're late."

Finn mentally groaned as Grant shoved the envelope beneath his seat. Great. Now he was part of a drug deal. Awesome.

The guy in the coat walked away. Grant checked his phone for the address, plugged it into his GPS, and they were off. Speeding south toward Crimson Point along the darkened coastal highway minutes later, music blaring, Grant and the front passenger laughing at whatever they were talking about.

"Can you let me off at the next turn? I'll walk home from there," Finn said, hating everything about this. Pissed off at himself for getting mixed up in it. Why hadn't he stood his ground?

"Nope. Later," Grant replied, and turned the music up.

Finn watched with a sinking heart as they sped past the last exit to Crimson Point and continued south. There was no moonlight tonight, a thick layer of cloud completely obscuring it. Out his window, Finn could just make out the whitecaps on the waves as they rolled onto the shore in the distance.

Two towns down the coast Grant turned inland and wound his way up into the hills. Eventually the residential neighborhoods gave way to a thick mass of forest covering the western slope. Where the hell were they going?

As soon as Grant turned onto a deserted dirt road, they were surrounded by massive evergreens on every side. The SUV's headlights cut through the murky darkness, the beams making the layer of mist hugging the ground shimmer like silver. When they rounded a curve in the road, Finn spotted another vehicle waiting there, taillights glowing like red, evil eyes in the darkness.

His pulse accelerated as Grant slowed to a stop behind it, parked and got out. Finn's whole body was tense. He watched intently through the windshield, uncomfortable as hell.

A middle-aged man got out of the other vehicle, spoke briefly to Grant, then took the envelope. He checked the contents, studied Grant a long moment and shifted, the SUV's headlights revealing the deadly black pistol shoved into the front of his waistband.

Finn swallowed, his mouth suddenly dry. Holy shit.

But just when Finn braced himself for the man to draw his weapon on Grant, instead he reached into his jacket and withdrew a smaller envelope, the right size for a stack of cash, and handed it to Grant. Then he said something else, grinned, and slapped Grant's shoulder before walking back to his vehicle.

Finn let out a slow breath of relief as Grant came back and got behind the wheel. "You guys hungry?" he asked as he reversed and turned the vehicle around, as if nothing out of the ordinary had just happened.

Finn didn't say anything, but Paul and the other guys gave enthusiastic responses. Grant retraced their route back to the highway and started north. Finn suffered through a stop at a fast-food place halfway back to Crimson Point, declining food and saying he wasn't hungry. Which he wasn't, because his stomach was all knotted up. He just wanted to get home.

"All right, I'll take you home now," Grant said, irritation dripping from every word as he got them onto the road again. "But just so you know, I can make room on my crew for both you guys if you're interested."

There was no way in hell Finn was getting involved any deeper in this shit, but when he glanced at Paul, he saw his buddy was giving him an encouraging look. Like he was considering it and wanted Finn to get in on it too.

Dude, are you serious?

"Money's way better than anything you'll make in Crimson Point," Grant added over the music as they sped through the darkness.

Finn kept his mouth shut, but Paul said he'd think about it.

For Finn there was nothing to think about. This was fucking insane, and even if he had been tempted to make easy money doing illegal shit, Finn lived literally next door to the sheriff. Also, his mom would freak the fuck out if she knew what was going on right now.

After what felt like an eternity, they finally reached his house and Finn allowed himself to take a full breath again. His mom's car was in the driveway, the multicolored lights he and Ryder had put up glowing cheerily in the night.

The moment the SUV came to a stop, Finn had his seatbelt off and the door open. "See you," he muttered, already climbing out.

"Yeah, man," Paul said. "I'll call you tomorrow."

"I'll call you too," Grant said with a smirk in his voice. "See if you've changed your mind."

I won't.

Without answering either of them, Finn shut the door and hurried around the side of the house, anxious to get inside. He sighed as the SUV disappeared around the corner, the thump of the bass echoing in the quiet.

He was so damn thankful for not being caught with those guys tonight. But there was no way he was hanging out with them again, maybe even Paul, and as of tonight he was cutting contact. Things would be awkward once school started back up and they saw each other again, but he'd deal with it later.

He nearly jumped out of his skin when his mom suddenly stepped out of the living room into the hallway. "Hey," she said with a smile, cinching the belt on her robe tighter around her waist. She seemed so happy to see him, it made something painful twinge in the middle of his chest. "Where've you been?"

Shit, had she been checking the app to locate him? "At Paul's. A guy from school gave me a ride home."

She nodded. "You know, you can have friends over here if you want. I won't bite, and I'll try not to embarrass you," she added dryly.

His face heated, guilt and shame bubbling up. He was never having those guys over here. Bad enough that they knew where he lived. He'd probably continue to play online with Paul, but he wouldn't hang out with him in person anymore. "Yeah. Maybe at some point," he lied.

"You hungry? There's leftover chicken and salad in the fridge."

"Nah, I'm just gonna go to my room." He took a step, stopped when his mom didn't move out of his way.

"Kay. Sleep tight," she said, and hugged him.

Feeling awkward, he stood there, the familiar scent of her perfume triggering a lump in his throat. He returned the hug quickly and let go.

She stepped back, giving him another smile that seemed a bit sad. "Well, goodnight. Love you."

"You too."

Escaping to his room, he shut the door and sat down on his bed, exhaling hard and feeling miserable. Moving here away from his home and friends had been shitty, but he realized it could be worse, and he had it a lot better than some. Sheriff Noah and Miss Poppy were cool. The sheriff's buddies were cool too, Jase, Beckett and Mac. But by far the best thing about moving here so far was meeting Ryder.

At that thought, his gaze strayed across his room to the bookshelf, where the few framed pictures were displayed. Some of him and his dad, and one of his dad in his dress blues. As far as Finn was concerned, his dad had been a hero long before he'd died in that fire trying to save people's lives.

Staring at his dad's face, his heart sank. His parents would both be so disappointed if they knew what kind of circle he'd gotten himself involved with here.

Shame burned hot in his belly, followed by a burst of resolve. He was the man of the house now. He needed to do better. Needed to grow up and make the best of things.

He needed to be the kind of person who would make his dad proud.

KYLE GLANCED over at his younger brother, sitting beside him in the front passenger seat of the pickup. "Is it him?"

Josh checked his phone. "Yeah. Got a location. Need to be there in twenty."

Kyle got them on the highway and headed north up the coast, following Josh's directions and smirking at the wisecracks about the street names in the area his brother made along the way. "Listen to this one: Blowhole Bottom." Josh busted out laughing at the latest source of ridicule he'd spotted on the digital map, a familiar, contagious laugh that made it impossible not to smile. "Who the hell names a road that?"

"Someone into blowholes."

Josh snickered. "Man, people around here have dirty minds."

"So you'll fit right in then."

"Look who's talking."

It never failed to amaze Kyle. Somehow, throughout everything that had happened to them, Josh had never lost his sense of humor. Not after their mom died when they were young. Not through the abusive, controlling life they'd lived after that with their dad and psycho bitch of a stepmom.

Even after they'd left home and been living in a shelter, eating at soup kitchens in between odd jobs they'd found to get by, Josh's smart-ass humor and wit had been the only bright spot in Kyle's life. He'd made it his responsibility to look after his brother a long time ago. This gig was the first big thing the organization had given them.

It had taken over two years to climb that ladder, and damn near a decade of risky shit before that, earning a rep that had finally gotten them noticed and recruited into where the real money was. The work was dangerous, but it paid well, and they'd almost saved up enough money to buy a house together down in San Fran.

They were low on funds at the moment, and this guy they were meeting always preferred to deal in cash rather than money transfers. In this business, anything that allowed them to fly under the radar was a good thing.

They made it to the drop point with plenty of time to spare, a spot out in a wooded area, high on a bluff above the highway. A few minutes past the appointed meet time, headlights turned the corner behind them.

Kyle squinted against the glare, relaxing slightly when he finally saw the expensive silver Audi sedan coming toward them. "Wait here," he told Josh.

Josh rolled his eyes. "Just because I'm your kid brother doesn't mean I'm a kid."

No, but it was Kyle's job to protect him, and he didn't trust the guy they were meeting. He walked toward the other vehicle, watchful.

The other driver stayed where he was, and as per usual, he had someone with him in the front seat. Sometimes it was his step-kid. Tonight, it was muscle.

Kyle walked straight up to the driver's side window, reassured by the outline of his weapon pressing into the small of his back, and waited while it lowered. "Hey. Got anything new for me?"

Victor handed over a thick envelope full of cash that Kyle tucked away into his waistband and covered with the hem of his shirt. "New shipment needs to be picked up and delivered," the guy said.

Good. He and Josh needed a big score like this. Human cargo always netted them big money. Another few, and they could finally have some real security for once in their lives.

Kyle pulled out a pen from his inside jacket pocket, along

with a receipt. He always wrote the info down rather than storing it in his phone, then flushed it right after the shipment was delivered. He was too paranoid about anyone finding his phone to risk storing important info on it. "Gimme the details."

Victor listed the contents of the shipment, along with a date, time, and location for both drop off and pickup. Kyle wrote it all down in his special shorthand. He was paranoid about concealing everything, so even if he were to drop a receipt, no one else would have a clue what his notes meant.

With the transaction complete, the Audi drove off, leaving Kyle to walk back to his truck. "So? When's the next shipment due?" Josh asked when he got in.

"Twenty-sixth." Three nights from now.

"Cool. I hate waiting around longer than that. Makes me twitchy."

Him, too. "Here," he said, pulling some cash out of the envelope and tossing it to his brother. The rest would go in the bank toward the down payment. "This'll get us through the next couple weeks."

But this next job would set them up for a lot longer than that.

SEVEN

Ryder's eyes flew open to reveal the unfamiliar room around him. His heart thundered in his chest, skin slick with sweat, and the echo of gunfire and explosions still ringing in his ears.

His gaze darted around the room, searching for any sign of danger. But there was none. Because he was in Oregon rather than a combat zone.

He sat up and exhaled hard, running an unsteady hand over his sweaty face. Shit, that one had been a bitch.

He swallowed, the ghostly images of the dream impossible to shake loose, triggering an avalanche of memories he fought every day to keep buried. He could see his Marines' faces so clearly in the moments before the attack. Men who'd served under him for months. Men who had trusted him with their lives.

He'd failed them, and their families. And today it was Christmas Eve. Their loved ones were facing their very first Christmas without their sons, husbands, fathers, brothers. Imagining their pain heightened his own suffering.

His stomach twisted, guilt slashing at his insides like

razor blades. Why? he wanted to scream. Why was he still here when they weren't? He'd been their captain. He should have died with the others.

He shoved off the bed as his stomach lurched, and stumbled into the en suite bathroom, immediately kneeling in front of the toilet. Tremors shook him, jolting all through his body, his breathing choppy.

Closing his eyes, he fought away the horrific images assaulting him. The screams of the wounded and dying all around him, mixed with the rattle of rifle fire. Of standing in the base hospital Emergency area, his wounded men just out of view. The staff forcing him backward, shoving him out the doors, preventing him from getting to his men. Even though he could hear two of them calling for him.

A chill snaked up his spine, bringing a hot rush of tears.

No. Stop. Stop thinking about it.

He used every trick he knew to empty his mind and focus on his breathing. As the minutes passed, gradually the horror began to fade. The shaking eased, and his stomach stopped churning. But he was clammy all over, cold.

Standing, he reached into the shower enclosure next to him and turned the water on hot. For the first time it registered how bright it was outside, silvery light coming through the window beside the sink.

He climbed in and stood under the hot spray, letting it pound over his back and shoulders in a pummeling, numbing rush. It had been a while since he'd had a nightmare that bad. This time of year was harder, the sense of loss and guilt sharper.

He didn't deserve to still be alive. Men much better than him had died that day, and the next.

The thought kept circling in his head, torturing him as he scrubbed himself, dried off and dressed. When he picked his phone up from the dresser in the bedroom, he saw it was already past ten, and it shocked him. He hadn't slept in that late in…years.

He grabbed a clean pullover and tugged it over his head as he walked down the hall toward the kitchen. On the way there, his gaze strayed to the closed pantry door.

He stopped in front of it. Stood there for a few moments, aware of the way his pulse sped up, his brain desperate for the relief it knew was inside. He pushed the door open, his eyes instantly moving past everything else inside, to the too-familiar bottle standing on the middle shelf in the back.

No, he told himself firmly. *Don't touch it.*

Then an insidious voice whispered in his mind. *Why not? No one will know. This one time more won't hurt. It'll help calm you. Help you forget, just for a little while.*

Yeah. Once more was okay. He needed it right now. And he was alone, so no one would ever know.

He was in the act of reaching for the bottle beckoning to him when his phone started ringing, startling him. A wave of self-loathing washed over him as he realized what he'd been about to do. The weakness that had made him cave so fast.

Saved by the bell.

Seeing Jase's name on the display, he answered, also seeing that he'd missed a call from his mom. "Hey, man."

"Morning. You got plans today?"

"Was just about to head out for a run." Not a total lie. He'd planned to run after he'd swallowed enough Jack to calm him down, then run later.

"Wanna meet up for some dune-buggying instead? The guys and I are finished helping our ladies get everything prepped for tonight and tomorrow, so we're meeting down at the rental place at noon. I can pick you up on the way, say eleven-thirty?"

"What guys?"

"Beckett, Noah, and Mac."

Ryder knew of them but hadn't met them in person yet. Jase had served under Beckett on a SF A-team. Noah was sheriff, and Mac was a former Royal Marine.

Staring at that bottle on the shelf now, his options were clear. Stay here and fail the no-booze test he'd set for himself, possibly even get drunk in the process, or he could get the hell out of here for a while and do something while hanging out with fellow vets.

It was a no-brainer. "Sounds good to me. We have room for one more? I'd like to invite someone."

"Yeah, sure. Who?"

"Finn, around the corner. Danae's son." This day and tomorrow had to be weighing on the kid as well, and from what Finn had said the other night while putting up the lights, he seemed to like and admire all the guys. He might even hero-worship them a little.

"Oh, great. See you in a bit."

Ryder put the phone in his pocket, then stared hard at the bottle for a long moment. "I don't need you," he said, hoping his brain got the message.

He wasn't an alcoholic. Wasn't addicted to it. Even so, he'd been starting to edge that way, and it would be all too easy to slide down that slippery slope. Jase's invitation couldn't have come at a better time.

Standing on the front porch of Danae's place a few minutes later, Ryder rang the doorbell and ran a hand over his close-cut hair. He'd come to invite Finn, but he was also hoping to see Danae. Her car was in the driveway, so she was probably at home.

She pulled the door open moments later, standing there in dark jeans and a form-fitting, raspberry-red sweater that hugged her trim figure and pert breasts. Her dark brown hair was pulled up into a messy bun at the top of her head, and the greeting smile she gave him made his heart kick against his ribs. "Hi."

Man, she was gorgeous. Those light eyes of hers were damn near hypnotic. "Hi. Is Finn working today?"

Her smile faded, replaced by surprise. "No, he's in his room. Probably still asleep. Want me to go get him?"

He should have called or texted instead of coming over, but he'd wanted an excuse to see her. "I can text him."

"Don't be silly. Come in." She stepped back and waved him inside, and he caught the rich scent of coffee on the air. "I'm just having my first cup of the day. Want one?" she said as she headed for the kitchen.

"Love one. Just black."

"Black it is."

He couldn't help staring at her ass as she walked in front of him. Trim but still curved and shapely, and it made him picture what her long legs would look like bare. Wrapped around his waist, or his shoulders while he held her hips steady and got her off with his tongue.

Oblivious to his thoughts, she poured him a mug at the counter and passed it over, her pale blue eyes lit up like stained glass shards in the morning light coming through the kitchen windows. "Happy Christmas Eve."

"Same to you." He clinked mugs with her, already feeling better, the memories and thoughts that had plagued him earlier vanishing like fog in the sunlight. He hadn't needed booze. He'd just needed to spend five minutes in her warm, calm presence.

"Have any special plans with Molly today?" she asked, taking a sip.

"Maybe later tonight. First, I'm heading out with the guys

for a while. I came over to invite Finn, if he wants to come hang with us. I'd have him back in plenty of time for dinner."

A soft, grateful smile lit up her face. "Oh, that's so sweet of you. I'll go tell him."

"Naw, it's okay. Let me text him and see if he's even awake." He pulled out his phone and sent off a quick one-handed text. *You up? I'm in the kitchen with your mom.*

He'd just slid it into his pocket when it chimed with an answer.

Hey. Gimme two minutes.

He grinned at Danae. "That got him up and moving."

"It's a Christmas miracle," she teased.

Sure enough, after only a few sips of coffee, a door opened down the hall. Heavy, flat-footed treads followed, then Finn appeared in the kitchen doorway dressed in boxers and what Ryder guessed was his dad's Marine Corps T-shirt, eyes bleary, longish hair standing up all over the place.

"Late night?" Ryder asked.

Finn grunted and crossed his arms. "Took me a while to get to sleep. What's up?"

"Jase and the guys invited me out for some dune-buggying. You interested?"

The sleepy look disappeared instantly, his lips curving into a grin. "You serious?"

"Yeah. I don't know if you're old enough for the rental place to let you drive your own, but you can ride with me. Jase is coming by in an hour. That work?"

He looked at his mom, then back at Ryder, the grin stretching into a smile wide enough to show teeth. "Yeah, it works," he said enthusiastically. "I'll go hit the shower."

As Finn hurried to the bathroom, Danae set her mug down and leaned against the counter to smile at Ryder. "This is really nice of you."

He shrugged. "I like him. And I thought it…might be good to get him out and take his mind off everything today for a bit."

Her expression sobered. "I think you're right. It's been a few years, but Christmas and birthdays are always the hardest now."

He was learning that firsthand. "How are you doing? This year."

She blinked as though his question had surprised her. It bothered him that she didn't have anyone to look out for her except for the friends she'd made here. "Better than last year, and a lot better than the year before that. But sometimes it still hits me hard. A movie on TV, or a decoration I pull out of a box. Little things. And boy, I miss how Terry didn't mind being the bad cop with Finn when he needed to. I hate that role."

He nodded, fighting the urge to reach out and touch her. To cup the velvety softness of her cheek and draw her closer, get lost in the crystalline depths of her eyes before covering those lush pink lips with his. "What made you want to become a vet tech?"

"I love animals. Always have. Originally, I had my heart set on vet school, but then I got pregnant with Finn and wanted a program that took less time and cost less, so vet tech it was. I love my job and it pays the bills, so it all worked out, and Sierra and I both do some volunteer work with the local shelter. Do you like animals?"

"Yeah, I like 'em. Haven't had many pets, though, except for a cat when I was little."

"I want to get us a cat. Whenever I go to the shelter, I keep waiting for a middle-aged or senior cat to come in for me to adopt. But I wanted to get us settled here more before I introduce another family member."

He nodded. She'd said it had been three years since her husband died. Had she dated at all since then? Was she even interested in it now? He *thought* she was attracted to him, but...

Her phone rang. She picked it up from the counter, shot him a guilty look. "It's my mom. I should probably take this, or she'll think I'm dead in a ditch somewhere."

"My mom's the same. Go ahead." He leaned against the counter to drink his coffee, listening to the sound of her voice as she walked into the other room. There was something soothing about it, matching her practical, put-together and responsible character. The way she spoke was unrushed. Calm.

He closed his eyes, let her voice flow over him. Within moments he began to notice the knot of guilt still lodged in his chest easing.

She was still talking to her mom when Finn came back in five minutes later, dressed and ready to go, hair damp from a shower. "You been dune-buggying before?" he asked Ryder.

"Since I was a kid. We've got great dunes close to where I grew up back in North Carolina."

"Cool. I've never done it, but always wanted to."

"It'll be fun."

Finn nodded, his excitement clear in his eyes, and Ryder was glad to see it. "You met the other guys yet?"

"Nope, but I've heard lots about 'em."

"They're all former military, except for Noah, but he grew up with Beckett, so he's just as good at stalking and shooting as the rest of them."

The kid seemed to really admire and respect people who had served. "You ever think you might want to enlist after you graduate?"

"I've thought about it. Still not sure yet. I'm thinking of

doing something with computers for my career. Programming or whatever. Maybe animation."

The two of them talked for a while longer, then Danae finally came back into the kitchen. Ryder had never dated a single mom before, preferring to avoid the complication that kids brought, but Danae and Finn had changed his thinking about that. He was damn tempted to ask her out.

You won't be here long enough to give her anything more than a few rolls in the hay. She deserves a lot more than that, and she might not be ready. Cool down, Marine.

Chastened, he focused on the conversation between her and Finn, unable to stop watching her. Every minute he spent in her company, he felt more drawn to her. He wanted more. More time with her. Getting to know her better. Find out what she liked to do, what made her laugh.

Find out what it took to make her melt under his kisses, his touch.

Before he knew it, his phone was ringing. Jase.

"Where you at?" Jase asked him. "I'm parked out front, but you're not here."

"I'm over at Danae's. Finn's gonna join us."

"Great. Be there in a sec."

Danae walked them to the door. She handed Finn his jacket, then fished a knit cap and a pair of gloves from a basket under the bench for him. "Have fun, but be careful if you drive," she told him.

"Mo-o-o-o-m," he groaned, rolling his eyes.

"What? I'm your mother, I can't help it." She reached up to tug the cap over his head, grinned, and wrapped her arms around his ribs. "Finn," she admonished when he stood there awkwardly. "Hug your mother."

Scowling, he gave her a quick pat on the back and immediately lowered his arms. Ryder bit back a grin.

Danae stepped back, giving Ryder a shrug. "Gotta steal hugs where I can these days."

He'd hug her gladly. Hold her as long as she wanted him to. And give her a whole lot more than that besides.

A horn honked outside. "And you be careful too," she told him with a saucy smile. "You bring my boy home in one piece. Dinner's at six."

"Yes, ma'am." He stepped past her, froze for a second when she placed a hand on the middle of his back, rubbing gently.

Their eyes met. Held.

If Finn hadn't been standing right there, Ryder would have turned and pulled her flush to him. Would have wrapped his arms around her and held that lithe body against his, then lower his head to nuzzle the side of her neck, breathe in her delicate scent like he had when she'd tripped at the base of the ladder.

She lowered her hand, gave him a smile that seemed a little startled, as if she'd been caught off guard by the spark between them just now. "See you later."

"You can count on it," he said, enjoying the way her lips parted in surprise to his words.

EIGHT

Ryder was looking forward to this.

"There they are," Jase said as the three of them strode into the rental facility. "Let me introduce you," he added to Ryder. "This is Beckett." He clapped a big, dark-haired and bearded man on the shoulder.

Beckett's complexion and features hinted at native ancestry of some sort, and there was a thick scar in his left eyebrow. "Ryder," he said, sticking out his hand. "Good to meet you finally."

"Same," he answered, shaking with him.

"I'm Noah," the guy in the middle said, shaking Ryder's hand next. He had brown hair and deep blue eyes. "Beckett's married to my sister, Sierra."

"Who my mom works for," Finn added.

Noah grinned and reached out to ruffle Finn's hair. "Good to see you, kid. You ready to rip up some dunes?"

"Hell yeah," he said with a grin, but it faded when he looked at the auburn-haired and bearded man standing nearby on crutches. "Are you really gonna ride out there? With that?" he said, nodding at the guy's leg, the bottom of a metal external fixator showing under the cuff of his sweat pant leg.

Molly had told Ryder all about the incident just before Thanksgiving, when he'd been caught in a landslide and buried alive. The fractures in his lower leg had been so bad, he was lucky he would be able to walk again.

"Aye. Cannae hurt it much more than it already is, eh?" His brown eyes twinkled as he reached past Finn to shake with Ryder. "Name's Aidan, but everyone calls me Mac. Welcome."

"Thanks, good to meet you."

"Go grab your helmets," Beckett told them, his years as A-Team commander evident in his natural air of command. "We'll meet you out back."

Ryder, Jase and Finn chose helmets and had a quick safety briefing that Ryder got the feeling was abbreviated because the others knew the owner and were frequent customers. "How old are you, son?" the owner asked Finn.

"Sixteen, almost seventeen," Ryder answered before Finn could.

"He got a license?"

"Learner's permit."

The man grunted, eyeing both him and Finn. "You break it, you buy it," he said, and walked off.

"I don't have my learner's yet," Finn whispered to Ryder on the way out.

"Don't worry about it."

Outside, the others were already standing beside their buggies. Finn's eyes widened inside his helmet as he stared at something over Ryder's shoulder. "No way, you brought your *dog*?"

Ryder turned to find Beckett holding an old dog that looked like a basset mix of some kind, its long ears trailing far below its chin. It sat cradled in Beckett's arms, staring at them out of droopy, red-rimmed eyes, his woebegone expression almost comical.

"Hell yeah, I brought my dog," Beckett answered. "Walter loves it. He's an animal out there." With that he reached into a backpack at his feet and pulled out a small helmet.

Finn laughed. "He has his own helmet?"

"Course," Beckett answered, carefully pulling it over the dog's head. "And custom doggles, too." He tugged them down off the helmet into place over Walter's eyes, and Ryder saw the dog's tail wag. "All right, speed demon, in you go," he said, placing Walter in the passenger seat and strapping him in.

Everyone else was already in his buggy, so Ryder led Finn around to the tandem one they'd been assigned. He climbed behind the wheel while Finn rode shotgun, and everyone started his engine. Beckett raised a hand, gave the signal for forward, and pulled onto the path leading out to the dunes.

Ryder looked over at Finn, a grin tugging at his lips. "Ready?"

The kid's eyes were sparkling, his teeth showing as he smiled. "Ready."

He ducked out behind Beckett. Noah was behind them, then Mac, and Jase brought up the rear.

They climbed the worn path up the hill dotted with drifts of beach grasses, the sound and salty smell of the ocean growing stronger. At the crest, the full force of the wind hit them, cold and damp. Below them, the gray-green ocean churned with barely controlled violence, big rollers tipped with crests of white as they crashed onto the water-darkened sand. On either side of them, rolling dunes of golden sand stretched out as far as the eye could see.

Beckett turned his buggy hard left and opened up the throttle, engine growling and rear tires sending up sprays of sand. Ryder followed, chasing after him as Beckett tore down the far side of the first dune. All of a sudden, a shrill howl floated back to them.

"Is that *Walter*?" Finn called out over the noise of the wind and engine.

"Guess so," Ryder said with a laugh. He wouldn't have thought the old guy had that much life left in him.

Grinning, he floored it to catch up, managed to pull alongside Beckett for a moment. The howling started again as they sped down the next dune, and when Ryder glanced over, he couldn't believe his eyes.

Old Walter was strapped in the passenger seat, head flung back, mouth wide open as he continued baying, long ears flapping behind him in the wind, doggles protecting his eyes.

Ryder glanced at Finn in disbelief, and they both burst out laughing. "This is the *best*," Finn shouted over the noise, pulling out his phone to capture it on video.

Beckett allowed them to keep pace for a few moments to let Finn get some footage, then shot them a challenging grin and yanked the wheel hard left, cutting away again.

After that, the chase was on.

Jase, Noah and Mac all caught up to them, and the next thirty minutes was spent jockeying for position, everyone trying to get past Beckett. It wasn't easy, but Jase managed to edge past him on the way up another dune, cutting him off and forcing him to turn aside at the last instant.

"Yes!" Finn shouted, throwing his fist in the air as they took the lead.

Near the top Ryder blocked Beckett from cutting them

off, narrowly avoiding colliding with Jase, and kept the lead on the way to the crest. Once they reached it, he stopped suddenly, making the others swerve around them.

"What gives?" Noah called out, pausing next to them.

"Just switching drivers," Ryder answered, and began unbuckling his harness.

Finn stared at him, wide-eyed. "Are you serious? I really don't have my learner's yet."

"Have you driven a go-kart before?"

"Well, yeah…"

"Then you can drive this." He got out, walked around the front and gestured to Finn. "Come on, take the wheel and get moving before they lose us for good."

Finn hopped out, raced around and strapped in behind the wheel. Placing his hands at ten and two on the steering wheel, he shot Ryder an uncertain look. "You're *sure*?"

"I'm totally sure." If they were in danger of rolling, colliding or getting stuck, Ryder would grab the wheel and correct him.

"Okay, kid, let's see whatcha got," Beckett called out, stopped a little ways down the dune from them.

"Aye, lead the way, lad!" Mac shouted, waiting near Beckett's vehicle.

"Take this downslope at an angle," Ryder told Finn, pointing in the direction he wanted them to go with the blade of his hand. "Then head toward the water and run along the edge of the sand where it's wet."

Finn started off hesitantly. Ryder leaned back in his seat, hands on his thighs as he prepared to enjoy the ride. "There you go, you got it," he said in encouragement as Finn slowly gained some confidence and put on a bit more speed, driving at a gentle angle down the back of the dune.

The front wheels touched bottom, and the terrain smoothed out for a bit. "That's right, now head to the water."

Finn did as he said, driving more cautiously than Ryder would have guessed most teenage boys would have. "Awesome," Ryder said once they reached the flat part of the beach near the waterline. "Now, hit it."

Finn's fingers flexed around the wheel, then he hit the gas. They shot forward on the sand, the back end sliding slightly. "It's okay, you're good," Ryder called out to him when Finn immediately let up on the gas. "Just ease off a bit until you straighten out when that happens, then hit it again."

This time they ripped forward without slipping. He could tell the moment Finn began to relax and truly enjoy himself. A smile split his face and his shoulders lowered.

The other guys pulled up alongside them in a line to the left as they sped along, all making rude gestures. Even Walter's expression was smug as he stared at them. Then Mac suddenly shot out in front of them.

"Whoa!" Finn shouted, yanking right when Mac cut them off and whipped past.

"Scottish bastard," Ryder said with a grin. "You gonna let him get away with that?"

The look on Finn's face said he would have, but then an evil smile curved his lips and he pressed down on the accelerator once more. Ryder let out a whoop and laughed.

The other guys took turns playing with Finn, pretending to veer at him and make him turn away. But the kid kept going, making the rest of them get out of his way instead, and finally they pulled alongside Mac.

Ryder and Finn both looked over at the Scotsman, who was somehow driving with his busted leg propped up on the passenger seat. "Ready?" Ryder said to Finn.

"Yeah."

Grinning, Ryder held up a middle finger. "Now."

Finn shot forward to cut around him.

"Now shimmy the wheel back and forth!" Ryder told him. Finn did, and Ryder glanced back in time to see the rooster tail of wet sand that sprayed up over Mac.

"Haha, *yes*! Suck it!" Finn shouted, then cackled like a maniac as he took off down the beach.

Ryder laughed along with him, clapping him on the shoulder twice. "Good work, son. That'll teach him."

They spent the next hour trying to spray sand on each other, and Finn was confident enough to brave the dunes when Beckett turned inland and started back. By the time they returned to the rental place, covered in sand, it was starting to get dark, a layer of mist creeping over the dunes and clinging to the ground.

Ryder pulled off his helmet to look at Finn. "Have fun?"

"The *best*," the kid answered, face glowing with pride and the touch of the chilly wind as he unbuckled his harness. Once he climbed out, he received hearty thumps on the back and some hair ruffling from the other guys.

"How's the leg?" Jase asked Mac as the other man hobbled out to grab his crutches.

"Still broken, wee man," he said with a big smile, cheeks flushed from the cold.

"Does Tiana know you came out with us?" Noah asked dryly.

Mac's smile faded a little. "Not exactly. She thinks I'm gettin' the messages in town."

Everyone laughed, and Mac took it good-naturedly. He winked at Ryder. "I'm married to a pregnant redhead. What she doesn't know won't hurt me, aye?"

On the way back to Crimson Point they stopped for a quick snack at a place overlooking the water. Ryder felt the best he'd felt in a long time. He was comfortable with these men. Felt like they understood him. Because they all knew nobody went to war and came back the same.

He stuck to water, didn't even allow himself one beer, and was glad to find he wasn't tempted or envious that the others had drinks. His thoughts turned to Danae, anticipation stirring at the thought of spending more time with her, hopefully tonight. That he was preoccupied with seeing her again soon instead of craving a drink proved he wasn't too far-gone after all.

Jase stopped at Finn's house first. The level of disappointment that hit Ryder when he saw the driveway was empty surprised him.

"Thanks again," Finn said as he climbed out of the back seat. "That was awesome."

The smile on the kid's face was contagious. "It *was* awesome. And you did great," Ryder said.

"Yeah, but just remember—none of us are gonna take it easy on you next time," Jase teased. "No more rookie leeway."

It was only a twenty-second drive to Ryder's place, but it felt like longer, every yard taking him farther away from where he wanted to be. "He's a good kid," he murmured.

"Yeah, because he's got a great mom."

No kidding. Finn wouldn't realize it yet, but hopefully in time he would realize how good he had it, how amazing Danae had been to shoulder everything and raise him alone after losing Finn's dad. "Is she at work, maybe?"

"Maybe. More likely she ran out to grab some last-minute groceries or something." He stopped in the driveway, the front porch light on. It should have looked warm and welcoming, but the thought of being alone in there suddenly felt depressing. "You sure you don't wanna come over tonight?"

"Yeah. Thanks anyway."

"Okay, but if you change your mind just come by. Otherwise, see you tomorrow morning."

Christmas Day. "Yeah, what time?"

"We'll probably be up by six at the latest. So say, eight?"

"Eight it is."

Inside the cottage, he hung up his jacket, his mind on Danae. He was aware of the time constraint he was facing with her, but there was something about her that drew him, and he was already more interested in her than he had been in anyone for a damn long time. He would feel things out over the next few days, see if she was even interested in him or any kind of romantic relationship again.

Today had ended a helluva lot better than it had started. He'd needed to get out and do something fun, and the guys had been great. Spending time with Finn and seeing that big smile on the kid's face was the best part.

He pulled out his phone when it chimed with a text, hoping ridiculously hard that it was Danae, checking in with him. Giving him an excuse to go back over there and see her again.

Instead, the message made his heart lurch and the blood drain from his face.

Hi, Captain Locke. It's Alison, Roy's wife. I just wanted to say Merry Christmas, and that we're all thinking of you. I know the next few days will be hard on you too. You'll be in our prayers. Take care.

The message was kind. Far kinder than he deserved, yet the words were like a KA-BAR to the heart.

His chest constricted, making it suddenly hard to breathe. He winced. God, he was a selfish asshole. She and eleven other families were grieving horribly right now, struggling with the absence of their fallen Marines, and he'd been out spending the day having fun to make himself feel better.

The words on screen began to blur, his mind carrying him back in time against his will to the worst day of his life. To the explosions, the rattle of gunfire. The wall of heat as the blast wave threw him backward. The acrid burn of cordite and scorched metal in his nose.

He'd been far enough away to escape any real damage. But his men hadn't been as fortunate.

Cold sweat popped out on his face, his back, under his arms as his heart rate accelerated. He was trapped back in time, staring down into a pair of fear and pain-glazed green eyes. Alison's husband. A mortar fragment had gone right through his body armor, piercing his chest.

He gazed up at Ryder, terror and agony contorting his face. "Don't let me die," he'd begged in a ragged voice Ryder could still hear. "Cap, don't let me die."

He had done everything in his power to save that Marine, and the others. Had stayed next to him on the helo back to base, squeezing his hand tight and talking to him until his voice gave out.

Alison's husband had made it to the base hospital. He made it through surgery.

Only to die within hours of coming off the table.

Ryder blinked and his gaze refocused, the letters of the message becoming clear once more. *Thank you*, he made himself type back. *Y'all are in my prayers too.*

Not that that did anyone a damn bit of good.

He set the phone down on the coffee table, feeling wooden, a crushing pressure squeezing his ribcage. The terrible silence of the empty cottage settled around him, thick and oppressive.

You shouldn't be here. Shouldn't still be alive when they're all dead. You were their Captain. They counted on you.

He'd made a mistake. Had to have missed something in the intel report prior to leaving for the op. How the hell else could he have taken his men straight into an ambush?

He shot up from the couch, a wild, frantic feeling tearing through him. He wanted to scream. Throw something. Put his fist through the wall.

He wanted to hurt. He *deserved* to hurt.

He couldn't stand it. Couldn't handle the crushing guilt and responsibility. But there was nothing he could do to stop it now. Nothing except…

Without even realizing where he was going, he found himself ripping open the pantry door. He shot an unsteady hand out to grab the bottle he couldn't resist a moment longer, desperate for relief. To escape the guilt and pain.

His fingers shook as he opened it, tears scalding his eyes. As the first big swallow burned down his tight throat, his mind had already embraced the oblivion awaiting him.

NINE

The look on Josh's face when Kyle handed him the large, wrapped box was priceless. "You said we weren't buying for each other this year," Josh said, taking the present anyway.

"I know. That's why I'm giving it to you tonight instead of tomorrow, so it's technically not a Christmas present."

One corner of Josh's mouth lifted as he shook the box gently. He looked just like he had when he was a little kid, sheer excitement dancing in his eyes. Back when their mom had been alive and they'd still celebrated Christmas. God knew they hadn't during the years they'd been forced to live under their father's roof. "It's pretty heavy. What did you get?"

"Open it and find out."

Josh tore off the paper and opened the tape holding the cardboard box together. His expression turned to shock as he stared at the contents, then he lifted his astonished gaze to Kyle. "No."

Kyle grinned. "Yep."

"No," Josh breathed, hurriedly pulling out the laptop, his

smile almost as contagious as his laugh. "You asshole," he said, shooting Kyle a mock glare.

"That's me. Asshole King."

"Who lives on Blowhole Bottom," Josh teased, then sobered and shook his head. "Guessing you didn't steal this?"

He chuckled. "Nope. Paid full damn price for it, so treat it with respect."

"I will." Josh stared at the closed laptop, smoothed a hand over its shiny silver surface. "These are expensive. I thought we were tightening our belts for the house."

"We are. But if you're heading to college after that, you're gonna need a decent laptop. Besides, this'll help you get started on your applications."

A smile spread across Josh's face. "You're the best, man. Asshole King or not." He got up, came over and caught him in a back-slapping hug. "I'll pay you back."

"Nah, forget it. You deserve this." Deserved a hell of a lot more than Kyle had been able to give him until recently.

He sipped his coffee and watched his brother set up the laptop, enjoying Josh's obvious excitement, and feeling a welcome sense of hope. For the first time in forever, the clouds appeared to be about to lift for them.

Josh was smart. Had so much damn untapped potential and could easily be the computer engineer he'd always dreamed about becoming if granted the opportunity. Money would buy him that.

The rest of the world looked at them and only saw a couple of thugs. But that was going to change after a few more jobs, at least for Josh.

His little brother was going to leave this thug life behind and make something of himself. That was enough for Kyle.

DANAE CHECKED her phone again for what felt like the tenth time in the past hour. Still no response from Ryder to her text asking how the day had gone for him, Finn was holed up in his room online with his buddies, and she was sitting out here alone on Christmas Eve.

Determined to do something productive, she got up and went into the kitchen to prep tomorrow's breakfast—a casserole made with cut-up croissants, ham, cheese, eggs and veggies. She assembled two of them, a larger one for her and Finn, and a smaller one for Ryder.

Taking him a casserole wouldn't make her look desperate, right?

She berated herself. It was a freaking casserole, not a marriage proposal. He would be going to see Molly and family in the morning, but even if he didn't cook it tomorrow, he could save it for another day.

She covered them with tinfoil, popped the large one into the fridge to sit overnight, then put on her coat, boots and gloves and stepped outside with the smaller casserole. Broken clouds hung above, revealing patches of indigo sky, sparkling with stars, the moon making brief appearances as the wind pushed the clouds across its pale face.

Turning the corner at the end of her street, she saw light coming from the windows at the front of the rental cottage, and Ryder's rental vehicle parked in the driveway. He had to be home. Sleeping maybe?

She rang the doorbell and waited, ordering herself to stop being nervous. There was nothing to be nervous about. Even so, butterflies fluttered around in her belly.

When he didn't answer, she rapped on the door twice, then stood there for another minute. She couldn't leave the casserole on the porch. The raccoons, foxes and coyotes in the area would be at it long before Ryder found it.

Just as she turned around and started down the stairs, she caught sight of a shadow moving across the length of the living room window. Her pulse kicked when the lock on the door turned. Ryder pulled the door open, and the greeting smile froze on her lips.

He leaned against the doorframe, squinting and blinking at her. And she could smell the strong, cloying scent of booze on him from where she stood. "Ah, hi," she said cautiously. "Is...this a bad time?"

"Kind of, yeah."

He was drunk, she realized with a start. And he didn't look happy about it. She'd better leave. "I just brought you a breakfast casserole to pop in the oven."

"Oh. Thanks." He straightened and reached for it.

She handed it over, and her heart sank when their eyes met. Pain. Pain and self-disgust. "Are...you okay?" she couldn't help asking.

He stared at her for a second or two, doing that slow blink, then frowned slightly. "Yeah. You wanna come in?"

His accent was stronger than normal. "Umm..." She should probably just go home and let him sleep it off. But that look in his eyes stopped her. Something haunted and lonely, two things she understood all too well.

She couldn't walk away if he was hurting. What the hell had happened after dropping Finn off? Finn had said they had a great time. "Sure, just for a minute."

She took off her boots on the rug inside the door while he carried the casserole to the kitchen and put it in the fridge. "You want anything?" he asked her.

"No, I'm good." But he wasn't. A half-empty bottle of Jack and an empty tumbler sat on the coffee table.

She eyed him as he came back out to the living room and lowered himself onto the couch with a sigh. She tried to shift the mood to something more upbeat. "Finn showed me some pictures from the dune-buggying. I especially loved the video of Walter." She paused, trying to read him. "Seemed like you guys had a great time out there."

"Yeah, it was fun."

So what the hell had happened between then and now? Finn had said they'd gone for a snack after, but something must have happened, because Ryder had come home and dived into a bottle. "Pretty sure that's the most fun Finn's had in three years, so thank you."

"No worries. He's a great kid."

She tilted her head, studying him, unable to stand seeing him like this. "What's wrong?"

He averted his gaze. "I'm drunk."

"I see that. Did…something happen?"

His face tightened, his shoulders tensing beneath the thin cotton of his T-shirt. He looked worn-down all of a sudden, and it worried her.

He was quiet so long she didn't think he would answer, but then he finally spoke. "Got a message from the widow of one of my Marines."

"Oh." She waited a beat, continuing when he didn't elaborate. "Was it…bad?"

"No." He let out a deep breath. "That would have been easier though."

His words made no sense, but it was clear whatever had been said weighed heavy on him. And as the silence grew, she made up her mind to do something to help him. "It's nice out. Feel like going for a walk, maybe?" she asked gently. "Get some fresh air, clear your head a bit?"

Ryder sat up taller, ran a hand over his mouth and goatee, and finally looked over at her. She braced herself for rejection, then a burst of surprise hit her when he nodded. "Yeah, that sounds good."

While he got his coat and boots on, she quietly put the cap back on the bottle of Jack and put it away in a corner of the kitchen, then put his glass in the dishwasher. He was at the door when she came back, and she could see the shame in his eyes. "Thanks," he muttered.

"No problem." How often did he do this? She'd never heard Molly say anything about her cousin having a drinking problem. "Ready to go?"

The cool, damp air felt good on her face as they walked side by side up the moonlit street together. "There's a trail that leads through the woods to a scenic overlook about half a mile west. That sound okay?" she asked.

"Sure."

She took out the mini flashlight from her right coat pocket and pushed her left hand into the other one. They stepped into the entrance of the trail, the tall treetops sighing as they swayed overhead. Hints of cedar and fir carrying on the wind, mixing with the rich scent of damp soil.

They walked in silence for a bit, the beam of her flashlight lighting the path lined by evergreen sword ferns and the glistening, holly-shaped leaves of the Oregon grape bushes, water droplets on the deep green leaves making them sparkle like diamonds.

The silence began to make her uncomfortable. Danae glanced at him, wondering if she should ask him something to start the conversation, or whether to just stay silent. "What did the message say, can I ask?"

"She wished me a merry Christmas and said I'm in her prayers." He let out a short, bitter laugh. "I'm in *her* prayers," he repeated, as if he couldn't fathom why.

Or more like he felt he didn't deserve them.

Dozens of questions crowded her mind, but she kept silent as they followed the length of the winding path. If nothing else, the cold, fresh air would be clearing away the haze of alcohol by now. And at least he wasn't alone anymore.

Near the end of the trail, over the sound of the wind in the treetops, the ceaseless roar of the ocean began to seep in. "The overlook is just up there to the left," she told him, switching off her flashlight.

The moment they stepped out of the shelter of the trees, the wind rushed over them in strong, cold gusts. A break in the clouds revealed a stream of moonlight that painted the ground silver. The well-worn path widened, curving along the edge of the high cliff that overlooked the sea.

Far below, off in the distance, the town was nestled against the natural bay in the coastline, its lights glittering in the darkness. Huge waves crashed onto the rocks below them, tall, curling rollers that exploded into white foam that glowed in the moonlight.

The wild, rugged gorgeousness called to her, lifting her spirits. She was just sorry Ryder wasn't in the right state of mind to enjoy it fully.

He stopped next to her at a bench perched near the cliff's edge, the low, wrought-iron fence in front of it warning people to keep their distance, and sat. He stared out at the view for a long while, then finally spoke, his voice barely carrying over the wind and sound of the waves below.

"The woman who contacted me, her husband was killed with a lot of other Marines on a mission during my last combat tour overseas."

Oh, no... Hiding a wince, she looked at him, the left side of his face bathed in moonlight. He was hurting pretty bad, and that seemed like it hadn't been an easy admission for him. If he needed someone to talk to, she was willing to listen.

He kept looking straight ahead, a restless, agitated energy pulsing from him even though they were sitting still. "They were under my command. My responsibility."

Her insides tightened, sensing that whatever he was about to tell her was ugly. Raw. And, for him, still fresh.

"I was there when it happened."

She stayed silent, watching him. Aching for him. She hated to see him hurting, and today being Christmas Eve made it all the worse.

A muscle in his lean jaw flexed. "I was the only one who wasn't severely wounded or killed that day."

Sympathy swelled, and before she could second-guess herself, she pulled her hand from her pocket and curved her fingers around his forearm in silent support. The muscles tensed like steel beneath the sleeve of his coat, but he didn't pull away.

"My last contract finished a couple weeks after, and I didn't re-up. But I guess I... Guess I haven't been handling it that well since. Been drinking too much lately. I stopped before I came here. Thought I could kick it on my own. But that message tonight brought it all back. And I was weak," he finished, his voice flat, thick with self-disgust.

"Have you talked to anyone about it?" she asked, her voice just loud enough to be heard over the wind.

"Just you."

Oh, man. "Ryder, you can't be expected to have to carry all that alone. Have you thought about working with a therapist?"

He shook his head. "Can't risk any of this stuff winding up on record somewhere. I've got special security clearance because of the clients I work with, and I need to keep it if I want to stay at my job." He shifted on the bench, her hand still resting on his arm. "I'm okay while I'm working. It keeps me focused. But tonight…"

"You were alone, and it's Christmas Eve," she finished.

He turned his head toward her. Their gazes connected, and she saw a myriad of emotions flicker through his eyes. Guilt. Shame. Pain. A plea, to help make it stop.

She wished she knew how to help him.

"Yeah," he muttered finally.

She wouldn't press him for more or lecture him about what he should do to get help, or what kind of help he should seek. Instead, she squeezed his arm and looked deep into his eyes, wanting him to see that she understood on at least some level. "I'm sorry you're hurting. That kind of pain must be really hard to live with."

He held her stare, his body almost preternaturally still, surprise flashing in the depths of his eyes. And it might have been stupid of her, or just a fanciful illusion caused by the moonlight, but she swore she felt a connection kindle between them.

A cold gust of wind whipped over them, rushing down the zipped-up neck of her coat. She shivered and released his arm. "Should we head back before we freeze?"

He nodded and got up, walking right next to her on the way to the trailhead. "What happened to your husband?" he finally asked.

"He became a firefighter after he left the Marines. There was a three-alarm fire at an apartment complex one night just a few weeks after Finn's twelfth birthday. He was inside when the roof in that area collapsed. His guys managed to dig him free and get him out of the building, but his injuries were too severe. He died the next day." It would never not hurt, but it was easier for her to talk about now, and especially since Ryder had just opened up to her.

"I'm sorry."

She nodded. "Thanks. He was a good man."

Neither of them spoke again on the way back through the woods, but by the time they arrived at her house his eyes were totally clear, all signs of alcohol gone, and he at least seemed more at peace.

She faced him at the side door and gave him a soft smile, hoping the walk and talking to her had helped him at least a little. "Well, I hope you get some sleep tonight." Acting on impulse, she stepped closer and reached out to hug him, her arms going around his ribs.

He stilled for a heartbeat, then returned the embrace, pulling her flush to his chest to hold her. Close and tight, his cheek pressed to the side of her head.

Her pulse kicked, heat and desire pooling inside her at the feel of that long, lean and powerful body pressed to the front of her, the possessiveness of it making her bite back a groan.

She was tall but he had her by at least four inches or more, and yet their bodies were perfectly aligned. He turned his head slightly, his jaw now touching the side of her face, his short goatee prickling her cheek. His nose nuzzled her temple, his warm exhalations fanning her suddenly sensitive skin, unleashing a wave of heat and a cascade of goosebumps.

She pulled away and stepped back, trying to rein in her reaction, and gave him another smile. "Sleep tight."

He nodded, one side of his mouth lifting as he stepped back off the stairs. "You too."

She had a feeling she wouldn't sleep much at all. And that she would be thinking about him long after she crawled into bed alone.

TEN

Yo. Dude. You there?

Finn pushed his phone away on his desk, mentally rolling his eyes as he kept playing the computer game with two of his friends back in Seattle. Paul had been bugging him all damn night to get together.

He hadn't bothered responding, because he wanted to put some distance between them, and anything he said would seem like a stupid excuse and possibly make him seem weak.

"After this passage, turn left, then right twice," he instructed his friends through the mic in his headset. His character was team leader—a Marine Raider lieutenant, whose rank and unit he idolized—and their platoon was conducting a high-stakes recon mission.

His phone kept buzzing with new messages every couple minutes. Irritated, he finally glanced at it to see what Paul wanted now.

Where the hell are you?? It's important, I need to talk to you.

He ignored it, giving his full attention to his friends and the mission on screen. Might seem dumb to most people, but playing this kind of game was the closest he could come to connecting with his dad now.

Finn missed him so bad, especially right now, during the holidays. There were so many things he wished he'd asked his dad about his military service. He'd always just assumed he would have lots of time to ask them.

His phone rang, startling him. Paul. He hit decline and kept playing.

More messages began to pop up, one after the other. Annoying, but as he read them, he began to grow uneasy.

Are you brushing me off?

Grant's been asking about you. Wondering why you've gone dark.

He's pissed. Thinks you might narc on him.

You can't narc on him, man. You don't want to cross him. Or Victor.

Who was Victor, the stepdad? Finn wouldn't narc on Grant, or whoever Victor was. He was smarter than that. He just wanted clear of that shit, and if Paul couldn't pull away from that crew, then he got the axe too.

But as he read the latest text sent from an unknown number, the blood drained from his face.

You better not talk about us to anyone. Or about what you heard or saw. We're watching you. If you talk, we'll know. And then you'll pay.

It was accompanied by a gif of a shadowy figure pulling back the edge of a jacket to reveal a pistol.

What the fuck? He grabbed his phone, distantly aware of his friends' voices in his headset. "Finn. Yo, team leader, what gives?"

"I gotta go," he blurted, and set his headphones aside, staring at his phone. That last text had to be from Grant, or someone connected with him. What did he mean, they were watching him? *Who* did he mean?

Unnerved, he got up and crossed to his window, overlooking the front yard, and pulled the edge of the curtain back a few inches. The decorations he and Ryder had put up on the lawn and trees glowed in the darkness.

The street was empty. There was no one out there that he could see. But the woods across the road were a perfect hiding spot for anyone wanting to set up recon on his house.

An icy tendril crept up his spine and he let the curtain fall. He was suddenly thankful it was Christmas break, so he wouldn't have to see the guys at school until things had settled down.

He copied the text and picture and sent it to Paul. *WTF???* he added.

Paul tried calling him again. Finn refused to answer.

You gotta talk to him. Tell him you're cool, Paul texted moments later.

I'm out, he responded, then blocked what he assumed was Grant's number but saved the text, just in case. What a psycho.

A warning buzz hummed in the pit of his stomach. He thought of his mom, oblivious of what had happened, and either on the couch watching a movie or reading in bed. He didn't want anything bad to happen because he'd been hanging out with Paul and Grant. Hadn't meant to put himself in a dangerous position.

Unable to shake the worry, he left his room and walked down the hall, relieved when he saw his mom cooking in the kitchen. She looked up with a smile from where she stood in front of the stove, whisking something in a pot, her cheeks bright pink. "Just took a walk with Ryder and I'm half-frozen. Want some hot chocolate?"

"Sure," he said, playing it casual. It was his responsibility to make sure she was safe. His dad would have expected that of him, and Finn wouldn't let him or his mom down.

"Feel like watching a movie with me? Maybe Elf? It's tradition."

He shrugged. "Okay."

"Really?" She looked thrilled. "I'll make us some buttered popcorn too. Why don't you go get the movie lined up? Be there in a few minutes."

He went into the living room, his eyes automatically going to the large picture window behind the couch. Across the darkened road, the woods looked black and menacing.

Telling himself he was making a big deal out of nothing, he sat on one end of the couch and got the movie ready while popcorn popped in the background. A few minutes later his mom came out with a tray holding two steaming mugs, and a big bowl of fluffy popcorn.

"Marshmallows in the hot chocolates, and extra melted butter on the popcorn. Because calories don't count in December," she told him happily, handing over a napkin before sitting beside him.

The truth was, he'd been dreading Christmas for a while now, the loss of his dad sharper somehow. But even if he'd never admit it, it was kind of nice to sit here with his mom and do this like they used to when he was younger. He liked that sense of tradition and doing things they had done while his dad was alive.

He rested the hot mug on his thigh and started the movie, digging into the buttered popcorn with his free hand. They'd seen Elf what felt like a hundred times, but his mom still laughed in exactly the same spots as she always had, and he found himself grinning a couple times too.

He was so engrossed in the movie, his back to the

picture window, that he only belatedly heard the roar of an engine as a vehicle raced up their street. It was so out of place he turned his head to look out at the street and spotted the dark shape of a vehicle hurtling past the house, its lights off.

He jumped as two loud bangs rang out, sloshing hot chocolate all over as his mug tumbled to the rug.

His mom cried out, whirling to face the window, but Finn grabbed her, shoving her down on the floor and flattening himself beside her, his heart thudding wildly.

Gunshots. Holy fuck!

The vehicle screeched to a stop somewhere up the street. Finn could hear it turning around with a squeal of its tires on the damp road, then it sped back past their house. He tensed, hand on his mom's back to keep her flat, bracing for more shots.

Thankfully, the vehicle sped past and the sound of it faded into silence.

Shaken, he didn't dare move as his mom turned her head around to stare at him, wide-eyed. "Did they just *shoot* at us?"

He didn't answer, his heart a jackhammer in his ears, waiting. Praying the vehicle wouldn't come back.

A minute passed as they lay flat on the floor. Then another. And another.

Finally, his mom pushed up into a sitting position. He got to his feet, his legs strangely weak. Holy shit. Someone had just shot at their house. And he had a sickening feeling he knew who it had been.

Suddenly someone pounded on the side door, almost making him jump out of his skin.

"Danae? It's Ryder. Open up."

"Oh, God," she breathed, and rushed for the door. Finn

followed, fear crawling through him. He wanted to be wrong about what had happened, but he was afraid he wasn't.

Ryder stormed inside, scanning both of them, in full operator mode, like he was ready to take on anyone threatening them. Finn felt safer already. "Are you both okay?"

"Yeah," Finn managed as his mom nodded.

Sheriff Buchanan appeared behind him in the open doorway. "Y'all okay?"

"Yes," his mom said, wrapping her arms around herself. "We were sitting on the couch, watching a movie. Then the car raced up and someone took a couple shots."

The sheriff's gaze cut straight to Finn. "Did you see anything?"

His stomach grabbed tight. He'd seen enough to convince him that it could have been Grant's vehicle, but he was too afraid to say and have to admit everything that had happened. "No. It was dark, and the car didn't have lights on."

The sheriff's face was grim. "Stay here while we check it out." He glanced at Ryder and the men disappeared out the door, shutting it behind them.

His mom stood in the foyer, a hand pressed to her chest. "God." She crossed to him and put her hands on his shoulders, her eyes searching his anxiously. "That was so damn scary. What kind of lunatic drives around shooting at houses like that?"

He didn't resist her hug, actually welcomed it, relieved that neither of them had been hurt.

She took his hand and took him to her room, where they both perched on the edge of the bed and waited for the others. About twenty minutes later the sheriff and Ryder announced themselves and came in. Finn and his mom met them in the hall.

"Mid to large-size SUV from the looks of the tire marks,"

the sheriff told them, Ryder at his shoulder. "Did a hard one-eighty between your house and ours. No bullet holes in your house and no broken windows, but I'll take a better look tomorrow when it's light."

"Thank you," his mom said. "So you think it was just random?"

The sheriff and Ryder both looked at Finn for an instant, and his heart nearly stopped. "Do *you* think it was random?" the sheriff asked.

Did they suspect it had something to do with him or people he'd been hanging out with? For an instant he nearly blurted out the truth. "Yeah."

"No problems with anyone recently, maybe at school or anything like that?"

"No." His pulse was hammering in his throat, and he was convinced the sheriff could see it.

Then Sheriff Buchanan nodded once. "I'll know more once I get a better look in the daylight. You both okay to stay here tonight? You're welcome to stay with Poppy and me if you want."

"Or with me," Ryder offered.

Part of Finn wanted to accept and go to Ryder's. But he didn't want to seem scared, and sure as hell didn't want to admit his suspicions, because it would implicate him too and his mom would be disappointed. That was the last thing he wanted to go through on Christmas Eve.

"Thanks, but we're okay here. Right, Mom?" he asked.

She hesitated, then nodded. "Yeah, we're okay. But thank you both."

"If you change your mind, let me know," Ryder told her, watching her in an intense way that Finn picked up on. "I'll come get you."

She saw them both out, bolted the door, then released a

deep breath and faced him. "On that note, I need a hot bath. And possibly a large glass of wine." She strode for the kitchen and wet a cloth under the tap, and he realized she was going to clean up the mess in the living room where he'd spilled his drink.

Finn took the cloth from her. "I'll clean up. You go have your bath."

The startled smile she flashed him made his heart hurt, guilt twisting in his belly. "Okay, thanks. Love you. And I know you're a big, strong guy now, but if you want to bunk with me later, you can just crawl in whenever." She gave him a quick hug and headed for her room.

Finn set to work in the living room, scrubbing the spilled hot chocolate and melted butter out of the rug and off the couch. Every so often he glanced out the window, still a bit worried the vehicle would come back.

Now that the fear and shock had passed, he was getting angry. That had been so fucked up. He'd never imagined getting involved with a dangerous group of kids here in this dead-end town in the middle of nowhere.

If Grant had fired those shots, he'd done it as a clear warning to keep his mouth shut. And Finn couldn't shake the awful feeling that it wouldn't be the last one.

ELEVEN

As predicted, it didn't take Savannah long to warm up to him.

Within twenty minutes of Ryder arriving at Jase and Molly's place on Christmas morning, Savannah was racing around the room, squealing in delight as her parents handed out present after present. She looked at each one for approximately three seconds after she opened it, then dumped it and ran off to do something else in her little reindeer socks, curls bouncing.

"You guys went all out, huh," Ryder remarked in amusement. He'd never seen so many presents for a single kid, especially such a young one. He was glad to be here though, to spend more time with his cousin and get to know Jase and Savannah. Growing up, he and Molly had spent most holidays together with their moms, so this felt nostalgic.

"Yeah, okay, so we went a little overboard this year with the gifts," Molly said with a laugh. She was still in her robe and had dark circles under her eyes, but her smile was pure maternal love.

He hadn't slept much last night either, unable to turn off

that innate part of him demanding he keep Danae and Finn safe, and be ready if that shooter came back. They hadn't, but it still bothered him that it had happened in a small town.

It seemed way too coincidental to be random. If it hadn't been random, why had they been targeted? An angry patient from Danae's clinic? Something to do with Finn?

"My God, look at this mess," Jase muttered in disbelief, staring at all the new toys lying discarded by the Christmas tree, and the wreckage of torn wrapping paper and boxes littering the living room floor. "Where the hell are we gonna put all this stuff, anyway? We've already filled the two sets of new shelving and storage cabinets I built."

"I dunno. Somewhere." Molly bent to grab one of the few remaining presents under the tree, pushed to her feet and handed it to Ryder with a smile. "For you."

He put on a light scowl as he accepted it. "You said we weren't doing presents."

"We're not. Just this one."

He tore off the bright red, holly-sprigged wrapping paper to find a printed photo album with the title: COUSINS ARE CHILDHOOD PLAYMATES WHO GROW UP TO BE FOREVER FRIENDS.

The cover shot was of him and Molly at her wedding to Carter years ago. Her in a gorgeous white gown, Ryder in his dress blues, their arms around each other, big smiles on their faces. "You made this for me?" he asked, and began looking through it. Must have been a lot of work, digging out these old photos and compiling them into a digital album.

"I did. Was feeling sentimental."

She'd done it in chronological order, starting when they were infants. The first picture was of them in diapers together, taken outside during the summer, chocolate ice cream smeared all over their faces. From there it chronicled various family holidays and get togethers throughout their childhood into their teens.

"Oh, man, I haven't seen any of these before." He couldn't wipe the smile from his face as he took them all in. There were a lot of happy memories, and he cherished them. Cherished Molly and her big heart.

He vowed to himself to make a better effort at staying close after this. The title on the album was exactly right. She was more than a cousin. She was one of his most trusted friends.

The number of photos tapered off sharply once he graduated and joined the Corps, because they hadn't seen much of each other after that, but she'd included pictures of him in his cammies that he'd sent her during various deployments.

At the end there was a picture of her holding newborn Savannah in the hospital shortly after giving birth, with his face grinning on the screen of a tablet in her free hand. He remembered that video call vividly, and how proud Molly had been to show him her daughter despite her exhaustion.

"This is amazing, Moll," he said, touched that she would make him this keepsake.

"I know." She hugged him. "Love you."

He squeezed her hard. "Love you too. And I'm gonna stay in touch more. Make sure I get out here to see you more often."

Molly gave him a soft smile. "I'd love that."

Apparently, not too fond of sharing her mother's attention, Savannah took a running leap and jumped on him. He laughed, catching her before her knee could do any damage to sensitive areas in his groin. "Is someone's nose out of joint?" The glare she was giving him was priceless—and pure Molly.

"Not *my* little angel," Molly said, reaching out to tickle her daughter's ribs. Savannah belly chuckled, then Molly scooped her up and blew noisy raspberries against her little neck. Shrieks and baby laughter filled the room, and there was no person on earth who wouldn't have smiled at that.

The happy, innocent sound, the cozy scene in front of the decorated tree, being here on Christmas morning with his cousin and her family... He hadn't realized how much he'd needed this visit. It felt like a lifetime away from where he'd been last night after he'd received that text.

His mind circled back to Danae, as it had since their walk last night.

I'm sorry you're hurting.

No one had ever said that to him before. No one but Chase had taken the time to simply acknowledge that he was in pain, without prying or pressing for more. It meant a lot to him that Danae had done just that.

She could have walked away as soon as she'd realized he was drunk. Instead, she had seen instantly what was really going on—that it was a coping mechanism to cover up an underlying issue. He was embarrassed that she'd seen him drunk. Mad at himself for succumbing so easily and giving in to the moment of weakness.

He'd been so sure he could do this by himself. Now he realized it was time to get help. He couldn't allow ego and pride to keep him stuck in this vicious cycle. He was also thankful Molly didn't know what had happened, and that Danae didn't seem the type to tell her.

When Molly stopped tickling her, Savannah whined and rubbed her fists against her eyes. "And there we go—post-Christmas gift-opening crash imminent," Jase said, busy stuffing torn paper into a garbage bag.

"Yep, and for Mom and Dad, too," Molly said, covering a yawn. "Let's get this video call done with the Meemaws before this little angel goes down for the count."

They called Molly's mom first, then Ryder's. With both sisters on the split screen, huge smiles on their almost identical faces as they talked and laughed and made a fuss over Savannah, it felt almost like the Christmases he and Molly had enjoyed growing up.

After the call ended Ryder stood, not wanting to make Molly and Jase feel like they needed to stay up and visit when they were all clearly beat. Besides, he was impatient to see Danae again. "I'm gonna head out anyway. Y'all go have a nap."

"Okay. Sure we can't talk you into coming to dinner at Beckett and Sierra's later?" Molly asked, shifting Savannah onto her hip.

"Thanks, but I'm gonna check in on Danae and Finn, see what they're up to tonight."

Molly raised her eyebrows. "Oh, really."

He smothered a chuckle. "I like them." Danae especially. It was impossible not to, and impossible not to respect the life she was trying to make for her and her son. And it was getting harder and harder to remember that he should keep his distance from her, since he was leaving in less than a week.

"I like 'em too." She gave him a speculative look, then leaned over and kissed his cheek. "Call you later."

"Bye, Savannah-banana." He ruffled her dark curls, shook Jase's hand, and left.

The sun was out, bright, golden beams of light flooding through the clouds as he drove back toward the water and up the hill to Danae's neighborhood. Everything was so green here still.

Finn opened the front door as Ryder was getting out of his rental. He was wearing a bright red Santa hat with flashing lights on it. "Merry Christmas."

"Merry Christmas," Ryder answered with a big smile,

glad to see Finn getting into the spirit of the holiday. That had to make Danae happy. "Come on in."

"You sure I'm not intruding?"

"I'm sure. Got a new gaming system I was just setting up. You wanna play?"

"Sounds good." He stopped on the rug inside the front door, his gaze fixing on Danae as she stepped out of the kitchen, wiping her hands on a dishtowel. She had on an emerald-green sweater that hugged her breasts and trim waist, and black tights that outlined her long, gorgeous legs in a way that made his tongue stick to the roof of his mouth.

Lord have mercy, those legs and the things he'd like to do between them...

"Hi. Merry Christmas," he said once he unstuck his tongue.

"Same to you. Were you over at Molly's?"

"Just got back. Savannah's worn them all out, so they're hitting their racks, and then going over to Beckett's place for dinner later."

She cocked her head. "And you're not?"

"No." He'd feel weird, showing up at a big Christmas dinner like that.

"Want to have dinner with us instead?"

The smile started in his heart and spread across his face. "Love to."

Her smile flashed, making her gorgeous, pale eyes sparkle. "Great, then you can help me in the kitchen. You too, Finn. You'll have plenty of time to game after."

It was the best Christmas afternoon he'd spent in forever. The three of them worked together to get everything prepped, following Danae's instructions—or orders. She was like a hot drill sergeant, and he got a kick out of seeing that side of her.

By the time everything was in the oven or setting up in

the fridge, Finn was dying to get to his new system. Ryder helped wash dishes, then played with him for an hour. When Finn's friends came online, Ryder left to find Danae.

She looked up from her spot in the living room couch in front of the window and lowered her ereader to her lap, those long, tights-encased legs stretched out before her and a pair of fuzzy pink socks on her feet. He was reminded again of the shooter last night, and how easily she and Finn could have been hit if the bullets had come through the glass.

"Guess we won't see Finn for a while now, huh?" she remarked with a wry twist of her lips.

"Nope, he's about to go into gaming hibernation." He took the seat on the end of the couch rather than sit across from her, wanting to be close but not crowd her. "Get any sleep last night?"

"Took me a while to fall asleep initially, but I wound up getting more than I thought I would."

"You should have stayed with me. Or let me bunk here on the couch." He'd wanted to but hadn't wanted to overstep.

"It was fine. They didn't come back, and Noah was over first thing this morning to check things again. The security camera caught the make and model of the vehicle, but not the plate. He found two casings on the road, but not the bullets themselves." She studied him. "What about you? How did you sleep?"

"Okay." He rubbed his hand over the back of his neck. This had been bothering him all day. "Listen, about last night. I'm sorry you saw me like that."

She shrugged like it was no big deal. "Just as long as you're okay."

He wasn't, though. And he was beginning to come to grips with that. "Thank you for listening."

"Anytime."

God, she was sweet. And sexy. It was taking all his willpower not to draw her close and kiss her the way he'd been imagining. "I'm going to talk to someone."

Her delighted smile warmed him from the inside out. "That's fantastic, good for you."

He was dying to kiss her. To lean forward, cup the side of her face in his hand and taste those soft, pink lips. Pull her flush to his body, feel her melt into him, and drown in her.

The only thing that held him in check was the time limit they were facing. She'd been through so much, had managed to rebuild her life after losing her husband, and he didn't want to cause her even a moment's more pain by starting something he couldn't stay and finish.

A timer started beeping in the kitchen. Danae set her ereader aside and stood. "That's the turkey. Guess we should give Finn the twenty-minute warning."

"I'll get him." Chances were good Finn wouldn't give him any attitude.

Finn came willingly enough, and by the time he got to the table everything was ready and waiting. All three of them sat down together, Danae said a quick grace, then everyone dug in.

Roast turkey, sour cream mashed potatoes, veggies baked in cheese sauce with a crispy breadcrumb topping, homemade chunky cranberry sauce, the best stuffing he'd ever tasted, plus gravy and hot, buttered rolls. The food was incredible, the company even better.

After a fruit and nut salad mixed with whipped cream, he sent Danae into the living room to enjoy more of her book, and coerced Finn into helping him clean everything up.

When he finished wiping the stove and countertops forty minutes later and turned around, Danae was standing in the opening, grinning at them. "Thanks, boys. We need to leave soon, by the way—I told Sierra we'd be at her place by seven for pie."

Finn groaned, shoulders slumping. "Do I *have* to go?"

"Not you. I was talking to Ryder."

Those piercing, pale blue eyes held him prisoner. He hadn't wanted to go, but if she was asking him there was no way he could say no. "Sure, I'll go with you."

Her lips curved up. "Good. We'll take Professor Plum."

Her five-door, purple MINI Cooper. A five-minute drive around the point, they arrived at a big, Victorian-style house perched up on the top of a cliff overlooking the sea. The driveway was full of vehicles. "Wow, cool place," he said, peering up at the distinctive roofline.

"I know. It's been in Beckett's family since the late 1800s. And the inside's even cooler. Come on," she said, climbing out. He caught up with her, carrying the bottles of wine she'd brought.

Red and green lights glowed all around the wraparound porch railing, filled out with swags of evergreen branches, and big cedar wreaths with sprigs of holly graced the doors. Danae walked up the steps to the side porch, knocked on the screen door and walked in.

"Merry Christmas!"

A chorus of the same answered from inside. A sea of faces greeted them, and Ryder was quickly introduced to Sierra, then Mac's wife Tiana, and Tiana's young daughter, Ella.

The old, cozy house smelled of Christmas spices and evergreen. A wood fire burned cheerfully in the hearth in the living room, a fully decorated natural tree twinkling in the corner.

"So glad you changed your mind and decided to come,"

Sierra said to him, giving his shoulder a squeeze. "Been dying to meet you."

"I think we have someone else to thank for his sudden change of heart," Molly said, a twinkle in her eye as she glanced meaningfully at Danae.

"What?" Ryder said, feigning hurt. "I just wanted to spend more time with my favorite cousin."

"Uh huh." Molly pushed him gently toward the kitchen. "Go pour that woman a glass of wine."

"Anyone else want anything?" he called out.

"I wouldn't mind a wee dram," Mac said above the hum of voices.

The mention of whiskey gave him pause for a second, but he went to the antique wooden sideboard where various bottles of booze were laid out and was happy to note he didn't want any of it. He delivered the wine to Danae, then took Mac his whiskey and visited with the guys for a while.

A while later, Sierra stood and clapped her hands to get their attention. "Dessert time."

Everyone sat down to dessert at the long, rectangular table, and demolished a series of cakes and pies made by Poppy. Beckett passed out homemade eggnog spiked with rum. Ryder took a soda instead, and Danae had a mug of mulled wine.

He couldn't keep his eyes off her. Even while engaged in conversation with someone else, his gaze kept straying to her, drawn to her with a magnetic force he had no interest in fighting.

Being in a room with so many people he barely knew wasn't entirely comfortable, but Jase and Molly were there, and being able to watch Danae was a pleasure all in itself. She sparkled every bit as bright as the tree in the corner of the room, her smile and laugh lighting up the room.

"So, how are things going?"

Yanked from his thoughts, he glanced beside him at Molly, who was giving him a sly look. "Going good."

"Yeah? You got any news you wanna share?"

"Nope."

Her expression turned bland. "Liar."

From across the room Danae's gaze met his, and a spark flared hot and bright in his gut.

"Walter needs his walk now," a small voice called out, bringing the chatter to an abrupt halt.

Ella stood over by the side porch door with Walter. Someone had dressed him in a red Christmas sweater and put fake reindeer antlers on his head.

Ella tugged on her jacket, surveying the adults expectantly. "I can't go on my own. Who's coming with me?"

"Good idea," Molly said, grabbing Savannah as she raced by, trying to get to Walter. "Time for a group walk."

Danae crossed the room to him, all long legs and trim curves, her eyes glittering with the reflection of the lights on the Christmas tree. All Ryder could do was stare, his pulse kicking hard in his throat. "You want to go with me?" she asked him. "I'll show you the lighthouse."

He would walk through a hail of gunfire to be with her. And his resolve to keep his hands off her was crumbling by the minute.

TWELVE

The trill of Ella's excited voice trailed back to them on the wind as the group marched up the hill together. She was out in front with Beckett and Sierra, pushing Walter along in his little buggy.

Tiana was a short distance behind them, keeping a slower pace alongside Mac, who hobbled along on his crutches. Noah and Poppy were next. Behind them, Molly and Jase had Savannah by the hands and were swinging her between them, her delighted shrieks and laughter ringing through the night.

Bringing up the rear, Danae smiled next to Ryder, their breath fogging in the cold air. "Love that sound, but glad I'm past that stage. Though parenting a teenager isn't a cakewalk either."

"I'd say you're doing a helluva job."

She glanced over at him. "Yeah? Well, then thanks." Most of the time it didn't feel like she was killing it as the single mother of a teenage son. But it was nice that someone thought so.

She tucked her arm through his and leaned into him a little. It was probably stupid of her given that anything between them would result in a dead end, but she wanted to get closer even though she knew it would mean heartache for her later. Having loved and lost, she understood better than anyone that you had to grab a chance at happiness when it came along—even if it could only be temporary.

She'd felt him watching her all evening, and the answering tingle inside her. She wasn't gutsy enough to make a move, however. She didn't want to seem desperate or needy.

"Walter seems to be enjoying himself," she said, watching as Ella dutifully pushed the buggy over the crest of the hill above. She was taking her training to be a big sister seriously.

"Not as much as when he was in the dune buggy."

She laughed. "Course not. Who could blame him?"

They reached the crest of the hill. A little ways ahead Mac was still keeping up with the others, but Danae deliberately slowed, wanting to have some privacy and steal Ryder away for a little while. "There's a trail just up here that'll take us around the point to the lighthouse."

"Lead the way."

They angled away from the others, cutting across a small grassy clearing between several stands of evergreens. She could feel the muscles in his arm flexing beneath her hand, and with every step the outside of his forearm brushed her breast, sending little streamers of heat through her.

What are you doing? a little voice demanded in dismay.

She silenced it and focused on the here and now. On Ryder. On how attracted she was to him, and how safe she felt beside him.

"It's such a perfect night." She tipped her head back to breathe in the cool, damp air. A three-quarter moon hung bright above them in a rich indigo sky, the sound of the ocean growing louder as they approached the pathway that wound around the edge of the cliff. "What do you usually do on Christmas? I mean, when you're back home in North Carolina?"

"Haven't been home for Christmas that much for the past decade. But usually I go to my mom's in the late morning, and Molly's mom and my grandma will come over after lunch and stay for dinner. I tried talking my mom and aunt into coming out here with me this year, but they're homebodies, and my grandma doesn't like to travel."

The wind picked up when they passed the screen of trees, and suddenly the wild, rugged beauty of the Oregon Coast lay spread before them.

In the distance, perched high on the end of the point, the Crimson Point lighthouse stood like a shadowy sentinel. No longer in use for shipping traffic, its light was only decorative, pouring a wide circle of amber and gold over the mist-slick rock around it.

"What a view," he said, curling his arm more tightly around hers.

The feel of his muscles turned her on, and it was a thrill to know that could still happen. "I know you've got lighthouses back home, but you have to admit, this one is pretty spectacular."

He made a sound of agreement. "The landscapes are totally different. This one is wild and...raw."

They walked past the lighthouse to the end of the point, and stopped in front of the safety railing, just out of the pool of light. The wind whistled around them on the exposed cliff edge, sharp and cold. Danae shivered and hunched down a bit, pulling her arm free of his to rub her chilled hands together.

Ryder stepped in front of her to block the direct force of

the wind and took her hands in his. Danae froze, her gaze jerking to his.

His dark eyes gleamed amber with the reflection of the lighthouse as he slowly raised her hands to his mouth. Her heart kicked hard against her ribs, her insides tightening in anticipation. With his big hands cradling hers, he bent his head slightly and blew on her cold fingers, then rubbed them between his own, never looking away.

Heat pooled low in her belly. She stood immobile, held by the force of his stare, the sensual glow there making anticipation fizz like expensive champagne.

"You shouldn't let me touch you," he said, releasing one hand to glide his fingertips through the hair at her temple.

She was having trouble concentrating. "No?"

He shook his head slowly. "I'm leaving in a week. And I've still got…personal issues to deal with."

She nodded, suddenly finding it hard to slow her breathing. He wanted her. She wanted him. They didn't need to make this complicated. "But that still gives us a week."

He stilled, her hands held securely in his, their faces inches apart.

His lashes lowered as his gaze dipped to her mouth. Tiny nerve endings in her lips began to tingle.

When he didn't move, just stood there until she thought he was going to pull away, he suddenly tugged her toward him and pressed her hands to his chest. Holding them there with one hand while the other came up to close around the nape of her neck.

She bit back a groan of longing. And before she could draw another breath, his lips were on hers.

Tender at first. Brushing. Testing.

More.

She curled her fingers into his coat and stepped into him,

lifting her face into the kiss with a moan filled with need. The hand at the back of her neck tightened, long fingers contracting in a sensual grip that made her head swim.

Holding her like that, he angled his lips across hers, learning the shape of her mouth. Caressing. Sucking gently first at her top lip, then the bottom, his tongue gliding over it like velvet before deftly sliding inside to touch hers.

Desire ripped through her, sending a rush of heat between her legs. Her nipples hardened, her body coming alive in a way it hadn't in over three long years.

There was no stab of guilt, no self-recrimination. Only joy, and the thrill of Ryder's tall, powerful body pressed to her, his mouth moving over hers in a way that made her knees wobble.

She made an incoherent sound, almost a whimper, and kissed him back, struggling to rein in the insane tide of hunger that gripped her. She didn't care if this made sense. Didn't care that they didn't have much time together. It had been so long since she'd felt like this and she didn't want to miss a second of it.

His hand left her neck, his strong arm coming down to band around her lower back and pull her even closer, his other hand still cradling the side of her face. As if he couldn't stop touching her. As if he couldn't bear to let go.

She shivered again as his tongue twined with hers, then retreated to glide across her lower lip. Teasing. Savoring, until she was ready to climb him and wrap her legs around his hips just to relieve the building ache between her thighs.

Closing her eyes, she let her head tip to the side as his mouth burned a path down the side of her neck, his lips and tongue hitting every sensitive spot that made her tingle and throb.

Then he stopped suddenly, his muscles tensing, his stillness momentarily breaking through the haze of arousal swirling in her mind. And over the rush of the wind, she heard indistinct voices in the distance.

They were about to be interrupted.

Disappointment flooded her as he eased his hold on her and raised his head. But the look in his eyes, the taut lines of his face as he stared down at her with pure, molten hunger made the breath catch in her throat.

"I want more. So much more," he rasped out.

Her mouth went dry at the stark hunger in his voice. Holy shit. The need pulsing through her shocked her.

She wanted more too, but they were about to lose all privacy for the time being.

As she turned to face the others, she couldn't help but wonder if the interruption was actually a blessing in disguise. Because if Ryder had just made the whole world fall away with a single, blistering kiss…

Maybe it was better not to experience the *more* she so desperately wanted.

THIRTEEN

Boyd Masterson mentally groaned when he saw the lineup from outside the door at Whale's Tale. He didn't come into town often, and he'd thought the day after Christmas would be quieter than normal, with everyone sleeping off their tryptophan and pumpkin pie hangovers this morning.

Wrong. There were already at least half a dozen people lined up at the counter, and it was barely seven thirty. Crimson Point had almost as many tourists now as it did during the summer.

He went in anyway, his stomach growling at the smell of cinnamon and coffee filling the interior. He'd already had his fill of socializing with his son and two buddies he'd brought with him to Boyd's place for Christmas, who had all left at oh-six-hundred. But he could suffer through a bit more if it meant having one of Poppy's fresh caramel sticky buns and a big cup of French roast to go with it.

She was behind the counter as always, a ray of sunshine with her bright, genuine smile, and the new kid was working the coffee machine. The group of six ahead of him looked like they were dressed for a hike. They placed their orders and took a couple tables near him to wait.

Poppy smiled at him as he stepped up to the counter, her blond hair coiled into a tidy bun at the top of her head. "Boyd, good to see you. What can I get you?"

"I'll take a sticky bun with—"

"Large French roast, double cream?"

He nodded, one side of his mouth turning up. Guess he came here more often than he'd thought. "Please."

She rang in his order and held out the credit card machine for him to tap his card on. "Did you have a good Christmas?"

"I did." It had been great to spend some downtime with his son. Travis's training and deployment schedule meant it didn't happen often. "You?"

"It was perfect. Finn's getting your coffee right now, and then if you want to go sit somewhere, I'll bring over your sticky bun."

He got his coffee and turned around to scan for an empty table. One of the female hikers wearing a bright turquoise jacket and dark-rimmed glasses passed by him as she backed toward the counter, deep in conversation with a man and woman she'd been sitting with.

Realizing they were on a collision course, Boyd shifted his coffee higher and started to move out of the way, but she suddenly turned toward him at the last instant.

He opened his mouth to give a warning, but too late.

She spun right into him, knocking into his shoulder. The sudden impact made his coffee slosh all over his shirt and down the front of her jacket, splattering his pants and shoes in the process.

Boyd covered a hiss as the scalding hot liquid burned his skin and caught her arm to steady her.

"Oh!" she exclaimed, jumping back with a look of horror

in her wide, golden-brown eyes. "Oh my gosh, I'm *so* sorry." She reached past him to grab a handful of napkins from the counter and started wiping at his shirt as he tried to retreat, the coffee still burning him.

She stopped and looked down at his shoes. "Oh, man, I got all of you." She pushed her glasses up higher on her nose and started to crouch down like she was going to clean the rest of him too.

Boyd stopped her with a hand on her arm. "It's okay, I've got it."

"Are you sure?" She peered up at him anxiously, soggy napkins dangling from her hand, her cheeks flushing pink. She was pretty, a light dusting of freckles stretching across the bridge of her nose and spilling onto her cheeks. "I'm really sorry. Are you hurt?"

He'd been hurt a whole hell of a lot worse than a light scalding plenty of times during his military service, but she seemed genuinely worried. "I'm okay." He softened it with a reassuring smile.

"I'll get you another coffee," she insisted. "What kind was it?"

"I've got it," Poppy said, coming to the rescue with a damp cloth in one hand and a fresh coffee in the other.

The other woman bit her lip as he began mopping at his shirt, and Boyd couldn't help but notice how soft they looked. Or how full they were. "Seriously, it's fine," he insisted.

"Okay," she said in a doubtful tone, then flashed him a grateful smile. "Hope your day improves from here."

"You too. Here." He handed her the damp cloth so she could clean herself up, then stepped out of the way for Poppy, who had already darted out from behind the counter to wipe the floor. "See you," he told her.

"Next sticky bun's on the house."

The other woman had gone back to her friends now. She was busy wiping at her jacket but looked up as he passed by. Their eyes met, and she gave him another apologetic smile. He nodded and headed out the door, prepared to stay away from town until the holidays were over.

∼

AFTER THE LONGEST and most agonizing wait yet, it was finally the twenty-sixth, and almost time for the meet up. Before heading out, Kyle checked his phone one last time for messages. Finding none, he pulled the receipt from his pocket and input the address he'd written down into his GPS app.

"Any news?" Josh asked from the doorway. He'd spent the past two days looking at various colleges in the San Fran area to apply to. Already looking ahead and making plans for his future.

Buying that laptop had been worth every fucking penny.

"Nope." And that's exactly how he preferred it. Straight forward. No complications to worry about or deal with. "Everything's still a go."

"How far away is the drop site?"

"About twenty minutes. Few miles southeast of Crimson Point, near where we were the other night."

"In the woods again?"

"Looks like. Let's roll." He always liked to get there early for something like this, to make sure everything was as it should be. Make sure nothing had been leaked to any outsiders looking to cause trouble, and that the meeting wasn't part of a secret sting by the Feds or cops to bust them.

A rival organization had recently made an attempt to move into the territory Kyle's group worked here on the West

Coast. He wouldn't put it past them to pull some shit tonight or on a future op. It always paid to be cautious.

He got his pistol and three extra loaded mags from the bedroom of the place he and Josh were renting for this job, and got in the moving truck with his brother. It was their preferred vehicle for this type of transfer. Nobody would look twice at it, and most importantly, it allowed them plenty of room to hide the shipment from view.

It also locked from the outside at the back, preventing their human cargo from escaping.

Josh didn't speak, uncharacteristically serious as he drove while Kyle navigated and kept a sharp eye out for any potential tails behind them as they left the secluded holiday cabin. It was set deep back amongst the trees, hidden from view from the road by the winding driveway that curved up the hill. He'd paid for it in cash, and the owner hadn't asked any questions.

"We good?" Josh asked when they got close.

The sun had set, and out here the darkness was already enveloping everything. There was no rain tonight. It was cold, a damp cold that went straight to the bone, and the fog was beginning to creep in, slowly gliding over the ground like a living blanket. "Yeah. But drive past the pickup point and then double back."

When he was as sure as he could be that they were still in the clear, his brother turned up the deserted access road deep in the woods and parked at the side. They waited there in the darkness for twenty minutes, until headlights glimmered through the trees behind them.

Kyle drew his weapon and waited, gaze pinned to the side mirror. He relaxed slightly when another moving truck materialized out of the shadows.

"Stay here," he told his brother, then got out. Reaching

into his pocket for the receipt, he quickly reviewed the challenge passwords. He'd flush it down the toilet as soon as they made it to their new digs for the night.

The other driver stopped behind them and turned off the lights. The passenger got out, nothing but a silhouette in the faint light seeping through the dense trees. "Have a good Christmas?" Victor's voice asked, using the pass phrase.

Nope. But the money he and his brother would make off this shipment would more than make up for that. "I like after Christmas sales better," he replied in turn, and started for the other vehicle.

Together he and Victor unloaded the cargo and transferred it to the other truck while Josh and the other driver kept watch. But just as Kyle pulled the last unconscious woman from the back of the other truck and draped her across his shoulder, he heard it.

Movement in the trees to his right. Then voices. Close.

Way too fucking close.

He froze as a light appeared suddenly, moving as it filtered between the tree trunks.

Before he could move, a dog burst out of the woods, followed by a man wearing a headlamp. The hiker jerked to a halt when he saw Kyle, staring, just as three other people emerged behind him. Then two more.

Fuck!

It was too late to hide everything. Too late to take off. The beam of that headlamp gave at least the first few people in the group a perfect view of Kyle's and Victor's faces.

Kyle dumped the woman in the back of the other truck and pointed his weapon at the stunned hikers as Victor did the same. They had to deal with this *now*.

God, he fucking hated complications.

WHEN WAS the last time she'd felt like this? A warm, floating sensation. Tiny, effervescent bubbles of anticipation in her tummy.

Danae had relived last night's kisses so many times throughout the day. Ryder had been on her mind nearly every waking moment, no matter how hard she tried to stop thinking about him.

Okay, it had been a long time since she'd had a first kiss, but… The way Ryder kissed was unforgettable. Confident, yet tender. Skilled, but controlled. She still couldn't believe how turned on he'd made her with only a few kisses.

But there was a problem.

Part of her was eager to see where this intense attraction went, and the other said she was nuts for even entertaining the idea. She'd made up her mind to be practical about this, like she was with everything else in her life. She understood he was leaving soon, and it was even more complicated because she wanted to hide any involvement from Finn, since he was already attached to Ryder.

None of that dimmed her attraction to him, however. Not even the sensible part of her could override that.

"Earth to Danae."

She jerked out of her reverie and focused on Sierra, staring at her from over on the other couch. Actually, Tiana, Molly and Poppy were all staring at her as well.

"Sorry?"

They were all lounging around in the living room of Poppy and Noah's adorable cottage, after spending a lazy afternoon together to relax and catch up after the holiday rush. A wood fire crackled in the grate in the corner, giving the fresh, beachy interior a warm, inviting glow that felt as cozy as a warm blanket.

Sierra smirked. "You were definitely daydreaming about something good. Or should I say *someone* good. Got something on your mind you want to share, maybe?" Her eyes held a sly gleam as she sipped at the mulled apple cider Poppy had made in the crockpot.

"Ooh, what?" Poppy said eagerly and sat up straighter, wineglass in hand. She'd invited them all over in a bid to put a dent in all the food they had left over from the days leading up to Christmas—both from her café and things she'd made at home. "I feel like I've done nothing but bake and work every waking hour for the past month. I've earned some juicy gossip. Tell."

"No gossip," Danae answered, cursing her fair complexion when her cheeks warmed.

Tiana cocked her head, eyes narrowing. "You're blushing."

"What? No, I'm not. Red wine always makes me flush, and the fire's warm."

"The fire—on the other side of the room," Sierra said with a snicker. "Riiight."

Poppy gave Danae a pleading look. "Please tell us."

"No, it's nothing. Just short on sleep, I guess." There was no way in hell she was coming clean in front of Molly. Talk about awkward. *Yep, Moll, I've got the hots for your cousin and made out with him last night by the lighthouse.*

Poppy's smile disappeared, her blond eyebrows drawing together in concern. "Are you still worried that shooter might come back?"

"Well, maybe a tiny bit." It bothered her, for sure. It seemed unlikely that anyone would wander out here into her neighborhood by chance and decide to take shots at her place for kicks. "Finn was pretty shaken up too, even if he doesn't like to admit it."

"I'll bet," Tiana said.

"I tried talking to him more this morning, but he just shut down and has been avoiding me ever since."

"He's probably talked to his friends, though, so that's good," Molly said.

"I guess. I haven't even met any of his new friends yet. Don't even know their names, because he's been totally secretive about who he's been hanging out with here. I hate that."

Poppy set her wineglass on the coffee table and curled up into the corner of her cream-colored couch, hugging a sapphire-blue velvet pillow to her stomach. "You know, Noah has talked about a reported increase in criminal activity in the area over the past few months. Not in Crimson Point, but to the north. Mostly low-level stuff, but there has been some teenage gang involvement."

"Gangs in this neck of the woods?" Tiana said, looking equal parts shocked and skeptical.

"He didn't say too much," Poppy added. "But it's definitely out there. He thinks it's likely tied to a larger-scale criminal element in the drug trade. Not that I think Finn would ever get involved in that kind of thing," she added hastily, waving a hand at Danae to reassure her. "He wouldn't hang out with people like that."

She hoped the hell not. She'd raised him better than that. But he was a teenager in a new town, and she could see him wanting to fit in. She would talk to him about it tonight, just to keep lines of communication open and let him know that she was concerned and looking out for him.

"Let's change the subject," Sierra said. "I'm sure everything's fine with Finn."

"Okay, I'll go," Tiana said, her mismatched gaze leveling on Danae as she put a hand to her small baby bump. "Exactly what were you daydreaming about before? Or should I say, who?"

More flushing. Dammit.

"Is it Ryder?" Sierra guessed. "It has to be Ryder."

"What?" Danae managed, fighting the urge to squirm. She could feel Molly staring at her.

"Oh, please," Sierra said, laughing. "We all have eyes, we can see what he looks like, and we know he's already been hanging out at your place a few times."

"Mmm, yeah, tall dark and commanding," Tiana said with a mock shiver of delight. "And knowing firsthand what being with an alpha male is like, I bet he's like that day *and* night."

"Hey, read the room," Molly protested as the others all laughed. "That's my cousin you're talking about."

"Yeah, and he's *hot*," Poppy told her.

Danae didn't know how to answer, but her face was on freaking fire. No one had seen them kissing last night, right?

Looking for an escape, she made a show of looking at her watch and got to her feet. "Well, I should get going. I need to head into the clinic for a bit."

Sierra blinked at her. "Are you kidding me? It's the day after Christmas, and there are no patients overnighting right now, so even I took the day off. Whatever it is, it can wait until tomorrow."

Danae shrugged. "I want to get a few things finished up before I start in the morning." She turned to Poppy with a smile. "Thanks for the wine and goodies."

"Please, take some with you," Poppy insisted, jumping up to rush into the adjoining kitchen. "Teenage boys have hollow legs and endless metabolisms, and Noah and I have way more here than we could ever eat. He's already taken most of it into the station."

"All right, I won't pass up your homemade treats."

"I need to get going too," Molly said. "I *love* working night shift." Sarcasm dripped from every word. "I'm just gonna check on Savannah," she called out to Poppy, who was going to watch Savannah until Jase came back to get her. He'd been out with Ryder all afternoon. "I'll leave her diaper bag up there next to the playpen."

"Sounds good."

Molly disappeared up the staircase, returning a few minutes later as Poppy emerged holding four cookie tins and a big smile. "Butter tarts, Nanaimo bars, sugar cookies, and some apple strudel. Finn's favorites from the café." She handed two to Danae, and two to Molly. "Nurses need sugar rushes to get them through the night, right?"

"We totally do," Molly said with a grin, and hugged her.

"Finn thanks you," Danae said. "My thighs do not." She hugged Poppy goodbye and turned for the door, only to stop when she saw Molly already there holding her coat out to her. "Um, thanks," she murmured, and her fears were confirmed when Molly stepped outside with her and shut the door.

"Hope they didn't embarrass you too much. They mean well," Molly said.

"I know. It's fine." She really didn't want to talk to her about Ryder, if that's why Molly had come outside.

Molly tilted her head slightly. "Are you okay?"

She blinked. "Yeah, why wouldn't I be?"

"Just with…the holidays. I know it's harder right now, and I'm not sure where you're at emotionally. Or whether you've even thought about dating again."

She hadn't thought about it at all until Ryder had moved in next door. Though she understood why Molly was asking.

It wasn't just because her cousin was potentially involved, it was because Molly was a widow as well.

"I'll be honest, I never expected to want to date again, but… I think I might be ready now." It was like Ryder had woken her from a deep sleep or something.

Molly nodded, empathy filling her eyes. "You know he's leaving next week, right?"

"Yes."

"Ryder's a good man. But he's…wrestling with some things that happened during his last tour."

"I know. He told me."

Her friend's hazel eyes widened in shock. "He did?"

"Well, not much, and not in detail. But some." She didn't dare tell Molly that she'd found him drunk that night.

Molly recovered from her surprise and summoned a smile. "Huh. Okay, then. Guess I didn't need to say anything."

"I appreciate you looking out for me. And I don't want you to feel awkward around me after this. He's leaving soon, so maybe nothing will happen anyway."

She nodded. "Just don't want to see either of you get hurt, that's all."

"I know. Now gimme a hug."

They embraced, and while it was sort of a relief to have her attraction to Ryder out in the open, as she drove to the clinic, a sudden realization gave her pause. After what he'd told her the other night, she was already emotionally invested. Attached.

Even going into this fully aware that their time together had a firm expiration date, it was still going to hurt like hell when he left.

FOURTEEN

Kyle raced after the hikers, intent on stopping them and tying them up somewhere safe so that he and his brother could make a getaway with their cargo. Victor and his partner for this job were up ahead, almost lost in the trees now, and Josh was behind him. The dog he'd seen was barking its damn head off somewhere up by the road.

It was hard to see. The guy wearing the headlamp had turned it off the moment he'd run away, but there was enough ambient light filtering down through the trees that Kyle could still see figures running through the brush.

"Take the three on the right!" Victor shouted back at him and Josh. Then a shot rang out, loud in the forest. Someone cried out and stumbled up ahead.

Kyle veered right, crashing through the underbrush. Two people bent to scoop up the fallen one and tried to carry him. He couldn't let them escape.

Kyle put on a burst of speed, gained on them easily as their burden slowed them down. He flew at the figure on the left of the trio. They both landed hard. A woman cried out and tried to pull Kyle off him. Josh appeared, ripping the woman away.

A fist hit the side of his face. Kyle grunted and grabbed the guy's arm, flipping him onto his stomach and wrenching his arms behind him. The instant he had the flex cuffs on, he stood, dragging the prisoner with him, ignoring the man's struggles and shouts.

The wounded guy was still on his feet, trying to stumble away from them.

Josh had the struggling woman subdued. She was screaming now. "Hold her and shut her up." He shoved her at Kyle, then went after the wounded guy.

He clapped his hand over the woman's mouth. "Shut up," he snarled, giving her a hard shake that made her freeze.

Josh got the wounded guy and came back, his pistol aimed at the guy's back. With all three secured, Kyle breathed a little easier.

He and Josh forced them back to the trail, muscling them in spite of their struggles, shouts and curses, and started the trek down toward the beach. He could hear Victor and the other guy farther down the hill.

He and Josh followed the trail, unsure whether Victor and the other guy had captured the remaining three. They had to find a good spot to tie them up. Somewhere out of view and far enough off the trail that it would take a while for anyone to find them.

Hopefully, not until at least daybreak. By then he and Josh would be halfway to the California state line.

The sound of the distant waves began to echo through the trees from the other side of the dunes. At the bottom of the trail Kyle dragged the woman and man out of the trees to find Victor and his partner waiting on the edge of the dunes, holding pistols on the other three bound prisoners.

"You got them all?" Victor demanded.

"Yeah," Kyle answered.

"Bring 'em here."

Kyle forced them up beside the others and drew his pistol to hold them there while Josh half-carried the wounded guy into place and dumped him on the sand.

Just as Josh began to turn away, Victor started shooting.

Kyle whirled around in time to see the first person fall, while everyone else started screaming and running. Scattering across the beach.

"Shoot 'em, shoot 'em!" Victor screamed, firing over and over.

Fuck! Kyle whirled and raised his pistol to shoot, narrowly avoiding the shot that streaked past and struck the man trying to flee near him. The guy jerked and slammed into Kyle, knocking him off balance. He scrambled to his feet and looked up.

Caught in the melee, Josh suddenly stumbled and went down.

"Josh!" He raced over and dropped to his knees beside his brother. Josh's face was a pained grimace, both hands pressed to his side. Jesus, they'd shot him.

"Just skimmed me," his brother gasped out.

Kyle's hands fumbled with Josh's jacket and shirt. Screams and gunshots continued to echo all around them as he tried to see the damage.

It was too dark to see how bad the wound was, but he could feel the warm stickiness of blood on his hands.

Then, suddenly, it got eerily quiet.

Kyle was too preoccupied by his brother's wound to care. "Lemme see."

"Don't touch it," Josh hissed, shoving him away.

Kyle regained his balance and rounded on Victor, who

was dragging a limp body back toward them. "You fucking idiot!" Hopefully the wound wasn't too bad, but whoever had fired that bullet could have killed Josh.

"Shut up and help us bury them," Victor snapped.

Kyle glanced around, stunned at the carnage. All six hikers now lay either dead or dying on the sand.

Shit. They couldn't be left out here in the open. Someone might see them and call the cops before Kyle and the others had bugged out of here.

Cursing under his breath, still trying to process what had just happened, he hurried over to the closest body, grabbed the wrist and started dragging it back across the dune. The wrist was slender, and when he looked down, he saw the woman's long, dark hair trailing on the sand.

His stomach lurched. He looked away and towed her to where Victor and his partner had already rounded up the others. Letting the limp arm drop, he began scooping sand over her.

Out of the corner of his eye he saw Josh drop to his knees.

"*Josh*." He raced over, knelt beside him and hooked an arm around his shoulders. Josh was breathing hard and shallow, awful groans of pain coming from him. "How bad is it?"

"I'm not okay," he said between clenched teeth.

Kyle blanched. "I'm getting you out of here." He wound his arm around his brother's waist and hauled him to his feet, Josh's cry making him cringe.

"Where the fuck do you think you're going?" Victor yelled.

"He's fucking *shot*," Kyle shouted back, and hurried Josh back to the trail, heart hammering in his throat.

Holy shit, this was a nightmare. He hadn't wanted to kill any of them. He'd only wanted to capture and bind them up so they couldn't report him and the others to the cops until they were safely out of the area.

Now six people were dead, and Josh was hurt bad.

He no longer gave a shit about anything else, not even the unconscious women in the back of the truck. His only concern was getting his brother to safety and stopping him from bleeding to death.

~

IF SOMEONE HAD TOLD him two years ago while he was still in the Army that his biggest problem after retiring would be a coyote wreaking havoc in his yard, he would have laughed his ass off. Yet here he was.

Boyd crouched down and adjusted the brightness of his NODs to examine the new hole under the wire fence he'd recently put up around the chicken coop. Some people would use a flashlight, but after spending the past two decades serving in one of the most elite units in the US military, night optics devices were as familiar and comfortable to him as a flashlight was to the average person. And they also left both his hands free.

Telltale tracks in the damp soil leading up to the edge of the fence, but the size didn't quite confirm his suspicions about the animal responsible. Too small for a fox, and not large enough for a wolf or coyote, unless it was a juvenile.

The motion-activated sensor had picked up on a disturbance ten minutes ago, catching the culprit in the act of trying to dig its way under the fence. The one he'd sunk deep into the ground to prevent such a thing.

A few sections of the chain link had been bent and distorted. They weren't wide enough for a fox or coyote to get through, but they were more than adequate for smaller predators looking for a chicken dinner to slip through.

From inside the safety of the coop, he could hear his ladies clucking away from their nesting boxes. He'd closed up the coop for the night half an hour ago as it started to get dark, minutes before the sensors had alerted him about the predator. The animal had probably been watching him from the woods, waiting for him to go back into the cabin.

Straightening, he walked across the landscaped section of his backyard to the shed and grabbed a shovel and pliers, then returned to the fence to repair the damage. As he worked, the quiet settled around him, broken only by the chickens and night sounds from the thirty acres of woods that made up the sides and back of his personal slice of heaven.

An owl hooted somewhere in the distance, the low, almost mournful sound resonating softly through the trees. He froze, his hand tightening around the pliers when the sharp, unmistakable sound of a gunshot echoed from somewhere behind him.

He rose, turning to face the back of his wooden cabin, listening. There was something else. Something indistinct coming from down the hall. Voices. Shouting.

The frantic barking of a dog.

He strode for the cabin and took his pistol from the gun safe before stepping out onto the front porch, where he stopped. The dog was still barking. Not as frantic now and moving away from him.

Yet Boyd's gut told him that shot hadn't been from a hunter taking aim at a kill.

He walked to the end of his gravel driveway and paused again, scanning the distant trees on the other side of the road as he listened intently. He didn't see anything moving in the woods. And the barking had faded away now.

More shots rang out. A few, spaced pistol shots, coming from somewhere far away at the bottom of the hill. Then a heavier volume of fire.

Less than thirty seconds later it stopped as suddenly as it had begun.

He made the calculation in his head. At least two weapons. Maybe fifteen to twenty rounds total. Definitely not hunters.

Unless they had been hunting human prey.

Pulling out his phone, he hurried across the empty road. "Multiple shots fired," he told the 911 operator, then gave her the approximate location, his name and address. His NVGs gave him a perfect view of the woods in front of him.

There were no more shots. No screams or shouts, and no hint about the dog.

As soon as he ended the call he slipped into the trees, moving quickly and quietly through the thick underbrush on his way to a trailhead he used regularly. Just as it came into view, something ran across it and disappeared into the brush. The size of a small dog. Or a coyote.

He withdrew his weapon and started down the trail, all his senses attuned to what was going on in front of and around him. But when he reached the overlook point halfway down without hearing or seeing anything else suspicious, he stopped.

Nothing moved except the treetops. Nothing disturbed the hush of the forest.

Holstering his weapon, he turned around and started back, convinced that the area he considered to be his private haven had suddenly become something far more sinister.

FIFTEEN

"So, what's Becca Sandoza really like?" Jase asked him as they cruised down the coastal highway, heading north back to Crimson Point. "The media paints her like she's standoffish and snobbish."

"She's not," Ryder answered. "She's a total sweetheart, she just hates having her privacy invaded, and the stalker incident this fall made her even more wary."

"No doubt. Is it weird? Having your best friend engaged to a movie star?"

"It was at first. Not anymore." Chase and Becca were great together.

And he'd be lying if he didn't admit thinking about getting together with Danae.

He'd thought about her constantly since last night, after they'd been interrupted at the lighthouse. She had driven him home soon after. He'd kissed her again in the driveway, and the way she leaned into him, the way she melted in his arms had made him want to drag her inside and lay her on his bed, strip her and devour every inch of her.

Somehow, he'd made himself get out of the car and go

inside his cottage alone. He'd held off on going to see her earlier, spending the day with Jase instead, and texting her a couple times.

The time apart hadn't changed anything on his end. He wanted more. But since he would only be here a few more days, he needed her to be sure she was okay with that before they took things any farther.

"How well do you know Danae?" he asked after a lapse in the conversation.

"Pretty well. I mean, not as well as Moll does. Why?"

"Has she dated anyone since her husband died?"

"Don't think so." Jase shot him a knowing grin. "Why, you interested?"

Hell yes, he was interested. How could he not be? He hadn't dated in a while either. Nothing serious anyway, and the occasional hookup. "Just wondering."

"She's great. But what about you? How are *you* doing?"

"Me? Fine."

"Okay."

Of course Molly would have said something to him about her concerns.

The incident on Christmas Eve had shaken him. He realized he couldn't conquer this on his own, and Jase would understand better than most what he was going through. "When you got out of the military, did you ever…talk to anyone? About stuff."

"Yeah, I talked to Beckett and Carter. A lot."

"But not a professional or anything?"

"Eventually. But not until after Carter died. Moll pushed me until I finally agreed to talk to a therapist. You wanting to talk to someone?"

He folded his arms, feeling awkward and embarrassed even though he knew Jase wouldn't judge. It was just hard-wired into him, the alpha male attitude of rub some dirt on it and move on.

But he wasn't moving on. Not really. He was stuck and needed to do something about it before it ruined his life. "Maybe."

"You could start with telling me or Beckett if that's easier," Jase offered. "I promise not to repeat anything to Moll."

Ryder appreciated that. He stared out the windshield at the darkened, winding road and the bank of fog they were driving through that dropped visibility to twenty yards ahead. It was sort of a metaphor. He felt like he was trapped in a fog bank too sometimes.

It was time to talk about this. And he was comfortable enough with Jase to try. "During my last tour, there was an ambush. I took a squad out to a remote village, acting on perishable intel about a possible bomb-making factory. It was a high-risk mission, because we'd been warned up front that we'd be all on our own, with no reinforcements if anything went wrong."

Jase made a low sound to let him know he was listening, and it helped Ryder keep going, even though his hands were balled into fists beneath his folded arms. "Command felt the target was worth the risk, and I volunteered to lead the mission on the ground. Helo dropped us at an LZ two miles out. We humped up the mountain on foot, taking our position about two hours before sunrise."

His heart beat faster, the images vivid in his mind. The green glow of the terrain and distant buildings in his NVGs. The smell of the earth, and the wood smoke from the village fires on the wind. "Everything we'd been told seemed to check out. But it turned out to be the opposite. By the time we reached the target building the enemy had sounded the alarm.

They came out of tunnels hidden below the village that no one had known about."

"Shit."

Yeah. His muscles were tight as wires, his chest tight as he continued. "We were surrounded and cut off within minutes. I radioed for help and was told it would be at least three hours before they could get anyone to us." He swallowed. "We took cover and held them off for as long as we could. Took our first casualty within the first five minutes, and after that it turned into a fucking bloodbath."

"Did you get the reinforcements?"

"Eventually. But by the time the sun came up, it was too late. I was the only one not dead or severely wounded." It was sheer dumb luck. There was no other explanation.

"Shit, I'm sorry."

Ryder nodded once, jaw tight, but the awful tension in his belly and chest was lessening a bit now that he'd said it all. Telling someone who had been in combat made it easier.

"There were still a few guys alive when we got to the base hospital. The staff wouldn't let me near them. MPs dragged me out of the building. Two more guys died before I was finally allowed back in. The other three were busted up so badly they were operated on and immediately shipped to Germany for more treatment. One lost an eye, a hand and his lower leg, and all I needed was some stitches."

"Did your command try to lay the blame on you?" Jase asked in a hard tone.

"No. But I don't know how to live with the guilt." And the next part was the hardest to admit aloud. "I got a text from one of my fallen Marine's widows the other night. A nice one. Then I got shitfaced. Danae showed up while I was passed out."

Jase winced. "Sorry."

"I...sort of told her about what happened. But not everything. I don't want to burden her with my shit." Didn't want to put those images in her head.

"I get it. How much are you drinking?"

Again, Molly must have told Jase her suspicions. "Too much lately. That's why I came out here, to go cold turkey away from everything back home."

"So what are you going to do about it?"

"Guess I need to see a pro."

"Yeah. Beckett had similar issues when he got out too. We all do. War is fucked-up and it always leaves a mark, even if the scars are invisible to everyone else. Beck's about as stubborn as they come, but even he finally reached out for help. He was referred to a psychologist who's a four-time combat vet, and really liked the guy, so I've seen him too. I can give you his contact info."

Ryder exhaled a relieved breath. There was hope after all. "Thanks. Can't hurt."

"No. And if you—" He broke off suddenly and hit the brakes.

Ryder's gaze shot to the figure emerging from the fog at the edge of the road ahead. Whoever it was, they were in bad shape and out here in the middle of nowhere.

"Jesus Christ," he muttered, quickly undoing his seatbelt and reaching for the door handle. He was out of the truck and rushing toward the person before Jase had even pulled over to park.

As he ran, the person became clearer. A woman in a torn, filthy turquoise jacket, the front of it smeared with blood, and her hands bound behind her as she staggered out of the fog toward them.

Holy shit.

Ryder slowed a few paces away so as not to scare her,

holding his palms out as he approached. She was gasping, trembling, more smears of blood on her jaw and cheek. "I'm going to help you," he said in a low voice just as Jase ran up behind him.

When she stayed put, he gently grasped her upper arm and turned her slightly. Some bastard had clamped her wrists together with tactical nylon restraints. She was clearly in shock, but the blood worried him most.

He scanned her quickly, trying to figure out if it was hers, but didn't see any obvious wounds. "Ma'am," he said when she didn't respond, her gaze unfocused. Next to him, Jase was already on his phone calling for help. "We're getting help. Are you hurt?"

She stared up at him, shaking, the anguish in her eyes slicing through him like a blade. "They're dead," she rasped out unsteadily. "They're all dead."

~

ONE LAST BIT of paperwork and she could go home, take a shower, and then hopefully spend the evening with Ryder once he got back.

Danae typed some notes into the program open on the clinic computer, eager to get this wrapped up. Since it was a small clinic, her duties weren't just limited to treating animals and helping with tests. She also did admin work and helped Sierra keep on top of the never-ending job of keeping supplies and inventory stocked.

She looked over her shoulder at the sound of the back door rattling, her fingers pausing on the keyboard. The clinic was closed, and she was alone in the back room. Was it Sierra? The lock was tricky, maybe her key was stuck again.

She stepped toward the door, only to jump and bite back a

scream as it suddenly burst open. A masked man came through it, his arm wrapped around another man, who was bleeding heavily from his side.

The first man's gaze locked on Danae. She backed away instinctively, heart in her throat, and it almost stopped beating when his gloved fist flashed up to point a gun at her. She stared at it in shock, a burst of terror streaking through her.

He kicked the door shut behind him and advanced on her. "You're going to stop the bleeding so I can get him out of here," he told her in a low, menacing voice, only his mouth and eyes visible, narrowed to slits in the mask holes. "Patch him up, right now."

He shifted his grip on the wounded man. *Now*," he barked when she didn't move.

She jerked and turned blindly for the supply shelf at the side of the room. He was blocking the back door, and she'd never make it to the other one across the room before he shot her. She was trapped. Had to do what he said, and then hopefully he'd leave.

Her hands shook as she reached for various things on the shelves, accidentally knocking boxes and supplies to the floor.

"Hurry!" he snarled, dragging the bleeding man toward the only flat surface in the staff room—the desk she'd just been working at. He swept an arm across the surface, sending her laptop crashing to the floor and scattering papers everywhere.

Some stupid reflex made her bend to pick some of the papers up. He snarled at her, snatched a crumpled blue receipt from the top of the fistful she'd grabbed. "Move," he commanded, stretching the bleeding man onto the desk.

Struggling to stay calm, Danae hesitantly moved closer and got her first look at her patient, who didn't have a mask on. He was young, maybe in his mid to late twenties, with short, dark hair and a few days of growth on his face. He was still conscious, but barely, his light green eyes unfocused, mouth slack.

Panic welled up. She was a vet tech, not an ER doctor. "What do you want me to—"

"*Stop* the fucking blood before he bleeds out," the first man snapped, lifting the pistol to aim it right at her head.

Her insides shriveled as she gingerly approached the wounded man from the other side of the table, too many thoughts flooding her brain all at once. There was no way for her to escape without risking getting shot. No one around to hear her if she screamed for help, and the staff room didn't have a security camera. Nobody knew what was going on. Nobody was coming to help.

She licked her lips, frantically gathering her racing thoughts and focusing on the task at hand. She needed to seem calm even if she wasn't. Couldn't risk doing anything to aggravate this situation or set the man off. "Pull his shirt out of the way," she said, surprised her voice wasn't shakier.

The man pulled the hem of the shirt upward, revealing what had to be a gunshot wound through his friend's lower ribcage. And she noticed a heavy black tattoo on the back of the gunman's wrist, moving up from his concealed hand to disappear under the sleeve of his jacket.

She pulled on surgical gloves and pushed the rising tide of fear aside, forcing her brain into work mode. *Just do what you can to stop the bleeding.* "Turn him so I can see if there's an exit wound."

"There is, and it's bigger."

The visual verified what he'd said. And a sudden, sinking sensation took hold. "He'll have internal damage. I'm not a veterinary doctor, I'm a tech, and he needs surgery. Even if I stitch up the wounds, it won't—"

"You stitch him up right the fuck now, or I'll put a bullet through your head."

God... She thought of Finn, of never seeing him again, and a new wave of terror broke over her. "Just...calm down, okay? You're scaring me, and I can't thread the suture needle when my hands are shaking like this. Put the gun down."

He lowered it slightly but didn't put it away. "Exit wound first," he ordered, turning the man farther onto his side. The wounded guy groaned and started to squirm. "Stay still. She's going to help you."

Trying to keep her hands steady, she injected the edges of the wounds with lidocaine first, then cleaned up the edges and prepped the suture needle. It took her three tries to get it threaded with the needle-driver, and all the while more blood was spilling onto the surface of the desk, spreading out in a pool. The sight of blood didn't usually faze her, but right now her stomach was churning.

It took eight stitches to close the exit wound, and four for the entry. By the time she was done, the man was barely conscious, his breathing choppy. She didn't know how much blood he'd lost in total, but he was in really bad shape.

"Give him something for the pain, and then something for infection, just in case," the man holding the gun ordered.

She grabbed some hydromorphone and Amoxicillin from the shelf, prepped syringes for both while guessing at the dosage for someone the patient's size and injected him. Then she packed gauze pads on both wounds and taped them in place around his ribs.

"That's the best I can do," she said, stepping back. What would he do now? *Leave. Please just leave*, she prayed. "But he needs to go to the hospital."

He fixed her with a hard stare, and the angle of his head allowed her to see the color of his eyes for the first time. Pale green, like the other man. Were they related?

Then he raised the weapon at her again, and every drop of blood in her body congealed, a scream of denial building in her throat. He was going to shoot her dead here in the middle of the staff room, even though she'd done everything he'd told her to.

No!

Her mind emptied of everything except for one, excruciating thought.

Finn. Her sweet boy. He was about to lose her too. Was about to be totally alone, with no parent to take care of him.

As she braced for the gunshot and the hideous pain, headlight beams flashed across the thin blind covering the square window in the door leading to the rest of the clinic.

The gunman cursed and shoved the gun into his waistband to grab the wounded man, lifting him over his shoulder. Danae spun around and darted into the closet. She flipped the lock and squeezed under the shelf in the far corner, cowering there in terror while her heart thundered against her ribs.

She jumped when the back door thudded against the wall a moment later. Then there was no sound except the pounding of blood in her ears over the sudden silence.

She didn't dare move yet, hardly dared to breathe as she waited there, covered in a film of cold sweat. Agonizing seconds ticked past, each one a small eternity.

Still no sound from the staff room. Had he left?

Gathering her nerve, she carefully unlocked the door and cracked it open a fraction of an inch to peer into the room. It was empty, the back door standing open, framing a dark rectangle of the parking lot. The only sound coming from outside was the restless churn of the ocean in the background, then came the squeal of tires from somewhere up the street.

Sagging with relief, she darted from the closet, found her purse lying on the bloodstained floor, and fished out her phone to call 911.

SIXTEEN

Noah came downstairs after his shower to find Poppy in front of the fire on the living room couch, with little Savannah in her arms. Poppy was humming softly and rocking the toddler, who was staring up at her with the slow blinks of a child on the verge of losing her battle to stay awake.

He stopped there at the bottom of the stairs and leaned a shoulder against the wall, watching them with a smile. With Molly at work, Poppy had volunteered to take Savannah until Jase got back to town with Ryder. Jase and Molly never had to worry about a babysitter with his wife around.

The scene was pure maternal contentment, and a deep tenderness welled up inside him. Poppy wanted a baby of her own so bad and would be a fantastic mother if and when that happened. They'd been trying for a while now, and she was starting to get disheartened that something was wrong. That it would never happen for them.

Noah tried to reassure her, and the trying part had been a lot of fun so far. But he didn't like seeing his sunflower so sad. After everything she'd been through, he would give her the fucking moon if she wanted it.

He pushed off the wall and walked over to her, catching her eye partway there, and her gentle smile, the sheen of tears in her eyes made his heart squeeze tight. He sank down beside her on the couch and brushed his thumb across the top of her cheek, skimming away the tears on her lower lashes. Savannah's eyes were now closed, her lips parted slightly, her little chest moving in a slow, even rhythm.

"You're a natural," he whispered. No surprise there.

Poppy sniffed and wiped at her cheeks with her free hand. "She's so sweet."

He took her hand and curled his fingers around it, waiting until those big brown eyes met his. "We'll get our turn one day. You'll see."

She put on a smile, but he could still see the sadness lurking in her eyes. "Yes."

He glanced at Savannah, who was limp in Poppy's arms. "Want me to carry her up to the guestroom?" They'd set up her playpen in there, and Poppy had already made it into a snug little bed for her with quilts and a pillow.

"Not yet," she whispered, staring down into Savannah's face.

Knowing his precious sunflower needed his love and reassurance, Noah stretched an arm around her shoulders and drew her into him, running a hand up and down her back while she laid her head in the hollow of his shoulder. Poppy snuggled into him, and the crackle of the fire were so relaxing, he smothered a yawn. His shift had started at seven this morning, and after a late night last night, his eyes started to droop too.

They flew open a minute later when his cell phone rang in his pocket. Savannah jerked, then went right back to sleep.

Wincing at the noise, he pulled away from Poppy, stood, and hurried into the kitchen to answer the call from dispatch. "Sheriff Buchanan."

"Just got a call from Danae Sutherland. Someone broke into the clinic and held her at gunpoint. She sounds pretty shaken up."

He started for the door, grabbing his holstered service weapon on the way. "When was this?"

"Maybe fifteen minutes ago. She hid in a closet until they left. She's still at the clinic."

"I'll call her myself. Heading there right now." Ending the call, he grabbed his sheriff's jacket from the peg near the door and turned to face Poppy, who was watching him worriedly from the couch. "Someone broke into the vet clinic and held Danae at gunpoint."

She gasped, gathering Savannah closer. "Be careful."

He stopped, strode back over to her and kissed her, then ran a finger down her cheek. "I will. Love you."

He called Danae on the way out to his vehicle, and she answered right away. "Are you safe?" he said immediately.

"Yes. I mean, I think so. He hasn't come back, but I'm afraid to leave the closet." She sounded shaky.

"Just stay where you are. I'm on my way to you, should be there in a few minutes."

"Okay."

"Why don't you tell me what happened?" He wanted to keep her on the line with him, just in case, keep her talking and help her feel less alone.

She was clear-headed enough to give him everything and provide clarification when he asked for it. By the time she was done, he was parking around back. The rear clinic door was wide open. "I'm here. You can come out now, but try not to disturb any evidence."

A patrol car turned into the parking lot a moment later, and a young deputy Noah had recently hired stepped out. Noah gave him a brief rundown of the situation, then took out his flashlight and began surveying the scene.

Through the open doorway he could see Danae standing in the staff room, arms wrapped around her middle. There was blood smeared all over the desk and floor, along with bloody boot prints and what looked like drag marks near the door and continuing outside.

"Call forensics in," Noah said to his deputy, then stepped inside, careful to avoid the blood. After making certain Danae was unhurt, he checked the rest of the clinic.

Just as she'd said, the damage and crime scene were contained within the staff room and exterior. "What about security footage?" he asked her, scanning the room. A few small boxes were scattered on the floor.

"We don't have one back here. Just in the reception area, and on the exterior."

"Can you access them for me? I need to take a look."

She nodded once, her face pale, and started for the door leading to the main area of the clinic. Noah followed, glancing at his phone when it rang in his hand. Jase. "Hey, I'm in the middle of something. Can I call you back?"

"No, we got a major situation here."

He stopped at Jase's grim tone, his muscles tightening. "What's going on?"

"A woman just stumbled out of the woods onto the road in front of us, torn clothes, covered in blood, hands bound behind her. She's in shock so we're not getting a lot out of her yet, but she says there's been a mass shooting near here, and that all the people she was with are dead."

What the hell? "Where are you?"

The location Jase gave was right on the southern city

limits of Crimson Point. He'd already called for an ambulance. "All right. I'm on my way now."

He ended the call, took Danae by the shoulder and explained the situation. He didn't like leaving her, but this new situation took precedence. "My deputy will stay with you and take your statement, and I've got more team members on the way. I'll check in on you when I can."

"Okay," she said with a brave nod.

On the drive south he called Poppy to tell her what was happening. "Jase is gonna be a while. Could you bundle Savannah up and go over to Danae's place? Finn needs to know what happened, and Danae will be home soon. I'd feel better if someone was there with her."

"Of course, but a mass shooting? Here? God, Noah…"

"I know." He didn't like the feel of this at all either. If it was true, it was huge, and his gut said it had to be linked to the recent rise in organized crime in the surrounding region. "Call you later, okay? Love you."

Flashing red and blue lights reflecting off the damp surface of the asphalt alerted him to the scene ahead, hidden just out of view around a curve in the road. Fog reduced the visibility to ten yards or so. An ambulance and a patrol car had both arrived before him.

He parked on the shoulder next to the guardrail and jogged over to where Jase and Ryder stood talking with the deputy already there. "Where's the witness?" he asked them, scanning the area.

"Paramedics are looking her over now," his deputy said.

"Any other reports come in?"

"Just one. From Boyd Masterson."

Delta vet who lived up the hill a mile or so from here. "What'd he say?"

"Said he heard multiple gunshots from down the ridge

earlier, about forty minutes before your friends found the woman on the road. Went down to investigate but didn't see anything. The timing lines up with what the female witness says."

"How many victims are we talking about?"

"Not exactly sure yet, but it sounds like around five maybe."

Damn. "Wait here," he said to Jase and Ryder. "I'll be right back."

He hurried to the ambulance, knocked on a closed back door and waited for the paramedic to move out of the way. The woman on the gurney sat up, wrapping her arms around herself. She looked to be in her thirties, her brown hair cut in a wedge-style, and her golden-brown eyes were dull with shock.

"I'm Sheriff Buchanan," he told her, keeping his distance so as not to crowd her. "What's your name?"

Her throat worked as she swallowed. "Ember."

"Hi, Ember." He scanned her quickly. There was a lot of blood on her clothing, face and hands, but it might not be hers. "How are you doing? Are you injured?"

"No. Not really."

"Abrasions, bruises and a small laceration on her wrist," the paramedic told him, draping a blanket around her shoulders. "Vitals are all good, but her core temp's down a bit."

He kept his gaze on Ember. "Mind if I come in?" When she nodded her assent, he climbed up and sat beside the gurney on the padded bench built into the side. "Can you tell me what happened tonight, Ember? Starting with who you were with."

She drew a deep breath, let it out in a shaky rush and clenched the ends of the blanket in her fists. "I was…hiking with my brother, his wife, and the rest of the group."

"Who else was in the group?"

"The guide, and two others. We were hiking along a trail through the woods a little while ago, almost back to the van where the guide had left it on an access road earlier. But when we reached the road, we saw men loading unconscious women into moving trucks."

Noah kept his expression impassive, but he was already piecing the scene together. "And they saw you?"

"Yes." She swallowed again, lowered her gaze. "We turned around and tried to get away from them, but they chased us down."

"How many men?"

"Three. Maybe four. No, four. They had guns. They shot at us," she said with a shudder. "The guide was hit. My brother and I tried to carry him with us. They threatened to kill him if we didn't stop, so we did. They bound our wrists behind us and marched us all down the hill to where the woods gave way to the beach." She pressed her lips together, her body rigid.

"And then?" he asked gently.

"Then they lined us up and started shooting," she choked out, a sob shaking her. "Over and over. Everyone started falling around me. My brother knocked me over when he was hit. He fell on top of me and I..." She covered her face in her hands, her shoulders jerking. It took her a minute to regain her composure enough to finish.

Noah reached out and took hold of her hand. It was ice cold, her fingers trembling.

She sucked in a ragged breath, blinked up at the ceiling. "I was too scared to move. I thought if I didn't move, they'd think I was dead. I thought the others were doing it too. Then the men started covering us with sand. They were arguing the whole time. I think one of them was wounded."

And two men had burst in on Danae not long afterward, one of them shot.

"They all took off before they could bury us. And when I finally dared to move, I realized all the others were d-dead. Incl—including my brother," she finished in an anguished whisper.

Noah squeezed her hand, holding on tight. "I'm so sorry, Ember."

She made a high-pitch sound and turned toward him, her arms reaching out, and there was no way Noah could pull away. He gathered her to him and held on tight, anger and sadness warring inside him.

He'd seen a lot in his time as a cop, but thankfully had never had to deal with human trafficking or mass murder until now. The mention of her and the others being buried reminded him too much of what had happened to Poppy, but there was something else nagging at him as well.

This past September, he'd been alerted by a concerned citizen about a possible kidnapping/sex-trafficking ring in the area. Noah had met with the man, who had reportedly seen someone loading two young women into the back of a moving truck a few miles east of Crimson Point.

But he and his team hadn't been able to find any evidence and hadn't turned up any more leads. He'd passed the intel on to the FBI just in case, hoping it might help in some missing persons cases in the area, but he hadn't heard anything about it since. After tonight... There was no denying they had a major problem in the area.

It turned his fucking stomach to think of that kind of shit happening anywhere near his town. That previous incident had to be connected to tonight. And with five murders tonight, his department was now in the middle of a major crime investigation.

When Ember quieted and leaned against him with an exhausted sigh, Noah gave her one last squeeze and eased her upright. "Can you give me the names of the people you were with, and a description of the men who attacked you?"

She told him what she could. "I got a picture of one of them on my phone. It's probably not that good, but I think I at least got the plate number of the moving truck. Your deputy has it. I think the screen's cracked though."

"That's okay." He tucked the blanket more securely around her. "The paramedics are going to take you to the hospital now, and one of my deputies will meet you there to take your statement. I'll be by later tonight to see you. In the meantime, I want you to know I'm going to do everything I can to find the men who did this and bring them to justice. You have my word."

She searched his eyes for a second, then nodded. "Thank you."

Hopping out of the ambulance, he found Jase and Ryder standing nearby. "She all right?" Ryder asked.

"Not really, no. Her brother and sister-in-law were murdered right in front of her." He stopped. "It's gonna be a long night. Tell Poppy I probably won't be home until late morning when you see her."

"Sure," Jase said.

Noah could feel their gazes on him as he walked over to join his deputy, planning out the next steps that needed to be taken. Starting with finding the site of the murders, and the rest of the victims.

SEVENTEEN

Ryder stepped up to the back of the ambulance with Jase just as the paramedic was about to shut the rear doors. Ember was lying down again, a blanket draped over her. She turned her head and met Ryder's gaze, looking exhausted.

"My cousin Molly—his wife," he added, pointing a thumb at Jase, "is working in the ER tonight. We called her to say you were coming in. She'll be there to meet you as soon as you get there."

"She'll take good care of you," Jase added.

Ember nodded, grief etching her face. "Thanks."

As the ambulance drove off, he and Jase strode over to Noah, who was on his phone next to his vehicle. Noah ended the call as they reached him. "Where did Ember appear on the road?"

"Down this way," Ryder said, taking the lead. He walked to the area where he'd seen Ember step out onto the road, using the light on his phone to look at the ground. He found her footprints in the soil at the edge of the shoulder. "Here."

"We're stretched thin tonight. I'm calling in everyone I

can, but it'll take them a while to get here. I need your help finding the other victims." Noah took over, leaving his deputy behind to meet the others, and led the way using his flashlight. "Stay clear of her tracks."

Ryder followed, with Jase behind him. It was fairly easy to spot the route Ember had taken up the hillside. The ground was waterlogged from recent rain, holding the shape of her footprints. Partway down the brush covering the hill got thicker, and they lost the trail.

"We'll pick it up again at the bottom," Noah said, and kept descending.

The bushes gave way to a thick band of forest as they neared the bottom of the hill. A steady breeze blew between the trunks and picked up when they made it to the edge of the dunes. Noah stopped and pointed his flashlight, searching around for footprints in the sand. "I'll go right, you guys go left. Just make sure you don't disturb any evidence."

Ryder and Jase started south, both of them using the light on their phones to check the ground. They found some small animal tracks. Then, up ahead, Ryder spotted an area where the sand had been churned up.

"Over here," he said to Jase.

As they neared it, more evidence became visible. Various sets of footprints in the sand, all leading in different directions. He and Jase stopped, not wanting to damage any of the prints, and Ryder's light caught on a slight mound in the sand in the midst of the tracks.

A human arm stuck up through the sand.

"Holy shit," he breathed, shining his light on it.

Standing next to him, Jase stuck his fingers in his mouth and let out a shrill whistle to alert Noah. "God damn, they just dumped them right out here in the open."

Noah ran up a minute later. Silent and grim, he took in the

scene with them, the high-powered flashlight illuminating a scene straight from hell.

Someone's hiking boot was visible beneath a thin layer of sand. A patch of bright blue jacket. And the clawed-out area where Ember must have dragged herself out.

Noah quickly went to work locating all the victims and checking for pulses. Ryder wasn't surprised when he straightened and shook his head a few minutes later.

Imagining what had happened here made Ryder sick and filled him with helpless rage. He'd seen shit like this in Afghanistan, Iraq and Syria, but never here at home.

He could hear Noah in the background on the phone, talking to a Special Agent Dunham, telling him about the crime scene. Within an hour, this whole area would be crawling with Feds.

Noah finished the call. "Feds are on the way. You guys better head back up top. But hey," he said, grabbing Ryder's arm as he turned away. "Do me a favor and check on Danae. I don't want her and Finn to be alone right now."

The words sent a chill down his spine. "Why, what's the matter?"

"I came straight here from the vet clinic. Some guy busted in with a wounded man and held her at gunpoint, made her stitch his buddy up. Probably would have killed her if he hadn't been scared off at the last minute."

"*What?*" He bristled, all his muscles pulling tight. Some asshole had threatened Danae and pointed a weapon at her? What the *fuck?*

"Jesus," Jase breathed. "Is she okay?"

"Yes. But Ember told me she thought one of the attackers was shot in the confusion. They must have gone looking for medical supplies and saw the vet clinic, wanting to avoid a hospital visit."

"I'll stay with her." Ryder spun away and took off through the woods with Jase right behind him.

Protectiveness and rage twisted inside him as he pulled out his phone to call her. No answer.

He ran back through the woods and up the slope with Jase right behind him. He needed to get to her as fast as he could. Make sure she was okay, and make sure he was there to protect her until those murderous bastards were caught.

~

"THAT WAS the scariest thing I've ever been through in my life," Danae said, now seated on her couch in the living room with Poppy and Finn.

She'd only just arrived home a few minutes ago after giving her statement to one of Noah's deputies. Poppy and Finn had been waiting for her at the door, both worried sick.

"I'll bet," Poppy said, handing her a mug of hot decaf tea. Savannah was fast asleep in her stroller over by the kitchen doorway, dreaming sweet, innocent dreams and oblivious of the evil in the world that Danae had glimpsed firsthand tonight.

"Thanks." She snuggled deeper into the corner of the couch and leaned into Finn a bit.

She swallowed, struggling to push back her emotions. Every time she thought about that gun pointed at her the last time, the moment when she'd thought her life was about to be snuffed out, and that Finn would be all alone in the world, it made her tear up.

Finn pulled a tissue from the box on the coffee table and handed it to her.

She flashed him a quick smile through her tears and

dabbed at her eyes. "I'll be okay," she whispered, thankful he was sticking next to her.

Headlights cut across the front window, and she recognized the vehicle. "It's Sierra," she murmured, and Poppy jumped up to let her in.

Sierra rushed through the door, her eyes fixing on Danae. "Are you okay?" she demanded, coming over to crouch down and take her hands, forehead knitted in an anxious frown.

"Yes." Physically, anyway. But that was a damn miracle, because she'd seen the intent in the man's eyes. He had been about to kill her. If that car hadn't pulled up exactly when it had... She shivered.

"You only told me the main parts on the phone earlier. What else happened?"

She explained everything as quickly as she could because it was Sierra's clinic and she deserved to know. "And then they left," she finished, not wanting to go over it again. She was tired, the adrenaline crash and emotional toll hitting her hard. While she appreciated her friends' concern and show of support, she wasn't up to visiting right now.

Sierra rubbed Danae's hands to warm them, her blue eyes full of worry. "Beckett's at the clinic right now. He's going to put cameras in every room—except the washrooms."

"Hopefully the exterior ones out back caught enough for the police to ID the guys. Or at least the wounded one, since he didn't have a mask on."

"I'm just so sorry it happened at all," Sierra said, hugging her, then sat on the loveseat across from them and began talking to Finn.

Danae started to drift into a sort of fog. Sierra and Poppy both fussed over her, bringing her food, more tea, covering her with a blanket. Finn stayed next to her, not saying a word, and a twinge of guilt hit her. She'd moved them here for a fresh start, and now this nightmare had happened.

She raised her head from the couch cushion when another vehicle pulled into the driveway. "That's Jase," Poppy said, and went to open the door.

But it wasn't Jase who strode in, it was Ryder. His gaze locked on her from the doorway, his face so full of concern it made her throat tighten. Finn moved aside and Ryder was there in four strides, sinking down beside her and drawing her into his arms right in front of everyone.

She burrowed in close, squeezing her eyes shut against the rise of tears as he held her tight to his chest. She didn't care that the others were watching, or that Finn no doubt realized there was something going on between them. Didn't care what anyone thought or what conclusions they came to. With Ryder holding her she finally felt safe, and she didn't want him to let go.

"Are you all right?" he asked in a low voice. Jase was here too, gathering Savannah from the stroller. "I called as soon as I heard, but you didn't pick up."

She nodded, afraid that if she tried to speak she would just choke up. Instead, she soaked up the comfort of his embrace, his strength and protection, not lifting her head from his neck until she had herself back under control again.

He leaned back a bit and set a hand on the side of her face, studying her in concern. "Noah told us what happened."

"You saw him?"

He glanced at Jase, then focused back on her. "Something else happened tonight. Something big, and it's probably connected to the guys who broke into the clinic."

"What is it?" Poppy demanded before she could.

"Mass shooting south of Crimson Point," Jase answered.

"He said to tell you he probably won't be home tonight, but he'll call when he can."

Danae's fingers curled into the front of Ryder's jacket, fear curdling her insides as he told her more details. Human trafficking. Innocent bystanders being chased down and executed. Burying them in the sand as they lay dying. The lone survivor crawling out of the shallow pit they'd been dumped into.

She swallowed, her mouth suddenly dry, pulse pounding in her ears. It was horrific. Unthinkable. And—

Shit, oh shit...

"I saw the wounded guy's face," she managed, her voice shaking a little. "I think that's why the other one was going to kill me." Was it possible he would come after her again, to keep her from helping the police identify them?

Ryder's face was somber. "You're going to have to take extra precautions from now until they're caught. It's likely anyone involved in what happened tonight has fled the area and won't be coming back, but you need to be careful anyway."

A phone rang, breaking the taut silence. "It's Beckett," Sierra said, looking at her phone, and answered.

She spoke to him for a minute, then ended the call. "He says the security cameras only caught brief glimpses of both suspects, and no clear image of the one without a mask. The sheriff's department is going to have you work with a sketch artist in the morning to help ID him."

"Okay." She released her hold on Ryder's jacket and sat up straight. "Anything else?" she asked with a tired sigh. She wasn't sure she could take anything else.

"Yeah, either I'm staying here tonight, or you're coming back to my place. Both of you," Ryder added, looking at Finn.

"We should go," Jase said to the others, tipping his head toward the door before speaking to Danae. "But if you guys need anything, just holler." He carried Savannah to the door, her stroller in his other arm, and Poppy and Sierra behind him.

"I'll be home if you need me," Poppy said, then ducked out.

"And I'll have my phone on me all night," Sierra added. "I'll call to check in on you tomorrow after you've had some sleep."

When they were gone, Danae groaned and slumped against the couch cushion. "God, what a night."

Ryder reached out and pushed a lock of hair back from the side of her face, his dark, intense gaze on her. "Do you want to stay here tonight, or go to my place?"

The Christmas tree glowed cheerfully in the corner, the contrast to her current mood jarring. It didn't seem like Christmas at all anymore, and between the shooting on Christmas Eve and tonight's horrific events, she was starting to feel like she and Finn would never find a new normal ever again.

"I want to stay here." This was her home. Finn's home. She wanted to be in her own space, have her things around her.

Ryder nodded once. "What else do you need?"

To get warm. She was still chilled in spite of the hot tea and blanket. Cold to the marrow of her bones, and every time she thought about that gun pointed at her that last time, it shook her. "A hot bath."

Hopefully followed by lying wrapped in his arms for the rest of the night.

EIGHTEEN

Finn stayed put on the couch, trying to come up with an excuse to leave the room without him looking like a heartless dick. Holy shit, tonight had been crazy. It scared him to know he'd almost lost his mom tonight.

He was trying not to look at her and Ryder. She was still perched on his lap, and Finn just wanted to escape to his room now. They were clearly into each other, and probably just wanted to be alone right now. Finn wasn't sure how he felt about that beyond surprised, and being glad that Ryder was here to make sure she was okay.

Except a giant, burning knot had formed in the pit of his stomach when he'd heard Ryder talk about the mass shooting. Hearing what had happened to his mom was upsetting enough, but the rest of it…

His mind kept circling back to that night at Grant's house. Everything he'd seen and heard since. Including the shooter on Christmas Eve.

The warning buzz inside him kept growing louder and louder, until there was no way to ignore it. He had to say something. But not to his mom. He didn't want to upset her more than she already was, and maybe—hopefully—he was wrong about this.

"I'm gonna go take a hot bath," she said, and finally got off Ryder's lap as she pushed to her feet.

"I'll run and grab a few things from the cottage, then come right back," Ryder said to them.

Finn stayed where he was, bouncing his knee as the anxiety kept growing, using the time alone to think through what he wanted to say. He could totally be wrong. Maybe there was no connection. But if it turned out there was, he couldn't live with himself if he didn't come forward now.

Ryder came back less than five minutes later with some rolled-up clothes and locked the door behind him. He seemed surprised to see Finn still there in the living room, watching him. "Everything okay?"

"Yeah, I just… Can I talk to you about something?"

"Sure." Ryder came into the room, set his stuff down on the coffee table, then sat on the other end of the couch. "What's up?"

Finn pushed out a breath. "What you said before, about the murders, and the woman who saw guys loading women into trucks."

Ryder's gaze sharpened. "What about it?"

He rubbed his hands over his thighs, struggling to fight the growing unease. "It could be nothing. I mean, I might just be paranoid and jumping to conclusions, but… I think a guy I've been kinda hanging out with could be involved in it somehow. On a low level." He hoped it was a low level. "And his dad or stepdad too."

Ryder's eyebrows crashed together, his expression foreboding. "Explain."

"Grant is a senior. We're not friends, but I met him through my buddy Paul. Not that we're gonna be hanging out again after this," he muttered under his breath. "Anyway, he deals drugs. Or at least I'm pretty sure he does."

"How do you know?"

"I saw it. The other night. I was there, in a spot out in the woods south of here when he did a drop."

Ryder's face darkened. "And?"

"At Grant's place there was a local paper on the table, with a front-page story about a missing senior from my school." He paused. "Some of the guys said she probably just ran away again. But then Grant's stepdad or whatever said something that sounded weird, and he and Grant smiled at each other like there was an inside joke. Or a secret."

Guess we won't be seeing her around these parts anytime soon.

"What did he say?" Ryder demanded.

Finn told him, then fell silent and folded his arms across his middle, feeling ill. Shit, what if he was right? What if they knew exactly what had happened to that girl? What if she'd been kidnapped because she was an easy target due to her history of running away from home, and been trafficked? What if Grant and the man were in on it?

"What else?" Ryder said, jaw tight.

"It all just felt wrong. And they live in this big, fancy house. Grant has a brand-new SUV, and the stepdad or whoever has a new Audi. I think it's all drug money. Or worse." He swallowed, watching Ryder. "What if they're involved in this, and know the guys who killed those people tonight and threatened my mom?"

Ryder pulled out his phone, the look on his face deadly, and the pressure of the lump in Finn's throat made the backs of his eyes sting. "You need to tell Noah. Now," he said, holding his phone out to Finn.

"I didn't know he was a drug dealer," he insisted, panicking. He didn't want Ryder or anyone else to think he was involved with that shit. "Paul just said we were invited to hang with Grant and the others, and next thing I knew we were in the SUV with them, on the way to a drug deal."

Ryder's expression softened slightly. "No one's blaming you. This isn't your fault. But you can help make it right."

"But what if I'm wrong? What if Noah investigates them and it turns out I'm way off? They'll know I ratted on them. You don't mess with Grant. He was already pissed at me because I cut contact after I saw the drug deal. The guy had a gun. Grant probably has one too, and—" He stopped.

"You think it was Grant who shot at your place on Christmas Eve," Ryder finished incredulously, putting the pieces together.

Finn nodded, completely miserable. He should have listened to his instincts that night and stayed at the movie with Carly. He never should have gone with Grant.

Ryder set a hand on his shoulder, squeezed slightly. "Hey. Like I said, this isn't your fault. But you have to report it. Trust Noah to handle this."

"I *do* trust him." Oh, man, Sheriff Buchanan was gonna be so disappointed in him when he found out who he'd been hanging with, and that he hadn't spoken up sooner about his suspicions after Christmas Eve.

His *dad* would have been so disappointed in him.

He pulled in a ragged breath, blinking back tears.

Ryder's hand remained on his shoulder. "If it turns out you're wrong, then no harm done—but I don't think you are. And if you're right, then this could give Noah and his department a break in the case." He nodded at him, dark brown eyes steady. "Call and tell him everything you just told me. I'll stay with you if you want."

He definitely wanted Ryder here. "What about my mom?"

He glanced down the hall toward her closed bedroom door. "I don't want her to know about this right now, in case I'm wrong. I don't want to stress her out any more than she already is."

"Fair enough. You talk to Noah, then you can wait until morning to tell your mom. We can tell her together if you want. But you're going to have to tell her."

Relief washed over him. At least Ryder wasn't mad at and didn't seem disappointed in him. And he didn't have to do this all on his own. "Okay."

Gathering his courage, Finn took the phone and made the call.

∼

RYDER GLANCED up from his phone when Danae entered the living room, dressed in flannel PJs and a fuzzy pink robe. Finn had finished his call to Noah ten minutes ago and retreated to his room for the night.

Ryder had promised not to say anything to Danae about it for now. Noah was going to call Finn with an update in the morning, and then Finn could sit down and talk to her. With Ryder, if Finn wanted.

"Guess my son's disappeared into his cave for the night?" she asked, standing by the end of the couch.

"Yeah, he needed to decompress, I think."

"Well, that makes two of us." She tightened the belt around her waist, flicking him an uncertain look, as if she wasn't sure what to do now that they were alone.

"C'mere," he said, reaching out to grasp her hand. He tugged her toward him, gathered her up and sat her across his lap, banding one arm around her back and stroking his free hand through her hair. She'd had one hell of a scare tonight, and he wanted to give her all the comfort he could. And to be honest, after what he'd seen, he needed it too.

Danae sighed and cuddled into him, her unspoken trust making his whole chest tighten. Damn, she was already burrowing past his defenses and into his heart. He couldn't pull away from her now when she needed him, though, and didn't want to anyway.

"Does it ever get any easier?" she asked softly after a few minutes.

"Does what get easier?" She smelled so damn good. A subtle mix of soap and perfume and woman.

"Getting over having a loaded weapon pointed at you."

He stopped stroking her hair and wrapped both arms around her, drawing her closer. With her warm weight resting against him and her ass in his lap, he was already half-hard, but determined to ignore the rush of hunger in his blood. "No," he admitted. "And it's gonna take a while for the fear to fade." The sooner those assholes responsible were arrested, the better.

"I was afraid you were going to say that."

He wished he could make this easier for her somehow. "Is there someone else you want to talk to? Your parents maybe?"

"It's just my mom now. I already talked to her on the way home. I'll talk to her again tomorrow. Right now, I just want y—this," she amended quickly.

It felt like a giant fist squeezed his heart that she wanted him here and wanted to be close. "I'm not going anywhere," he murmured against her temple. "Wanna watch a movie or something? Be good to help take your mind off things a little."

"Sure." She grabbed the remote, flipped through the channels and stopped. "Hey, it's Becca Sandoza."

"So it is." But all he cared about was Danae. He shifted her onto her side, stretching out behind her and drawing her into the curve of his body.

She groaned and cuddled in tighter, making him even harder. "Oh, God, I've missed spooning."

He looped an arm around her ribs and kissed the edge of her cheek. She must miss her husband like hell right now. And when Ryder left, she would have no one to hold her.

It twisted him up inside, denial and protectiveness roaring through him. He fucking hated what Danae had gone through tonight. Hated this entire situation, and that he wouldn't be here for her soon.

Leaving suddenly seemed unthinkable. How the hell was he supposed to leave her when she needed him? When he cared this much and was so into her?

He tried to watch the movie, but he'd seen it before, and he was completely preoccupied by the woman in his arms. He already cared about her, dammit. Didn't want her to have to face getting through this alone, and if Finn's suspicions were correct, the danger might be closer to home than she imagined.

Within half an hour he felt her body slacken and her breathing deepen. He lifted his head to look down at her face, and his heart tripped all over itself. She was asleep, so damn beautiful and kind, and shouldering so much all on her own.

Her eyes flew open when he eased his arm from around her waist, that startled, pale blue gaze piercing him. "Let's get you to bed," he murmured, dropping a kiss on her forehead.

She sat up, still half-asleep, and walked with him to her bedroom door. But when he stopped there, she faced him and reached for his hand.

He started to shake his head. This was a bad idea. He wanted her too damn much, and his need to comfort and protect were testing his control. The urge to lay her down on her bed and peel the robe off her, stroke every inch of her naked body with his hands and mouth, drive into her, claim her, had all his muscles tensing.

"Stay with me," she whispered.

There was no fucking way he could deny her when she looked at him like that, her plea blending with the fear she was trying to mask. And Finn was in his room, online with friends. Ryder could hear his voice coming from behind the closed door down the hall.

He relented with a nod, pulse thudding as Danae led him into her room, and then to her queen-size bed. She reached for the belt on her robe. He stopped as lust punched through him. She even managed to make flannel PJs look hot.

"They're not sexy, I know," she said with a wry smile. "But they're cozy."

He shushed her by stepping forward, cupping her cheek in one hand, and brushing his lips across hers. Just a fleeting caress.

She inhaled sharply, her pupils dilating in the lamplight until they all but swallowed the pale irises.

More arousal flooded him, combined with a possessiveness that shocked him. Nope. They weren't going there. Not now. Especially not tonight.

"Lie down," he said in a low voice. He would get in and hold her, nothing more.

She got into bed and came up on an elbow, watching him as he pulled the covers back on his side. "You don't have to if it makes you uncomfortable."

He bit back a humorless laugh. Uncomfortable? Maybe because of the suddenly tight fit of his jeans, but that was all. "I want to."

He kept all his clothes on as he crawled in next to her, an

added barrier in case his resolve weakened. Before he could even stretch out, she turned toward him and plastered the length of her body to his.

He closed his eyes and bit back a moan, the feel of her even in those flannel pajamas making it hard to remember he was only here to hold her and make her feel safe.

Her sigh gusted against the base of his throat, her breath warm against his skin. "Thank you," she whispered.

He held her close, one hand buried in the luxurious thickness of her hair. "Try to sleep now, sweetheart. I've got you."

She eventually drifted off, but he only allowed himself to doze off and on. Twice she startled awake during the night, her body rigid with fear. Both times he murmured to her in a soothing voice and stroked her hair and back until she fell asleep again.

Faint gray light eventually began to seep around the edges of the wide blind on the window, signaling daybreak. She was on her stomach now, facing away from him with her long hair trailing over the pillow, still sound asleep.

Ryder pushed up on an elbow to study her, giving himself until it began growing brighter outside. Then, carefully, he eased from the bed and crept out the door. Finn probably wouldn't be up for a while yet, but Ryder didn't want to take any chances of the kid finding him in bed with Danae.

He settled himself on the couch and lay there staring up at the ceiling, at war with himself, intensely aware of the clock ticking down on his time in Crimson Point.

The last thing he wanted was to walk away now. He wanted to be here to protect Danae until the danger had passed.

But it didn't matter what he wanted, because duty would tear him away in only a few more days.

NINETEEN

"Can't talk right now, Pop," Noah said as he got out of his vehicle in front of the large log cabin built in a clearing high up on the hill southeast of town.

"I just wanted to make sure you're okay," Poppy said, her voice worried.

"I promise I'm fine," he said, wanting to reassure her. What he'd seen and heard last night was weighing on him though.

"Is there anything I can do?"

"Yeah, just check on Danae for me later. How was she last night?"

"Scared. Ryder stayed the night with her and Finn. I haven't talked to her yet this morning. I'm going to take some muffins over there in a bit and see how she is."

His wife was a total sweetheart, and he knew exactly how lucky he was to have her. "That's good of you." He eyed the front door ahead of him. Boyd would already know he was here. Had probably known the instant Noah's vehicle had come onto his property half a mile down the road.

"Noah?"

"Yeah?"

"Did they… Did they really bury those people while some of them were still alive?"

He stopped walking, his hand tightening around the phone. Shit, Ryder must have told her. Not realizing it would trigger so much darkness for her.

"Yes." He paused, hating that this had dredged up the nightmare she'd endured at the hands of an elusive serial killer Noah almost hadn't identified in time. "You okay, sunflower?"

"I'm… Not really," she admitted, her voice unsteady.

He wished he was with her right now. "We're going to find who did this, and make sure they face justice."

"I know."

The sadness in her voice sliced at him. Being sheriff meant duty getting in the way of family sometimes. "I'll be home as soon as I can. I love you."

"Love you too. Just be careful."

"I will."

Ending the call, he walked up the wooden steps to the front door of the cabin and raised his hand to knock. Before his knuckles made contact, the latch lifted, and the door eased open.

"Sheriff." Boyd Masterson wore a flannel shirt with the sleeves rolled up to his elbows, revealing the tats on both forearms. His short, dark hair was graying at the temples, and damp from a recent shower.

Although he was almost fifty, Boyd was fitter than most men twenty years younger. He'd lived alone up here for the past two years now, and while he wasn't all that sociable, he was a reliable source for anything that happened in this area. "Long night for you, I'm guessing," he added, green eyes studying Noah.

"Yeah." He was dead on his feet, and so were his deputies. Between the situation with Danae and the mass murder, he'd been forced to call everyone in, including support personnel. They'd spent all night combing the area around the grave, searching for whatever evidence they could find. At least they'd been able to rescue the unconscious women they'd found dumped into the back of the moving truck.

Boyd tipped his head toward the back of the cabin. "Just made a fresh pot of coffee if you want some."

He almost groaned. Normally he stopped in at the café on his way to the station, but he hadn't been back to town yet. "If it's not any trouble."

"Not at all. Come on in."

He followed Boyd into the kitchen, a cozy, rustic room in the log home he'd built up here in the hills, far away from the town and everyone in it. Boyd was a loner, but he was a good guy, and he'd served many years in the Army. His son was currently serving as a PJ with the Air National Guard.

"What do you take in it?" Boyd asked him, filling a mug at the counter.

"Cream, if you've got it." He took the mug with a murmured thanks and waited for Boyd to invite him to sit down at the circular table in the middle of the room. A log fire was burning in the fireplace a few feet away.

"Feds are on scene now," he said when they were both seated. "Got here at oh-six-hundred and have officially taken over the investigation." But this was his home, his town, and he wanted to find out everything he could on his own to assist with the investigation.

"You want to know what I heard last night."

"I do."

With a calm voice and stoic expression, Boyd relayed

what happened. His years of combat experience were evident in his eyes, and the way he spoke and carried himself.

"What time was this?"

"Right around seventeen-twenty."

It matched exactly what Ember had said in her statement. She'd been much more clear-headed this morning when he'd gone to see her at the hospital, but she would never be the same and had a lot of healing to do. Once the Feds were finished with her, she would go home to Seattle and begin planning a funeral for her brother and sister-in-law.

"How is the survivor?" Boyd asked, taking Noah by surprise. That information hadn't been officially released yet. The Feds were going to issue a statement in the next few days once they had a handle on things.

"How did you know?"

Boyd lifted a broad, flannel-clad shoulder. "Rumors floating around."

Someone from the hospital, maybe. Noah couldn't legally tell him much about the situation, however. "There was a female survivor. She's cooperating fully with us. But the other five people she was with last night were all murdered."

Boyd nodded, his vivid green eyes somber. "Even a hermit like me hears the rumors. This is too big for Crimson Point. Has to be related to organized crime."

Also bang on. "We're looking into that now, along with the Feds. But there's definitely been criminal activity in this area recently. Thought you should hear it from me, so you were aware."

"I appreciate that."

Boyd Masterson could more than handle himself if anyone dangerous stumbled onto his property. Anyone who made the mistake of tangling with him would soon regret it. "Thanks for the coffee. I needed it."

"Sure. Take one to your deputy outside."

He carried the filled travel mug to his deputy, waiting out in Noah's department-issued vehicle. "His statement matches Ember's exactly," Noah said, exhausted and looking forward to a hot shower and seeing his wife. He didn't want her to be alone right now. Maybe he'd call Tiana and ask her to go over until he got home.

"What's that guy's story, anyway? I heard he's like a strange mountain recluse or something," he said to Noah.

"He's a highly decorated former Delta operator who's more than earned some peace and quiet." Considering everything Noah knew about him, he was just thankful Boyd was an ally and not his enemy.

～

JOSH DIDN'T LOOK TOO good this morning. In fact, he looked like shit.

Kyle studied his brother, worried. Josh had been nearly unconscious by the time Kyle had been able to bring him back here last night and carry him inside the cabin. Josh had slept for a few hours, then woken, and he'd seemed a bit better. More alert.

Now he was sleeping again, but his face was pale except for his cheeks, which were flushed dark pink. Kyle put his palm to his brother's forehead and cursed silently. Fever. Maybe an infection starting.

The bleeding was still under control at least, and the stitches were holding. That woman had given Josh shots for pain and infection, but they'd both probably worn off by now. Kyle would have given anything to hear one of Josh's wisecracks or see his brother grin. Anything to reassure him that Josh was going to be okay.

Last night had been one fuck-up after another. They'd picked that area for the transfer specifically because it was so isolated and because they hadn't used it before. There was no way anyone should have been out there at that time of night in the middle of winter, and after those hikers had stumbled upon them, things had gone from bad to worse.

He rubbed a hand over his stubbly upper lip, more stress piling up with every passing hour. They shouldn't be here. They should have been hours down the coast, well across the California line by now, on their way to San Fran. But he couldn't move Josh yet. It was too dangerous in his brother's condition.

Shaking out a few pain relievers from the bottle he'd found in the bathroom earlier, he picked up the glass of water and put his hand behind Josh's neck. "Hey, wake up."

His brother's eyelids fluttered open weakly, a grimace pulling at his mouth.

"You've got a fever. You need to swallow these pills."

"Tired," Josh mumbled, shivering. "Hurts."

"I know. But get these down you, then you can sleep again."

He helped Josh with the pills, waited until he'd swallowed a few more sips of water, then eased his head back onto the pillow and covered him with the quilt. Josh was out within moments.

Kyle stood and began quietly pacing the length of the small cabin. He definitely wasn't moving Josh today, and since they didn't have any food or medicine, he needed to pick up some supplies.

He reached into his pocket for his phone. When he pulled it out, a crumpled receipt fell to the floor. The one from last night when he'd written down the info from Victor, containing payment details and the next drop point.

But when he unfolded it, prickles of alarm skittered across his skin. The back was blank. And the receipt was for some medical supply place he'd never heard of.

"Fuck," he whispered, the blood draining from his face as the implication hit home. His receipt must have fallen out of his pocket at the vet clinic last night. The woman had knocked a bunch of papers onto the floor, and when she'd gathered them up, he'd seen the receipt sitting on top and grabbed it.

He'd grabbed the wrong goddamn one. The woman must have his. He'd seen her absently stuff the papers into a leather bag on the desk.

He glanced at his brother's still form, furious with himself. And scared.

He needed that piece of paper. The information on it. Without it, there was no way to find or access the money, and no way to contact the person he and Josh were supposed to be meeting for the next shipment in four days.

There was no way to contact anyone from the organization. He and his brother, Victor and his partner, they were all radioactive now. Disavowed by the people who held the power to protect and end them.

He had to get that slip of paper back. No matter what it took.

TWENTY

Finn rubbed his damp palms over his jeans, dreading the upcoming conversation with every fiber of his being. He'd already talked to Sheriff Buchanan about everything. Now he had to come clean to his mom.

As promised, Ryder was here, sitting in the easy chair across from him. Finn had found him on the couch when he'd come out of his room an hour ago. "You wanna eat something first?" Ryder asked him.

"Nah, I'm good." More like he wasn't hungry. His stomach was too upset right now to even think about food.

His mom appeared in the hallway and stopped on her way to the kitchen. She glanced at them both. "Morning."

"Morning," Finn mumbled. Shit, he hated all this. Should have just come clean on Christmas Eve. Maybe then his mom wouldn't have been held hostage and almost killed. Maybe those people wouldn't have been killed last night.

Every time he thought about it, he felt sick.

She frowned at them. "Something wrong?"

"Kind of."

Her eyes cut to Ryder. When he didn't say anything her

expression turned pinched, and she sat on the couch beside Finn. "What's going on?" She searched his eyes worriedly.

He blew out a breath. "The other night. When someone shot at the house. I think I know who did it."

She stared at him in alarm. "Who?"

"A guy from school. A senior. His name's Grant. Paul introduced me to him. We've...hung out a couple times."

She didn't say anything. Just kept staring. And the fear and disappointment in her eyes made him feel like shit.

"At his place I met his dad, or stepdad, I'm not sure. Anyway, I could tell the guy was bad news. He hinted about things that made me nervous. And then Grant... He drove me home, but basically, I found out he's a drug dealer. Well, at *least* a drug dealer."

She sucked in a breath, anger bleeding into her expression. "*Finn.*"

"I know. I was stuck because I was in the vehicle with them at the time. He and his dad, or stepdad, basically offered me a job. I said no. But it was other stuff they said. About a missing girl from school. I didn't think too much about it at the time, but now... I think it's more than drugs."

He rushed on, wanting to get this all out. "I cut contact with them all after that. On Christmas Eve they basically threatened me, warning me not to snitch on them." He wasn't going to show her the text with the gun gif. She was worried enough as it was. "Not long after that, the shooting happened."

His mom put a hand over her mouth. "Oh my God. Oh my God, you need to tell—"

"I've already told Sheriff Buchanan. He took my phone so they could use the evidence on it."

She lowered her hand, swallowed. "So this guy and his

dad, or stepdad, they might be involved with what happened to those people last night?"

He shrugged. "Maybe. I dunno. But like I said, I cut all contact with all of them. Even Paul."

The disappointment in her eyes was worse than if she'd yelled at him. "Finn…"

He hung his head. "I know, and I'm sorry. I would never have hung out with Paul if I'd known he hung out with guys like that. And I'm sorry I didn't tell you, especially after what happened Christmas Eve."

A long, tense moment of silence followed. Then she sighed. "All right. Come here." She held out her arms.

His throat stung as she hugged him. Her forgiveness meant everything.

After a moment she pulled back to look him dead in the eye. "Is that everything? Or is there more?"

"That's it. I swear."

She hugged him again then sat back, shaking her head. "God, when I think about you having any link at all to people like that…" She stopped, calmed herself. "Thank you for telling me." Then she looked over at Ryder. "I'm guessing you already knew?"

He dipped his chin. "He told me last night. I promised to let him tell you this morning."

Finn cringed inside at the way that sounded out loud. But hell yeah, telling his mom had been a thousand percent harder than telling Ryder.

"Okay," she said in a tone that rang with finality and got up. "I'm having leftover pumpkin pie—with extra whipped cream if anyone wants to join me."

As she walked to the kitchen Finn let out a slow breath, all but sagging back into the couch. Ryder got up, stopped on his way by to lay a hand on Finn's shoulder. "Proud of you," he said, squeezing once before going to the kitchen.

Those quiet words, that squeeze, made warmth spread through his chest. Made him think of his dad, and what he would have thought of all this.

I'm sorry, Dad, he said silently, hoping he could somehow hear it. *I screwed up, but I've done everything I can to make it right now.*

He hoped it would be enough.

~

"EXCHANGE THIS SHIRT FOR A LARGE, got it," Ryder said from the passenger seat beside her, and took the bag holding one of Finn's Christmas gifts that she handed him. "Anything else?"

She'd taken the day off to…process things before going back to work tomorrow. Ryder had insisted on running her errands for her while she waited in the car, and in truth she felt safer that way. "I placed an online order at the drug store. It should be waiting for me at the counter if you don't mind." Hopefully he wouldn't look in the bag and see the condoms.

She hadn't needed to use any since she and Terry first started sleeping together in senior year of high school, but if things kept progressing with Ryder the way she suspected, then she wanted to be prepared. And a small bottle of lube just in case, because hey, it had been a while.

"Sure." Ryder got out, paused before closing his door to give her a half-smile. "You okay?"

She was parked in the middle of a busy mall parking lot, in broad daylight. This was as safe as she was going to get without Ryder standing guard next to her every single second. "I'm good. Thanks for checking."

He leaned in, kissed her softly. "Back in a bit. Lock the doors."

She did as soon as he shut his, then watched him walk across the parking lot toward the entrance. It hit her just how emotionally attached to him she was already.

He'd slept in her bed for the past two nights, fully clothed, holding her, without making any sexual advances. Solely to make her feel safe. Both mornings she'd woken alone because he'd snuck out at daybreak, not wanting to cause any awkwardness with Finn who was under enough stress.

How was she supposed to stay emotionally uninvolved with a man like that?

Laying her head back, she closed her eyes to rest while the radio played quietly and tried to empty her mind. Things had been so insane, but she refused to sit at home and dwell over what had happened the other night any longer. On top of dealing with Finn's bombshell about Grant and the stepdad guy, she had worked with the sketch artist yesterday, and done two more interviews with the FBI.

They were continuing the investigation and any potential links to Grant's stepdad—whose name was Victor—and had assured her that the suspects who had broken into the clinic were most likely long gone from the area, along with the other two men involved in the murders. Even so, Ryder had shifted into straight-up bodyguard mode and insisted on being her shadow wherever she went.

Besides, living in fear wasn't an option for her. Crimson Point was her home now, and this was her *life*. She wanted to reclaim it and get things back to normal as soon as possible. Even if she dreaded stepping through the clinic door tomorrow morning and having everything flood back.

The rattle of a shopping cart made her open her eyes. An

elderly woman was pushing it to a cart return nearby. But then a weird sense that she was being watched made her look up.

It felt like her heart stopped for an instant as she locked gazes with the man standing across the parking aisle from her. The way he was staring at her—shock and recognition—set off her internal radar. He was tall and powerfully built. Short, dark hair. Pale green eyes.

A warning prickle made the hairs on her nape stand up. He kind of reminded her of—

Her gaze dropped to his hand, holding a bag. And her heart lurched when she saw the heavy black tat on the back of his wrist.

Jerking her eyes back up to his face, she started to reach for her phone to call for help, but the man whirled away and rushed through a row of parked cars.

"Shit," she breathed as she lost sight of him, digging her phone out of her purse to dial 911, her pulse pounding.

He might come back. She couldn't sit here and wait for Ryder.

Just as the emergency operator answered, Danae started the engine and sped away, relaying what had just happened. "It was the man who held me at gunpoint two nights ago. I'm sure of it." She was breathing too fast, her hands trembling on the wheel, gaze darting to the rearview and side mirrors every few seconds.

"Ma'am, try to stay calm. Where are you right now?"

She would call Ryder as soon as she finished this one, but she couldn't sit here a moment longer. "Just leaving the mall." She turned out of the parking lot and sped up the road, watching for any sign of being followed.

It wasn't likely. That guy would no doubt be trying to get the hell away from here. Still, she wasn't taking a chance.

"I'm going to drive straight to the police station and talk to Sheriff Buchanan in person."

"Okay, how far away are you currently?"

"About seven miles." Ryder would be worried as hell when he found out what was happening, but she couldn't focus on him now.

When no one followed her through the next light, she relaxed a bit, her heart rate easing. Damn, that had been scary as hell. She couldn't believe they'd run into each other. The FBI were definitely wrong about him leaving the area.

She stayed on the line with the operator as she drove, until she reached the turnoff to Crimson Point. She took it. "Okay, I'm technically in CP now. Still no sign of him. I should be at the station in—"

She broke off at the sound of a speeding engine coming up behind her, gasped and swerved her car as it whipped past her and cut hard in front. The abrupt turn caused her tires to spin on the wet road, sending her careening toward the sheer rock face of the cliff to the right.

She let out a yelp and brought the car to a stop, her front bumper just inches from the cliff face on the eastern side of the highway.

"Ma'am? What's going on?" The operator's voice suddenly sounded far away.

Danae couldn't answer, she was too busy staring in horror as the other car's door opened. The driver climbed out, and a chill snaked through her when she saw his face.

"Oh my God, it's him," she blurted, panic detonating.

She grabbed the gearshift and put Professor Plum in reverse, but there was nowhere to go. She was boxed in between the other vehicle and the cliff.

She darted a panicked gaze through the windshield, her

blood pressure nose-diving. "Shit, he's coming toward me—and he's got a gun!"

"Ma'am, I've dispatched officers to help you. Can you—"

She didn't hear another word, too busy undoing her seatbelt and hitting the trunk release, too afraid to try and exit through the side. Heart slamming into her ribs, she scrambled into the back and crawled out through the rear hatch, quickly closing it and hiding behind the trunk.

Fear crawled through her. There was nowhere else to run. Nowhere to hide. The man was coming for her. She had to run. Had to find—

She whipped her head around at the sound of a big engine approaching from behind. A semi-truck rounded the curve in the road and hit its Jake brakes, releasing a blast of sound from the exhaust valves.

Danae stayed crouched behind her vehicle, torn between running to the truck and being too scared to move. The rig driver blasted the horn. She jumped at the sudden burst of noise, but in the silence that followed she heard the sound of a door slamming shut and then tires squealing as the attacker tore away.

She closed her eyes and bowed her head, sucking in shaky breaths. *Oh god, oh god, oh god...*

"Hey, are you okay?"

She turned to the semi driver, now rushing toward her with a stunned look on his face. "Yes," she answered, shuddering. Now that the initial terror had faded, she was shaky, queasy.

"Let me help you," the man said, reaching down to help her to her feet.

She gripped his upper arms, grateful for the support. "Thank you," she breathed, her legs beginning to quiver along with the rest of her.

"Who the hell was that?" he demanded.

"Long s-story," she managed.

He walked her around the side of her car and opened the door for her. "Sit down. I'll call the cops."

"They're already on the way."

"I'll stay with you, make sure that prick doesn't come back."

Nodding, she kept the 911 operator on the line and texted Ryder with trembling fingers.

~

RYDER STEPPED out of the mall with a new shirt for Finn and Danae's order from the drugstore. But when he reached the right area of the parking lot, he stopped. Danae's purple MINI was gone.

He looked around, confused. Had she moved somewhere?

His phone rang in his pocket. Seeing Danae's number on the display made him breathe easier. "Hey, where are you? I can't see—"

"Can you come get me?"

He tensed, the tremor in her voice pushing him into immediate action. "What's wrong?" he demanded.

"The gunman from the other night saw me in the parking lot. I drove away immediately, heading for the police station, but he followed without me noticing and cut in front of me on the turnoff. He blocked me in and started coming toward me with a gun in his hand. A trucker showed up and scared him off, thankfully."

Jesus Christ... Urgency ripped through him, instincts screaming at him to get to her, now. "Did you call the cops?"

"I was on the phone to 911 when it happened. They're coming."

"I'm glad you're okay." His chest hurt. A tight, searing ache that wasn't easing.

"You're Ryder?" one of the cops said as he strode toward them.

Ryder nodded and kept hold of her while they filled him in on everything so far. The semi driver was showing his dash cam footage to the other cop. With any luck it had captured the make, model and license plate of the suspect's vehicle—and hopefully an image of the asshole's face as well.

When Danae had calmed and stepped back to wipe at her cheeks with the heels of her hands, he wrapped an arm around her waist and helped her to the waiting SUV. "We'll get someone to come get your car," he told her, bundling her into the back passenger seat. "They'll either meet us at the station or bring it home for you."

The driver took them to the station, Ryder holding her hand tight the whole way. "Want me to call Finn?"

"No, he's at work. Don't tell him yet, it'll only upset him more. I'll tell him after he gets home."

Noah was waiting for them at the station. He hugged Danae and took them into a quiet conference room in the back.

Ryder sat beside her while she explained what had happened and answered Noah's questions. The department would be reviewing security footage from the mall in addition to the rig's dash cam, and Noah would pass on everything personally to the FBI agents working on the larger case.

When they'd finished up, Noah drove them home. Beckett and Jase had parked her car in her driveway. Ryder told Noah to go to his cottage instead. He felt safer having her there for the moment.

Ryder followed her inside, watching her closely. Her

"Where are you?" he demanded.

She gave him her location, and the catch in her [voice] shredded him. Dammit, he never should have let her o[ut of] his sight. "I'm on my way right now, sweetheart. Just stay [put] and I'll be there in a few minutes, okay?"

"Okay." He caught the sound of sirens in the backgrou[nd.] "I gotta go."

He was relieved to know the cops were on scene [to] protect her. "All right. See you soon."

He hailed a ride and the driver sped along the wet road[,] the invisible vise around his ribs clamping down tighter wi[th] each passing minute. He called Noah's cell on the way, b[ut] the sheriff had already heard what had happened, and Ryde[r] ended the call just before reaching the turnoff Danae ha[d] specified.

His heart squeezed when he saw her standing with two deputies and another man who must have been the rig driver. The semi was parked in the middle of the north-bound lane, and the back bumper of Danae's MINI was close to the cliff face.

He shook his head, furious with himself for not sticking to her today. He'd only known her a short time, but she already meant something to him, and if anything had happened to her...

He got out behind the cruisers blocking the road and strode over. Danae broke away from the cops, walking toward him faster and faster. Steps away, her face twisted, shredding him.

Ryder caught her and pulled her to his chest, holding her tight. With her safe in his arms, he closed his eyes and dragged in the first deep breath he'd taken since she'd called.

She shuddered, her hands gripping the back of his jacket[.] "I was so scared," she choked out.

shock had worn off a while ago. She looked tired now, ready to crash.

He slipped an arm around her waist, sliding his other hand into her thick, dark hair. "What do you need right now, sweetheart?" he murmured.

She stared up at him with those piercing, pale blue eyes, and took his face in her hands. "You. I just need *you*."

Need slammed into him, hot and intense.

On its heels came regret. *I'm leaving soon. I don't want to hurt you. And I'm not in the best spot personally right now.*

But before he could utter another word, her lips were on his, obliterating all the thoughts from his mind—except one.

Making her his. Even if it was only for a little while.

TWENTY-ONE

She wanted this. Needed this. Needed *him*.

Danae took Ryder's head in her hands and kissed him, her heart pounding out of control, besieged by a chaotic mix of arousal and a frantic need for physical reassurance that she was truly safe.

He caught her to him with a low sound that seemed to come straight from his gut, his arm locking around her hips and pulling her tight to the length of that deliciously hard body. She wasn't going to overthink this. He was here and he made her feel safe and desirable. That was all that mattered right now.

Ryder shifted her, walking her backward until she came up against the wall, then broke the kiss to stare into her eyes. His expression was tight, dark eyes blazing with hunger. "You need to be sure," he said, his voice all low and raspy.

He was sweet to stop and check. "I am. So sure, I bought condoms. They're in the bag on the table."

One side of his mouth lifted in the hint of a smile. "I've got it covered, sweetheart."

She loved it when he called her that, his deep, dark drawl

wrapping around her like a caress. Then his mouth came back down on hers and she stopped thinking altogether.

No more fear. No more loneliness. Only Ryder, and the way he made her body come to life with his touch.

The way he kissed her made heat pool low in her belly. A slow, velvet stroke of his tongue against hers tightened her nipples and ignited a desperate throb between her legs. His arm locked beneath her ass and lifted her, bringing her core against the rock-hard bulge in his jeans.

She gasped into his mouth, wound her legs around his hips and held onto his shoulders as he carried her down the hallway and into his room, kissing her like he couldn't get enough of her. When they reached the bed, he laid her down and immediately came down on top of her, anchoring her with his weight. She moaned, melting beneath him.

He worked her sweater off, then her jeans, growling low in his throat as he stared at her delicate, pale blue lace bra and panties. But she wanted to see all of him too, was hungry to explore that muscular body she'd been fantasizing about.

She peeled his snug T-shirt up the length of his torso, over his broad shoulders and over his head, then pushed on his shoulders until he straddled her hips and came up on his knees.

She stared at his body, fascinated, flattening her palms on the hard ridges of his pecs and slowly exploring the delicious terrain revealed to her. Gentle at first, then bolder, another flash of heat rippling through her when she reached the taut lines of his abs and he sucked in a breath, making them stand out in sharp relief.

She traced them with her fingertips, followed the thin line of dark hair from below his navel to where it disappeared into his waistband, her gaze fastening on the thick, hard ridge trapped in the denim.

He pushed her hands away when she started to undo his fly, peeled his jeans and underwear off and tossed them aside. She didn't even get to see what he'd uncovered before he caught her by the shoulders and forced her flat on her back, his hands locking her in place.

"Been imagining this since the first time I saw you," he muttered, his mouth on the side of her neck.

Danae tipped her head to the side to give him room, her hands busy gliding up and down the smooth length of his back. Muscles bunched and shifted beneath her palms as he moved lower, the silken heat of his lips and tongue blending with the prickle of his goatee on her skin, sending chills throughout her body.

His hands slid beneath her to release her bra. He cupped her breasts, thumbs caressing her throbbing nipples. She grabbed his head, pulling him downward, fingers digging into his scalp when the heat of his mouth closed over one rigid peak. A moan spilled free, heat and wetness gathering between her legs as pleasure streaked through her.

Time seemed to dissolve. The confident, dominant way he held her in place pushed her arousal higher, combining with the sensual pull of his mouth. And when he finally reached between them to tug her panties down her thighs, those long, warm fingers skimming her slick folds…

"Ryder," she sighed.

He kissed a spot beneath her belly button, rolling her right nipple between his fingers and thumb. "So wet, baby. Let me make this good for you."

It was already way better than good. Her muscles quivered with every tender caress of his fingers, pulling needy sounds from her throat.

Gentle swirls. Teasing glances. The tantalizing pressure of

his fingertips barely easing inside her. Then again. And again, her clit swollen, aching.

She dug her fingers into his head, fighting to breathe. So much need. She was desperate. Frantic with the need to come.

"Shh," he whispered, his dark head dipping down between her legs. His tongue touched the crease between her hips and thigh, his lips caressing a path down to his slick fingers.

She bit her lip, her hips bucking when his tongue stroked the edge of her swollen clit. Pleasure swelled, each languid, velvety caress taking her closer to the peak.

"So soft," he groaned, sliding two fingers into her on the next stroke. Rubbing. Caressing. Adding to the heat, the delicious pressure building.

She whimpered, twisted, her body gathering in anticipation of the moment he sent her flying. *Please, please, please...*

"Do you want me in you when you come?" he murmured, the combination of his fingers and tongue making her mindless.

"*Yes.*"

His fingers slid free, but his tongue stayed exactly where it was, licking slow and steady, keeping her at a simmer while he put on a condom. So she hadn't needed to go to the drugstore after all.

She had just enough awareness to glance down as he settled into place between her thighs, reaching out to touch his cock.

He took her hand and closed her fingers around him, staring down at her with burning, dark eyes. God, he was thick. Her core clenched in anticipation, greedy for the moment when he filled her.

Ryder's jaw clenched as he watched her stroke him. He allowed her only a few, then dragged her hand to his mouth for a quick kiss and put it on his shoulder before bracing his palm next to her head and reaching down to guide himself between her legs.

Danae stared up at him, breathless, her heart pounding as his hips eased forward, lodging the thickest part of him inside her. She hissed and tried to lift her hips, but he kept her immobile, staring deep into her eyes while his fingers crept up to find her clit.

Her eyes slammed shut and a long, liquid moan came from her lips, the combined sensation indescribable. She clung to his shoulders as he lowered his weight onto her and began to move. Smooth, steady strokes, the length of his cock sliding over her G-spot while his slick thumb caressed her clit.

His mouth captured hers, drinking in her incoherent moans, tongue driving deep in time with his thrusts. Her orgasm swelled, rising higher with each motion of his hips.

She locked her legs around him, thighs trembling. Caught in the vortex, and trusting that Ryder would make sure he delivered the release she was dying for.

It wasn't hard and fast. Instead, it continued to build and build, promising something incredible. Release spilled through her in long, lovely waves, carried her on an endless tide of pleasure and warmth, fading slowly into ripples.

She heard his deep growl, managed to open her eyes. Ryder's were squeezed shut, his face taut. So gorgeous he stole her breath.

Taking his head in her hands, she drew him down into a deep kiss and rocked into him. He groaned and plunged both hands into her hair, squeezing tight as he rode her faster. Harder. Until he drove deep one last time and locked there, moaning into her mouth as he shuddered over and over.

Danae held him close, stroking his shoulders, his back, her body relaxed and her mind calm. Finally, he kissed her softly and let his head drop onto her shoulder.

She closed her eyes and sighed, feeling like she might float away if it hadn't been for his heavy weight anchoring her to the bed. "I didn't expect it to be like *that*," she whispered, a smile curving her lips. "I haven't been with anyone since Terry. I mean, I was hoping it would be good, but *wow*."

He came up on his elbows to peer down at her, his fingers stroking her hair away from her face. "I knew it would be," he murmured, then started dropping kisses across her face. Her nose and forehead. Cheeks and eyelids. Her lips.

Her heart quivered, the incredible tenderness making her throat tighten. *Oh, Ryder...*

"Don't move," he whispered against her lips. "Back in a second." He withdrew from her and disappeared into the en suite.

Crawling in beside her a minute later, he pulled the covers over them and drew her half on top of him. Cradling her head in the hollow of his shoulder, he draped her bent knee across his body and kissed the top of her head. "Sleep for a bit."

His embrace, the warmth of his body and the knowledge that she was completely safe while she was in his arms, allowed her to drift off. She stirred sometime later, was vaguely aware of him leaving the bed.

Slowly she awakened, already missing the warmth of his body as the memory of what had happened earlier came back in a rush. Ending with them winding up in his bed together.

A sinking sensation took hold, taking her mood with it. Before Ryder had walked into her life, she hadn't thought she wanted or was ready for a relationship. Now...

Damn. She'd gone into this determined to keep her heart

out of the equation, but now she realized how stupid and futile—and naïve—she'd been to ever believe she was capable of that. She wasn't the sort of person who could sleep with a man without being emotionally involved.

When he left in a few more days, it was going to feel like a breakup, and she already dreaded having to deal with the pain.

She sighed to alleviate the pressure expanding in her chest and rolled to her side. Now what? There was no way to pull back from him now, and she didn't want to anyway, even to spare herself pain later on.

No. She wanted as much of him as he would give her during the time they had left together.

Quiet sounds from the kitchen broke into her thoughts. She got up, quickly pulled on her clothes and walked down the hall. Ryder stood at the sink fully dressed, his back to her. Various bottles were lined up on the counter beside him. He was pouring the contents of one into the sink.

Liquor, she realized. Her heart squeezed at the significance of it.

He glanced up when she stepped toward him. Gave her a little smile as a stream of amber whiskey flowed out of the bottle and down the drain.

"No more excuses," he said, emptying the bottle and reaching for another one.

Danae stepped up behind him to wrap her arms around his waist, cuddling close and resting her cheek against his back. "Good for you," she murmured. "And for what it's worth, I'm proud of you."

He set the empty bottle on the counter and turned, his hands closing around her hips in a possessive hold that sent a thrill through her. "Thank you." His eyes were dark and intense as he watched her. "How're you doing, sweetheart?" He tucked a lock of hair behind her ear.

"Better when you're with me." *And I'm dreading the moment you leave me.*

He nodded, dropped a soft kiss on her lips. "Good. Now how about we empty the rest of these, then go pick up Finn from work and talk to him together."

∽

KYLE READ the news article he'd just found on his phone, cold prickling over his skin. Holy fuck, what were they going to do?

He'd thought it would take time for anyone to stumble upon the bodies they'd hastily buried in the dunes. At least a few days, enough time for Josh to regain some strength and then for Kyle to find them a new safe place to lie low.

But things were even worse than that.

He read it again, his pulse accelerating, beating in his ears over the drip of the rain off the eaves outside. There was a survivor.

One fucking survivor. And whoever it was, was talking to both the local cops and the FBI about them.

The scene had been messy. So fucking messy, because it had just happened all of a sudden. None of them had been prepared for it. There had been no time to plan anything when Victor had started shooting. No time for anything, or to even realize what the hell was going on.

Only reflex. Knee-jerk reflex that had left God only knew how much evidence and their DNA at the scene. Jesus.

Josh was passed out on one of the single beds. Instinct made him want to wake his brother, get him in the truck and get as far away from the area as possible right now.

But that wasn't going to happen. Because it wasn't an option. He wasn't willing to kill his brother to try and escape. If he moved Josh now, if Josh started bleeding inside again or the stitches burst…

No. Shit, he would never risk that. And he still didn't have the receipt with the intel they needed on it. So they were stuck here in this cabin, and a manhunt was about to explode around them.

He got up, went to the window and pulled the dingy curtain aside on the small window overlooking the tangled front yard. The cabin was built on a hillside, the dirt road barely visible from here through the screen of trees and tangled brush. Outside the whole world was wet and gray, everything dripping with rain.

"Kyle?"

He turned and crossed to his brother's bedside. "Hey." Josh's eyes were glazed with fever and pain. He was too damn pale, almost gray. "Feeling any better."

"No. What's going on? What were you looking at?"

"Nothing. It's all good." He pushed the hair off his brother's forehead, forced a reassuring smile. "Just need you to get well enough to travel again."

"Working on it."

"Yeah." He tucked the blankets more securely around Josh's shoulders. "Go back to sleep. Don't worry about a thing, I've got this."

Josh stared up at him for a long moment, then closed his eyes with a sigh.

Kyle went back to the window, his insides tangled in knots. He didn't *have* this. Not by a fucking long shot.

TWENTY-TWO

Kyle's eyes flew open in the dimness. Unsure what had woken him, he blinked up at the stained ceiling tiles of the rental cabin and listened to the sound of the rain on the roof. What time was it? What day was it?

"Kyle."

He jackknifed up into a sitting position at the rasp of his brother's voice, coming from the bed next to the window. "What's wrong?" Josh lay on his back, face pinched and ashen above the dark growth covering the lower part of his face.

He put a hand on his brother's forehead. It was burning hot. Hell. "Did you sleep?"

They'd been up most of the night, talking and making plans. It had been two days since he'd been spotted in the mall parking lot. Two days since he'd failed to get the receipt back from the vet tech. Now time was running out.

He needed that fucking piece of paper with the information about the money's location, the access code for the locker where it was stored, and details about the next shipment if they were going to be able to make enough to stay on the run for a while.

"Some." Josh grimaced, tried to shift. He had seemed to be improving last night, had even eaten a decent meal at supper. Now he looked bad again, and neither of them had gotten more than a couple hours' sleep.

"Wait. I'll help turn you." He reached beneath his brother's back and carefully turned him onto his uninjured side.

Josh hissed and went rigid, blanching.

"I'll get you more meds," Kyle blurted, rushing for the table in the adjoining kitchen.

He shook out four extra strength tablets that he'd bought at the drugstore the other day and helped Josh with the water glass. He pressed his lips together. Over-the-counter meds weren't nearly strong enough. He was going to have to get something stronger, and more antibiotics. Tonight.

"What happened to your truck?" Josh said weakly, his gaze fixed on the window looking out at the SUV parked in the driveway.

"Had to get rid of it." Either the vet tech or the semi driver would have reported his license plate, so that night he'd driven inland and found a used car dealership willing to do a straight-up cash deal for the compact SUV now parked outside.

Then he'd driven his truck to a spot high up on the cliff here on the coast, doused the interior with fuel, and lit the match before pushing it over the side. Even if the cops had already found it, there wouldn't be any prints or DNA to lift.

"You find out the woman's name and address yet?"

"Heard back a few hours ago." From a guy he'd contacted within the organization who was good at hacking databases. It had cost him a couple grand, but worth it. "Her name's

Danae Sutherland, and she's apparently renting a place in Crimson Point."

"You sure she has the paper?"

"Has to. Saw her shove a bunch of them into her bag at the clinic."

"How are you gonna get it back? You can't go to that clinic again. And you can't—" He broke off, sucking a breath through his teeth, his face twisting, hand pressed to his side.

"What's wrong?" Kyle demanded, tensing.

Josh glanced down and slowly removed his hand from his ribs. There was blood all over his palm, and the bandage was soaked with it. "Shit," he muttered.

Kyle ran to the bathroom and rummaged through the stuff he'd bought, returning with more gauze pads, tape, and a new tensor bandage. "Lemme see," he ordered, pressing down on his brother's shoulder to keep him still, then reached for the edges of the tape covering the dressing.

Blood spilled down Josh's ribs, the wound puffy and red. "You've popped some stitches," he told his brother.

"Hurts," Josh said, shivering.

Working fast, Kyle soaked some gauze with hydrogen peroxide and gently cleaned the wound, flinching when his brother groaned and swore. But there was nothing he could do to close up the edge of the wound. All he could do was pack more gauze over it and then bind it tight by winding the tensor bandage around his ribs.

"Keep pressure on it," he said, placing Josh's hand back on top of the tensor bandage. "And try not to move."

Josh groaned and closed his eyes, cheeks flushed, body shivering. Kyle pulled the blankets up to his brother's chin, the frantic urge to *do* something beating at him.

Taking him to the hospital remained a last resort. The

cops would have both their images on file by now, either from the vet clinic cameras or the ones at the drugstore. If he dropped Josh at the Emergency Room, they would arrest his brother as soon as he got there, and Kyle would have to run.

He couldn't risk them being separated or caught. If they were caught, that vet tech would testify against them and seal their fate.

Kyle's decision was easy. There was no way he was abandoning his brother.

There was also no way he could move Josh now without more medical treatment.

"I'm going out," he told Josh, stalking over to the door to pull on his jacket. If she'd already turned the receipt over to someone or thrown it out, he was basically screwed. He had to recover it, no matter what it took.

"Where? What are you gonna do?" Josh asked.

"Kill two birds with one stone," he answered, and shoved his pistol into the back of his waistband. "Don't move around while I'm gone. I'll be back soon, and we'll get that bleeding stopped." With help.

He would go to the vet tech's house. Get that paper back, then eliminate her and the threat she posed. But not before he used her to save his brother again.

~

"WHEN WILL YOU BE DONE?"

Behind the wheel of Professor Plum, Danae smiled at Ryder's question as she parked along the curb in a spot just down from the front of the clinic. Rain drummed against the roof, hood and windshield. "Around five-thirty or so. Why, you gonna miss me while I'm at work or something?" She'd taken the morning off for another meeting with the FBI, and then another with Noah.

"Hell yes, I'm gonna miss you," he growled, leaning over from the passenger seat to capture her lips in a searing kiss, one hand curling around her nape to hold her still.

He'd been all but stuck to her side since the incident at the mall the other day, even patrolling around the clinic while she was at work. They'd also spent a lot of "quality" time together since getting home from the police station the other day. Including last night, after sitting down to eat dinner together with Finn at the table.

And again this morning when she'd popped over to the cottage and found him just out of the shower.

Seeing him in nothing but that towel wrapped around his hips had inspired her. She'd walked in, shoved the door closed, and jumped him.

The towel had lasted all of three seconds, and then she'd sunk to her knees to take him in her mouth, her insides turning hot and molten at the way he'd grasped handfuls of her hair and eased in and out of her mouth. She had barely begun before he'd hauled her to her feet, stripped her, then bent her over the end of the couch and gave her a hard, intense orgasm.

As if sensing her thoughts, he pulled back to peer into her eyes, made a low, guttural sound at whatever he saw there. "If we weren't in the middle of the damn street, I'd slide my hand into your panties and make you come all over my fingers right here and now."

She shivered, heat rolling through her. "Tempting as that offer is, I'd rather wait until we're alone later. So you can use your tongue," she added in a naughty whisper. It felt so good to be a sexual being again. She'd missed it, and Ryder was a deliciously generous lover.

He grinned, chuckling as he kissed her again. "Can't wait." Then he sobered. "Sure you're okay with me leaving?" He had an online therapy appointment, and she completely understood him wanting the privacy of his cottage for it.

"Of course. Sierra and the receptionist are both inside." She wouldn't be alone. The FBI had informed her that the suspects had left the area now, and Grant's stepdad was long gone too. She hoped he never returned.

"I'll be back as soon as I can."

"I can't believe you're going to run back through the rain instead of taking my car."

"Gotta burn off some of this sexual frustration somehow," he answered, taking her hand and placing it on the bulge in the front of his track pants.

"You'll be soaked by the time you get back." It was already raining steadily, and the forecast called for a deluge to begin soon, along with high winds.

"Nothing a hot shower won't cure, and then I'll be back straight after."

Danae squeezed his erection gently, rubbing her palm over the swollen head, delighting in his low moan. She loved that she held the power to do this to him.

She'd made up her mind to live in the moment and enjoy every minute they had together, rather than live the next few days in dread, anticipating him leaving. "Don't burn off *too* much."

He nipped at her lower lip, sucked it softly, giving it a caress with his silken tongue. "Go, before you break my control."

She stood on the sidewalk to watch him jog away through the gray rain, admiring the view. The man was a specimen. When he was half a block up the street, she wolf-whistled, earning a grin he tossed at her over his shoulder that almost melted her knees, then forced herself to go inside the clinic.

The receptionist smiled at her from behind the front desk, on the phone with someone. It was so much easier coming in here knowing other people were around, though it was impossible to forget what had happened in the staff room the night of the attack.

Danae waved on her way through to the back, and Sierra gave her a bright smile when she came through the door. "Was that Ryder I saw run past a minute ago?"

She looked away and set her purse on the counter, ordering herself not to blush. "Yeah, he's running home. Insisted on driving down here with me, just in case."

"Well, he *is* a bodyguard."

Yes, he was. And his career would take him away from her soon enough. But she wasn't going to let herself focus on that now.

"He's being overprotective," she told Sierra. "Noah called last night to say a different department down south found a burned-out pickup belonging to Kyle Vanderhoff at the bottom of a cliff. His brother hasn't turned up at any hospital or clinic anywhere in the area either, so they're probably far away by now." The evidence made her feel a whole lot safer.

"Good." Sierra squeezed the top of Danae's shoulder on the way by. "Let's get to work and then I won't ask a million questions about you and Ryder making out like a couple of horny teenagers in your front seat a minute ago," she teased.

Danae blushed, and thankfully Sierra didn't bring it up again. By mid-morning they'd made good headway in catching up after the holiday disruptions. A new shipment of supplies was due in the next morning, and the first spay of the day arrived soon after Danae had finished prepping the O.R.

Ninety minutes later, Sierra came in as Danae finished

prepping for the next patient, perusing the contents of a file. "Hey, I'm missing the latest lab report from the oncologist for the Boxer mix coming in next. Have you seen it?"

"Yeah, it's in my—"

Crap. In her workbag, along with all the other files she had hastily shoved in there the night she'd been held up and needed to reorganize. It was sitting at home on her kitchen table because she'd been too damn preoccupied with getting over to Ryder's this morning for a pre-work quickie to remember to go back and grab it.

"It's at home. I'll run back and grab it."

"And the receipt for the new cauterizing machine?" Sierra asked.

"It's in there too." She glanced at her watch. There was still time to grab it and get back before she needed to prep the next patient. And Finn should be home too. "Be back in fifteen."

"Okay."

She rushed down the sidewalk, hopped into Professor Plum, and pulled a tight U-turn to head back up Front Street. It was raining in earnest now, the afternoon light already beginning to fade under the heavy gloom of the dark clouds. When she got home, the warm glow of the Christmas tree in the front room window looked so cozy.

She dashed through the rain to the side door. It was locked. "Finn?" she called out as she stepped inside.

No answer, and she didn't hear his voice coming from his room. Maybe he hadn't gotten home from work yet.

She wiped her shoes on the mat and rushed into the kitchen. Her leather bag was there on the table where she'd left it, along with a note.

Miss you already, it read in Ryder's bold, uppercase block lettering.

Smiling, she folded it and tucked it into her pocket, then opened her bag and double-checked to make sure the paperwork she needed was inside.

The side door opened behind her. She turned toward it, a greeting smile in place. "Hey, buddy—"

The words died on her lips and she took a hasty step back as a man's silhouette filled the hallway instead of her son's.

Kyle Vanderhoff. Aiming a pistol at her.

His eyes shot past her to the bag on the table, then the papers in her hand. "You're coming with me," he growled.

She backed up a step, terror clawing at her. How? How had he found her? He was supposed to be far away from here.

"Mom?"

She whirled, fear coating her insides like ice when Finn's voice reached her from down the hall. Kyle whipped around too, pointing his weapon toward Finn's room.

"No!" she cried, holding her hands palm out in a supplicating gesture. Instinct took over, demanding she protect her son. "I'll go with you, right now," she told Kyle, blocking the route to Finn's room with her body. "Just don't hurt him. Please."

Kyle stalked over and grabbed her workbag. "Put your purse and the papers inside," he snapped.

She did and let out a startled cry when he grabbed her by the back of the hair and started dragging her toward the front door.

"Mom!"

Her son's frantic shout sent a new wave of terror over her. "No, Finn! Stay back and get out of here!" she yelled, her heart threatening to explode.

Kyle hustled her outside to the SUV sitting behind her car, opened the passenger door and shoved her across the console into the driver's seat. "Drive," he snarled, still holding the gun on her as he slammed the door shut beside him.

Hands shaking, Danae started the engine and did as he said. Catching a glimpse of Finn's scared face in the window as she drove away, a measure of relief hit her that at least he was safe.

TWENTY-THREE

Therapy was damn hard work. Painful work. But the only way to make it work was to be totally honest during the process. Even if every instinct he had screamed at him not to.

Ryder put away his laptop, relieved the session was over. This one had been harder than the first one, yet also more freeing. He was starting to trust his therapist more. Able to open up to him about things he hadn't been before.

Chase called him as he was getting ready to head out and drive back to the clinic to wait for Danae to finish. When he'd come here for the holidays, the last thing he'd expected was to get involved with anyone. With Danae it was even more than that. He had never been this serious with anyone before, and never so fast. But it felt right. Now he didn't know what the hell he was going to do when he left.

"Dude, are you *serious* right now?" Chase said in a shocked tone when Ryder told him everything that had happened since they'd last spoken.

"I know. It's been...eventful around here."

"No shit. You okay?"

"I'm all right." Conflicted about leaving Danae to fend for herself, though. And even more so about the strength of his feelings for her.

He didn't know how he was going to walk away and go back to work like nothing had happened, or spend the next few months on the other side of the world in Australia without a chance in hell of being with her. But he'd signed a contract, and he would never leave Becca in a situation where she had to scramble to find protection at the last minute.

"You sure about that?"

Ryder couldn't help a wry smirk. Chase knew him better than anyone in the world. "Just worried about Danae and her son."

"I can understand that. Any word on the investigation?"

"Nothing new yet. The good news is, the Feds think the suspects have moved out of the area. Possibly into northern Cali."

"Good." Becca's voice sounded in the background, asking what was going on. "Tell you later. What about you, did you contact that therapist Jase told you about yet?" Chase said to him.

"Just finished my second appointment."

"Yeah? How'd it go?"

"Better than I expected. Plus, he's a Marine, so... I feel like he gets it." Ryder hadn't talked about the mission to him yet, but he liked the guy and didn't feel embarrassed talking to him about his situation anymore.

It helped a lot that the guy actually understood what it was like to go to war and see combat. "Got another one booked for the day before I come back. Also haven't touched a drop of alcohol since Christmas Eve, and I poured out the bottles I found here at my rental."

That had marked a definite shift in his mindset. But right

now, he was just looking forward to an entire evening alone with Danae. He wanted to spend as much time with her as possible before he left.

"Gotta go," he said to Chase, tucking his wallet into his back pocket.

"Wait, when am I gonna get to meet this lady of yours?"

Never, probably, and that made him sad as hell. "Later, man."

Not two seconds after he ended the call, someone pounded on the door.

"Ryder! Ryder, open up!"

Finn's frantic voice shot through him like an armor-piercing round. He ran to the door, ripped it open.

Finn's face was panicked, pupils constricted. "My mom," he panted as if he'd just sprinted over. "Some guy just busted into our house and dragged her off at gunpoint."

Shock hit for an instant, then instinct took over. He pulled Finn inside and shut the door. Fear for Danae was like a lead weight in his gut, but he couldn't let it take over. He had to stay clearheaded. Every second counted. "Did you see him? Where did he take her?"

"I didn't see him, but he was pulling her toward the side door as I came out of my room. She screamed at me to stay away, so I went back in and shut the door. I heard a vehicle take off outside a few seconds later and ran to the front window. It was a gray SUV. Small one." His eyes gleamed with unshed tears. "You have to go after them," he choked out. "You have to help her!"

Ryder yanked out his phone.

"I already called 911," Finn argued. "The cops are coming, but they're gonna be a while, and we can track my mom with the app on my phone." He held it out so Ryder could see. "They're already on the highway moving south of Crimson Point. We have to go *now*."

Ordinarily there was no way in hell he would take Finn with him in a situation like this. But he was right—they couldn't afford to waste a single moment. "Don't take your eyes off that signal," he ordered, racing for the bedroom to grab the pistol Noah had loaned him.

They jumped into his SUV together. The tires screeched as he hit the gas.

"Where are they?" he demanded as he tore up the street, struggling to maintain the calm he normally operated with under pressure. The wipers whipped back and forth to clear the rain beating down on the windshield.

"Still on the highway. Heading south." Finn gave him a general location and he could see the dot moving for himself.

Ryder sped for the highway and called Noah, immediately launching into what was happening when the sheriff answered. Finn kept watch on the location of Danae's phone, alerting them the moment the beacon turned off the highway.

Ryder kept his foot on the accelerator, racing after them through the rain, determined to save Danae.

Whatever that bastard wanted with her, there was no way he planned to let her live. And Ryder refused to accept that it might already be too late.

~

WHERE WAS HE TAKING HER? What did he want from her? He had to want something, or he would have shot her dead in her kitchen.

Danae's heart pounded a hard, bruising rhythm against her ribs, her palms cold and damp around the steering wheel as she drove through the pouring rain. "Where are we going?" she finally said. With the gun pointed directly at her side, she was hyperaware of his every movement, every twitch.

"To my brother," he growled out, gun in his left hand while he set her work bag on his lap with his right. "You're gonna fix him up like you did last time."

She didn't have any supplies, but didn't dare point that out, afraid that's what he was looking for in her bag right now. And that he would shoot her when he discovered she had nothing.

He ignored her, rummaging through her bag. What the hell was he looking for?

He glanced up, looking through the windshield. It was growing dark out now, and this stretch of road well off the highway was all but deserted, filling her with a sickening despair. "Left at the light."

A flashing four-way a quarter mile ahead, its red light blurred through the mist and rain. She made the turn, trying to figure out a way to escape. But with him holding that gun on her, anything she tried would be futile.

She thought of Finn. He would be frantic. Would have called for help as soon as she'd driven away. Someone would be out looking for her. Noah. Maybe Ryder.

She prayed they found her in time.

"Right at the next road, then first left," Kyle snapped.

Seeing no other option, she followed his instructions, her dread increasing as it became clear they were heading into a heavily wooded area away from any sign of civilization.

"Left at the end of the road." He pulled a piece of paper from her bag, unfolded it, and checked it in the light of the dash display.

The pavement ended abruptly. The SUV's tires bumped along the dirt road, puddles from the rain reflecting in the headlights. Tall, thick evergreens surrounded them on all sides.

Cold spread through her gut. Once he was finished with her, was he going to kill her and dump her body where no one would see?

"Take the driveway on the right."

She almost missed it. Even with the headlights on it was so damn dark out here and the rain made it hard to see.

The vehicle leaned sharply to climb up the steep, dirt driveway that angled out of view behind more trees. All her awareness was on that weapon in Kyle's hand. Once she stopped, she would have only a second to get out and run.

You'll never make it. The instant you try, he'll shoot you down, just like he did to those other people in the dunes the other night.

She cut off the terrifying thought, tried to slow the frantic slam of her heart, to clear her head so she could think. She had to make herself seem indispensable. Had to make him believe she could help his brother and pray she could stall long enough for help to arrive.

Up ahead, through the gloom off to the left, she glimpsed a small wooden cabin nestled amongst the trees. The end of the road.

"Park here, turn off the engine and hand me the keys," he ordered.

She did, still having no idea if her plan would work long enough to save herself.

Saying nothing, he hauled her out, grabbed her by the back of the neck, and forced her toward the cabin.

"Kyle?" a weak voice rasped from the shadows when they entered.

"Yeah. I brought help. Close your eyes." He flipped on a light, a single bulb in the center of the ceiling.

Danae's gaze fixed on the man lying on the bed at the far end of the room. The resemblance between him and Kyle was obvious now. His face had a grayish cast except for the bright red fever spots on his cheeks. The bandage on his side was soaked with blood, and more of it was dripping onto the sheets beneath him.

Kyle laid a hand between her shoulder blades and shoved her forward roughly. "Help him."

Short of an equipped room, she already knew there was nothing she could do. But she went to him anyway, desperate to buy time. Maybe the camera at the front of her place had caught Kyle's new license plate number, and the police were tracking it somehow. Or maybe Finn had managed to get a picture of it on his phone.

If she could just stall long enough, make herself useful enough and stop Kyle from shooting her, maybe someone would find—

Her phone.

She sucked in a soft breath, pulse skyrocketing. Her phone was in her purse, and she never turned it off, so Finn would be able to track her with it. Surely he would think to do that. Or Noah would. Or Ryder.

Just then, Kyle swore viciously. Cringing, she looked behind her to find him holding her purse in one hand, and her phone in the other. He glared at her, the malevolent look on his face freezing her.

He threw her phone to the floor and slammed his boot into it, over and over, until it was crushed to pieces. Danae bit back a cry of despair, the thread of hope she'd been clinging to snapping in an instant. Now there was no way for anyone to find her.

A deep, molten rage began to build inside her. This asshole had targeted her repeatedly. He felt entitled to threaten, use, and probably kill her. He'd fucking broken into her house and threatened her *son*.

His jaw flexed, one dark eyebrow rising in reaction to her hard stare. "Help him now, or I put a bullet through your gut and leave you in the woods for the animals to finish off."

For just a moment she thought about risking it. To attack him, take him off guard, and try to escape through the door.

But as enraged as she was, the saner part of her knew her only chance was to stall and give the police as long as possible to try and find her.

Pivoting, she walked over to the wounded man and knelt beside the bed. Kyle was right behind her, dropping a bag full of medical supplies at her feet. Nothing useful. Just various sorts of bandages, gauze pads and antiseptic…and a package of knock-off Steri-Strips.

Just stall. At least convince him you're helping.

She took his wrist and felt for the radial pulse. It was rapid and thready, his breathing fast and shallow. His skin was hot to the touch, and he was losing too much blood.

She lifted the wounded man's hand from his side and unwound the tensor bandage before peeling the sodden gauze from the exit wound on his back. Her heart sank when she saw it. Several of the stitches had torn, and the edges were inflamed and hot.

"Well?" Kyle demanded, shoving gauze and the Steri-Strips at her. Fucking gauze and Steri-Strips. Like she was supposed to stop this by taping the edges of the bleeding wound shut.

She took some gauze without looking at him and pressed it to the wound. The patient made a guttural sound and writhed in pain, but she didn't let up on her pressure. Even if she'd had a suture kit and antibiotics, they wouldn't have helped much.

"I can seal the wounds shut again and stop the bleeding temporarily," she lied. "But he needs surgery. You have to take him to the hospital. I'll keep pressure on the wounds while you drive."

And as soon as they reached civilization, she would jump out and run for her life.

"That's not happening," Kyle snapped, and kept looking through the papers he'd dumped out of her bag. What was he *looking* for?

She thought frantically of what to do. If she couldn't do something to help his brother, he'd just kill her. So she hid her despair and did what she could to staunch the bleeding. "How long ago did the bleeding start?"

"Hour and a half." He grabbed another slip of paper. A receipt, then read it quickly and shoved it into his pocket with a look of sheer relief on his face.

"Kyle."

She and Kyle both stilled at the patient's weak voice.

The brother was staring at Kyle, his fever-glazed eyes full of pain and fear. "Maybe we should listen to her."

"You know why we can't," Kyle argued, but she could see the doubt creeping into his expression, the torment in his eyes as he spoke to his brother. "We just have to get the bleeding stopped and give you a day or two to heal up a bit before we can get out of here."

He had no fucking clue what he was talking about. At the rate he was losing blood, the brother would be lucky to make it through the night. But she didn't dare say so. Didn't dare do anything but keep steady pressure on the exit wound and pile more gauze on top to soak up the blood.

"Just tape it shut and keep pressure on it," Kyle snapped, angrily shoving a pile of papers across the bed.

She needed to keep pushing him to take his brother to the

hospital. It was her only chance. "I can't control the bleeding for long. And even if I could, he would just keep bleeding inside. He needs an operating room."

The brother shifted. Froze suddenly, gasping as he clapped a hand over top of hers, but too late.

His movement had opened up the wound more. Blood spilled out from beneath her hands, soaking the wad of gauze she held in seconds.

He turned fearful eyes to his brother. "Kyle," he choked out.

Danae glanced over her shoulder. Kyle was pale, his throat working as he swallowed, gaze stuck to the blood soaking the bedding.

His gaze flicked to hers for a moment, and she could clearly read his indecision. His fear.

"Kyle," the brother pleaded again. "*Help* me."

Mouth pinched, Kyle shoved to his feet and pulled out his phone. "Stop the goddamn bleeding!"

"We have to get him to the hospital."

"I'm not taking you or him anywhere," he spat. He dialed something and put the phone to his ear, then leveled the pistol at her, the deadly look in his eyes making her heart constrict. "If he dies before the ambulance gets here, then so will you."

TWENTY-FOUR

"Where now?" Ryder demanded as he sped along the wet, darkened road. The rain was coming down so hard now it was a continuous wash on the windshield, limiting his visibility.

"It's gone," Finn said in a dismayed tone.

He snapped his head around to look at him. "What?"

"It disappeared." Finn frantically tried to reload the app. "The dot stopped at the location I gave you, and now it's just gone."

Fuck. "Tell me the last location again."

"To the left of where we are. Not far. Less than a mile." He was enlarging the map, trying to find more information. "There are no fucking street names out here!"

Without street names or an address, trying to find Danae out here in this weather made that single mile seem like a hundred. "Try again," he ordered, refusing to accept that they'd lost her.

"I am," Finn snapped, working away on his phone. "It's not fucking *working*."

Ryder held himself back from saying anything else. Finn

was freaked out. Ryder was the adult, and the one with the most experience. He had to stay calm. So he kept driving, searching for any sign of the gray SUV Finn had described.

Where are you? he demanded silently, scanning the muddy road ahead.

"There's a left turn up there," Finn said urgently, pointing. "Try that."

Ryder did, taking them higher up the hill. "Where now, do you remember?"

"Somewhere to the right, I think."

The road narrowed, turned rougher. They bounced along the uneven surface, splashing through puddles forming in the depressions.

Still nothing. No people, vehicles or houses. Just this dirt road winding through the woods.

Just when he was about to burst from frustration, the headlights picked up something on the ground in front of them. He squinted, peering through the rain and mist.

Tire tracks imprinted in the dirt road, now filling with water.

"Tracks!" Finn blurted, sitting forward in his seat.

"I see them." They looked fresh. Were they from the SUV Danae had been taken in?

They were out in the middle of nowhere, and close to the spot where the beacon had vanished. They also hadn't come across any other evidence of a single other soul being out here. And these tracks were fresh.

This had to be it.

He followed the tracks higher, then they turned right at a fork up ahead. He lost them for a few heart-stopping moments, until they suddenly cut left and disappeared into the brush.

A driveway.

Ryder slowed, peering up the bank above it, and glimpsed the shadowy outline of a cabin hidden there. Heart pumping, he hit the brakes and reversed, rolling down his window to crane his neck outside and get a better look up the curving, climbing driveway.

He glimpsed the back of an SUV. Could be brown or gray. "This is it," he said, quickly cutting the lights and turning around.

He parked across the base of the driveway, blocking it off to prevent the kidnapper from escaping, and quickly turned off the dome light. "Take your phone, stay on this road and find a safe spot where you get reception, then call Noah and tell him what's going on. Pull up our location on the map, take a screenshot and send it to him. Tell him to get his ass up here *now*. And don't make any noise when you shut your door."

"What are you gonna do?" Finn blurted.

There was no time to wait for backup. He had to do this now.

"I'm going after your mom."

Grabbing the pistol from the console, he threw open his door and jumped out, intent on rescuing Danae from that psycho.

∽

KYLE KNEW the moment his brother's heart stopped.

There was so much blood. Way too much. And Josh's breathing turned shallower and shallower. Until his chest quit moving.

He shoved to his feet, moving on pure reflex, and felt for a pulse in Josh's neck. Danae removed her bloody hands from where she'd been applying pressure on the bandages and shrank back.

Kyle ignored her, his full attention on Josh. "No," he rasped, grabbing his brother's shoulders and leaning over him. "Don't you fucking do this. Don't you fucking leave me," he croaked out, his voice breaking. He had the receipt back. They could finally get their money and move forward.

This had all been for their future. For the new life he'd promised Josh. Kyle couldn't bear losing him.

Automatically he started doing chest compressions, some part of him stubbornly refusing to accept the evidence before him. But even as he labored, he knew it was over. Josh's face was lax, the skin around his nose and mouth already turning blue.

He yanked his hands free and straightened, struggling to breathe through the pain. "Fuck!" he screamed, white-hot agony ripping through him like fire until he caught movement in his peripheral vision.

Danae, creeping toward the door. The bitch thought she could escape.

He grabbed his pistol from the bed and whirled, leveling it at her. It wasn't her fault Josh had died, but he didn't care. She would die too.

"No," she cried, throwing up a hand as she huddled into a ball near the door. "No, please—"

Just as his index finger tightened around the trigger, a brief flash of movement through the window made him freeze. He stepped to it, stood at the edge out of sight and carefully pulled back the curtain slightly to see outside.

A shadow was moving around out there, barely visible through the screen of brush around the cabin.

The rage that had been blinding him a moment ago was gone, extinguished beneath a wave of icy fear.

Someone was out there. Maybe more than one person. Coming for him. Because there was no sign of an ambulance.

He pressed his lips together and jerked his gaze back at Danae, still frozen in place near the door, watching him with wide, terrified eyes. The ambulance was on the way. Would be here anytime now. Then more people would show up and there would be no escape. He'd planned to take off just as he heard the sirens get close.

The hard, bitter truth hit him all at once.

His brother was gone. But he could still save himself—if he left immediately. And his captive would provide the perfect insurance against anyone wanting to shoot him. He needed her as a hostage. Needed her alive.

For now.

Shaking inside, he cast one last look at his brother. His stomach twisted, grief rising sharp and unbearable. But Josh would want him to escape. Would want him to get out of here and live.

He shoved everything down inside him and rushed at Danae.

She cried out and scrambled to her feet, grabbed the doorknob and twisted it. He caught a handful of her hair a heartbeat before she stepped through the open door.

"Where do you think you're going, huh?" he snarled, shoving the muzzle of the pistol into her back as he steered her outside.

Cold sheets of rain poured down on them. He blinked it away, struggled to see through the torrent, his heart and mind racing. But as he started toward the SUV, he spotted the outline of a vehicle blocking the end of the driveway.

He jerked to a halt, cursing bitterly, and glanced around. There was nowhere else for a vehicle to go but the driveway. He was going to have to escape on foot.

Danae made an enraged sound and twisted in his grip, digging her nails into his wrist. "Let me go, asshole," she snarled.

He jerked her sideways, making her stumble and struggle to stay on her feet as he darted for the darkened forest ahead of them, dragging her with him.

"Kyle!"

The male shout from not too far away behind him almost stopped his heart. A spurt of panic sent more adrenaline flooding through him, giving him added speed as he raced for the woods.

He whirled and fired blindly behind him. Danae screamed as the gunshots exploded through the darkness and tried to wrench away.

Kyle kept her between him and the man, his free arm locked around her ribs as he reached the trees and plunged headlong into the relative safety of the darkened forest.

TWENTY-FIVE

Danae stumbled after Kyle, unable to break free of his grip no matter how she fought. Hope tore through her, blending with raw fear. "Ryder!" she screamed, desperately clawing at the arm locked around her ribs.

He'd come after her. Had found her somehow. She'd heard his voice. But Kyle had just shot at him. Had he been hit? Was he back there bleeding to death on the driveway right now?

A branch slapped her in the face. She gasped, the sharp sting momentarily stunning her into silence.

They crashed through the underbrush at a breakneck pace. The ground was sodden and slippery, cold rain dripping down on them from the trees towering overhead.

Her foot caught on a fallen branch. She pitched forward. Kyle released her just as she fell, her palms skidding across the rough cedar needles covering the ground.

She had to get away from him. Barring that, she had to at least disarm him.

Gritting her teeth, she got up, planted her feet and dug her heels into the muddy ground, then twisted and grabbed the wrist of his gun hand. He cursed and tried to shove her off, but she moved in close, pressing her body tight to his to take away his leverage.

She was all instinct, all the fear and rage bursting free. Teeth bared, she dug her nails hard into his skin, a guttural snarl coming from deep in her throat as she pulled and twisted.

His fist slammed into the side of her head, stunning her, but she didn't let go. Getting that weapon out of his hand was her only chance of making it out of here alive.

She thought of Finn. How she couldn't leave him. How she couldn't let him suffer the loss of his only surviving parent. She strained with all her might.

I won't give in. I won't.

"God damn it," Kyle swore, and tried to rip her off him.

The sudden shift of his weight threw them off balance. She seized on it, leaning away. He stumbled but couldn't catch himself.

She grunted as she hit the ground on her side, Kyle's weight and momentum carrying her forward. And then they were falling. Slipping down an incline and crashing to a stop at the bottom.

Trembling, gasping, she struggled to her feet, forcing her knees to keep her upright.

"Stupid bitch!" Kyle roared. She could barely see him. He was twisting around on his knees, his arms moving back and forth on the ground.

He dropped the gun.

"Danae, run!" a voice shouted from above her.

Ryder. Heart pounding, she glanced upward, saw his silhouette outlined in the faint light coming through the trees above.

"Run!"

She spun to follow his order, her mind racing. The road. It had to be off to the left somewhere, and down the hill. An ambulance was on the way. She could flag it down and get help.

Her legs felt like lead as she pushed through the tangled underbrush. The forest was nothing but a mass of shadows before her. Branches snagged on her clothing, roots and branches hidden in the darkness forming tripping hazards at every turn.

She had only a second's warning when twigs snapped behind her, then cruel hands grabbed her, one arm locking around the front of her throat. She cried out at the sudden, terrifying pressure and tried to shove her hands between the steely forearm and her skin, panic clawing at her as her airway closed up.

Survival instinct took over.

She stopped struggling and kicking and sank her teeth into the closest flesh she could reach, biting down with all her strength.

Kyle bellowed and tried to shake her loose. She held on like an attack dog, adding her nails.

Blood hit her tongue, salty and nauseating.

A punch to the side of the face knocked her head around, bright spots exploding in front of her eyes. He hurled her away from him.

She hit the ground hard on her side, her head bouncing off the muddy earth.

Ears ringing from the blow, she raised her head, struggling to push up on her hands. A second later, a terrifying snarl came from behind her. Her head snapped toward it, a warning prickle racing over her skin.

Through the gloom, she barely caught the shadow as it launched itself at Kyle.

. . .

RYDER'S SHOULDER SLAMMED into Kyle's back, knocking him to the ground. Before the bastard could move, Ryder was on him, straddling his lower back and reaching for his flailing hands.

He'd lost his weapon somewhere back there in the muck when he'd fallen down the incline he hadn't been able to see. It was going to be hand to hand, and Ryder was so down for that.

An elbow caught him in the gut. He grunted, doubled over, his left hand grazing one of Kyle's.

Before he could grab hold of it, the man flipped sideways. Ryder went with it, rolling to get out of range. He leapt to his feet, scanning the area in front of him. Danae should be there, but it was so damn dark all he could see were shadows.

A low snarl was his only warning. He tensed, searching for his target, spotted the shadowy blur coming at him a heartbeat before it made impact.

Ryder leaned back as he caught Kyle around the ribs. He twisted, throwing him over his hip. Kyle went down hard, an audible thud reverberating through the ground.

Ryder dove at him, fueled by rage and adrenaline. This motherfucker had kidnapped and almost killed Danae. Ryder was taking him down hard.

A fist caught him in a glancing blow across the jaw, but the pain only cleared his head and sharpened his focus. He grabbed a fistful of Kyle's jacket to hold him still and drove his fist toward the asshole's face.

Kyle bucked beneath him at the last second, throwing off his aim. He wrenched his body sideways, taking Ryder with him.

Ryder locked both hands in Kyle's jacket, refusing to let

go. They rolled, flipping over and over, skidding down another hollow.

Ryder slammed sideways into a fallen log at the bottom, the momentum finally tearing his hands free of the jacket. He grabbed at Kyle, his fingers brushing over the back of his jacket as Kyle stumbled back.

"Ryder!"

Danae's worried cry from somewhere up above filled him with relief, but he couldn't answer, couldn't split his attention while he was hunting his prey.

An icy rivulet of muddy water spilled down his face. He wiped it with his shoulder, blinked to clear his eyes and adjust to the gloom surrounding him.

He could hear the bastard now, trying to run away to the left. Ryder chased after him, his gaze locked on the shadowy silhouette crashing through the underbrush ahead.

The low visibility and uneven terrain made the pursuit a challenge. He tripped twice, went sailing headlong and twisted at the last moment to absorb the impact, rolling to disperse the energy.

Popping to his feet, he kept going, his senses following every cracking twig and crunching step ahead in the shadows. Ryder gained on him, a surge of triumph exploding through his bloodstream as Kyle's outline finally became distinct less than ten yards in front of him.

The hair on his arms stood up as he closed in on his prey. *You're mine, motherfucker.*

He took six more running strides, then planted his right foot and dove at Kyle. He crashed into Kyle's back, knocking him flat to the ground, the impact heightened by Ryder's weight on top of him.

Kyle gave a loud *oof* and tried to twist away, but Ryder

had him now and wasn't letting him go. He barely felt the blows Kyle landed on him.

Seizing the collar of Kyle's jacket, he reared his right fist back and drove it down with all the strength in his core and arm. Pain radiated up his hand as Kyle's head snapped to the side, his body jerking.

Ryder pulled his fist back and hit him again, dead in the face. Bone crunched.

Kyle howled and fought to get free, but Ryder twisted the collar, compressing his airway, and delivered another punch.

This time Kyle went dead still and sagged, a garbled moan coming from his lips.

Breathing hard, Ryder paused, blinking icy streams of rain from his eyes as he squinted down at the man beneath him. He wasn't sure if Kyle was unconscious or faking it, but at least he was down and not moving.

Watching him closely, Ryder got off him, reaching down to feel for his pocket. His phone was somehow still there.

His jeans and shirt were soaked, and for the first time he shivered, the cold registering. He turned on his home screen and aimed the light down at Kyle. The fucker was out cold, blood coming from his nose and lips.

Shoving his phone away, Ryder gripped the front of Kyle's jacket and jerked him into a sitting position, then bent and levered him over his shoulders before standing. His adrenaline levels were dropping now, the almost superhuman strength he'd felt a minute ago fading fast.

He stared back through the woods, aiming in the general direction he'd come. "Danae?" he called.

"Up here! Are you all right?"

He didn't have the breath to answer, Kyle's dead weight and the muddy ground taking their toll on his tired muscles.

He wound up having to almost crawl his way up the second incline they'd fallen down.

As he neared the top, he caught the faint sound of a siren approaching in the distance. He hoped the hell it was Noah.

Rustling and snapping twigs alerted him to movement above him. He glanced up in time to see Danae there, trying to pick her way down.

"No, stay back," he warned, then paused to catch his breath. He didn't want her anywhere near him in case Kyle came to.

She scrambled back up to the top and turned around to reach a hand down for him. He shook his head, afraid he'd pull her down, but realized she couldn't see him. His feet slipped, sending him flat on his belly in the mud. Kyle groaned and stirred.

Setting his jaw, Ryder clawed his way up and cleared the lip, pausing there on his hands and knees for a moment.

"Are you okay?" Danae asked worriedly, hovering just out of reach. The sirens were closer now.

"Fine. Go back," he gasped out. "To the cabin."

She moved hesitantly, stopping to look back at him every few seconds. He pushed to his feet, the jostling making Kyle stir again, and hurried after her.

The gloom slowly began to lift as they neared the edge of the tree line, the deep shadows giving way to different shades of gray. Then flashing lights began to glow on the thick trunks they passed, and finally Ryder could see what was happening. An ambulance was parked in front of Ryder's rental at the end of the driveway.

He headed straight for it, dumping Kyle onto the ground. "Need something to cuff him with," he panted to the startled paramedic.

Taking the restraints they offered, he secured Kyle's arms

behind his back and straightened, his gaze automatically seeking Danae. She was over by the cabin door, talking to the other paramedic. She was covered in mud, blood and cedar needles, hair plastered to her head and her arms wrapped around herself.

All the remaining tension in his chest eased when he saw she seemed unhurt. He stopped and closed his eyes for an instant, drawing in a deep breath.

Thank God. He would never have forgiven himself if he hadn't gotten here in time.

TWENTY-SIX

The rain was still pouring down in a torrent. Soaked to the skin, shaking like she'd been submerged in ice water as the paramedic stepped into the cabin, Danae looked up to find Ryder striding toward her.

She took a stumbling step forward, a weird, high-pitched sound coming from her throat. "Ryder," she croaked, reaching for him.

Hard, strong arms engulfed her a heartbeat later. "Sweetheart."

He crushed her to his chest, one hand cradling the back of her head, pressing her face into the base of his wet throat. He was soaked too and covered with mud. He had to be as cold as her, but it seemed like she was the only one shaking.

"C-can't s-stop sh-shaking," she quavered, her breathing fast and shallow.

His arms tightened around her like warm steel. "Let it roll through you. Don't fight it, it'll only make it worse."

Her instinct was to resist, to be strong, but she did as he said, letting the shakes rip through her. Painful, wracking waves while her breath hitched. Ryder held her securely the whole time, his low voice murmuring next to her ear, until finally the earthquake faded into tremors and she was able to breathe almost normally again.

Trying to block out everything else around them, she clung to him and shut her eyes. "Get me out of here," she gritted out, her jaw trembling along with the rest of her.

Without another word he picked her up and started carrying her past the ambulance. She kept her eyes closed and her face averted, not wanting to see Kyle ever again. "Is he dead?" she asked.

"No. But a busted face is only a hint of the pain coming to him." He shifted her, leaning back a little as he started down the sloping driveway.

"Mom!"

Her head shot off Ryder's chest at Finn's voice.

Her anxious gaze settled on her son, running toward them. A sob broke free. Kyle had almost taken her from her boy. She had almost lost the chance to see him grow into the man he was going to be.

Ryder stopped and set her on her feet. She rushed for Finn, grabbing him tight, and he didn't pull away when she clung to him.

"Oh my God, what are you even doing here?" she demanded when she could find her voice again, horrified and yet desperately glad to see him.

"Ryder and I followed you using the locator app. Don't worry, I stayed out of danger the whole time," he added quickly. "Ryder, you get the bastard?"

Danae didn't have the heart to admonish his language.

"Yeah."

"Good." Finn's muscles relaxed.

More sirens screamed in the night, coming up the road, and within moments flashing lights lit up the darkness. She kissed Finn's cheek, squeezed him once more and let him go. "N-Noah's here," she said, relief flooding her. But she was still shaking like crazy.

Ryder draped a blanket around her shoulders. She hunched into it, clenching the ends together in her hands, shivering so hard her teeth rattled. "Can you go meet Noah and tell him what's happened?" he said to Finn, then gathered her close again.

She shuddered convulsively, her whole body jerking. It was like she was freezing to death, yet she wasn't that cold. She couldn't control the shaking. Couldn't seem to slow her heartbeat.

Gradually her heart slowed, and she regained control of her breathing. By the time the worst was over she ached all over from the strain, a powerful wave of exhaustion hitting her.

Ryder shifted her, easing his grip a little and ran a hand over her hair. "Noah's here."

She lifted her head and focused on Noah, coming toward them with rapid strides. "Is she all right?" he asked.

"Yes." Ryder jerked his chin toward the cabin. "One suspect's dead inside, and one's restrained in the ambulance."

Noah nodded. "Wait here, I'll be right back." He directed his deputies to follow him and disappeared inside the cabin. The paramedics followed soon after, bearing a gurney.

A few minutes later Noah returned. "Okay, tell me what happened. Danae, you start."

She drew a breath, reached for Ryder's hand and held on tight as she went over everything, beginning from the moment Kyle had barged into her house, and ending with fighting with him in the woods. She even remembered to tell him about the receipt Kyle had shoved into his pocket.

It left her feeling drained, a sort of mental fog creeping over her.

Noah recorded everything and took notes, then switched his attention to Ryder. "Now you."

Closing her eyes, Danae rested her head on Ryder's sturdy shoulder, soothed by his embrace and the sound of his voice. The interlude was cut short when a hand gripped her shoulder.

Noah's face was close, his expression sympathetic. "I'm going to have the paramedics check you, just to be sure you're okay. Then we'll take you back to Crimson Point. You'll need to give an official statement at the station, and then the Feds are going to want to talk to you. I'll see if I can postpone them until tomorrow."

"What about Finn?"

"He's a witness, so he'll have to come into the station with us. Ryder can follow us back in his rental."

She wanted to argue that she would rather she and her son be with Ryder instead of him, but realized Noah was just doing his job and following protocol. It was standard to separate the witnesses, to make sure they didn't corroborate on their story and the details.

Reluctantly she started to push the blanket off her shoulders, preparing to stand. Ryder hugged her close and tucked the blanket back around her. "Let me." He lifted her into his arms and started down the driveway.

A paramedic looked her over and cleared her to leave. Finn was already in the back of Noah's vehicle when she got to it.

Ryder carefully settled her in beside her son. "Take care of her," he said to Finn, then wrapped his hand around the back of her neck and leaned in for a kiss. "See you soon, sweetheart. I'll be right behind you."

She was aware of the telling look Finn gave her as Ryder closed the door but didn't feel like explaining herself or what was happening between her and Ryder. She wasn't even sure *what* was happening, and she was too damn exhausted to try and figure it out right now.

She almost fell asleep on the way back to Crimson Point. As soon as they arrived at the sheriff's office, Noah took her and Finn into an interview room, and Ryder into another. He got them something hot to drink, then began the process of taking their official statements.

They were still in the interview room when the FBI agent in charge of the trafficking case arrived. Danae bit back an irritated response when she was told that they were going to talk to her now. All she wanted was to go home with Finn and Ryder, have a hot shower, something to eat, then crawl into bed with Ryder and fall asleep in his arms. This entire ordeal had been a prolonged nightmare. She just wanted it over with and to put it all behind her.

She did as she was told, however, answering all the federal agents' questions as calmly and thoroughly as possible. In the meantime, Beckett had come to pick Finn up and take him home. He would wait there with him until she and Ryder got back. Because Ryder had told her he wasn't leaving without her.

"Is there any update on Kyle?" she asked later. More than two hours had passed since the FBI agent had taken over. She was past exhausted and wanted *out* of here.

"Kyle's not talking yet, but he will." The man paused, leaning back in his chair to regard her with sharp brown eyes. "I can divulge now that he and his brother were both linked to a larger organized crime ring operating up and down the West Coast."

"And were they involved in the trafficking incident when those hikers were rounded up and killed?"

"Yes. Although we're not yet certain if they killed any of the victims yet. We're still waiting on forensics and ballistics reports to confirm it either way. I can tell you they both left DNA at the scene."

It took almost another hour to go over everything else, then she was finally free to go. Noah escorted her out to the lobby. Ryder shoved to his feet and hurried over to pull her into a hug. "How you doing?" he murmured, his lips close to her ear.

"I'm so done."

"Take her home," Noah said to him.

"With pleasure." Wrapping an arm around her shoulders, Ryder led her outside into the well-lit parking lot.

She drew a deep breath, pulling the cold, salt-tinged air into her lungs. "It's so quiet out here," she murmured, that strange sense of numbness coming back.

"I'll have you home and bundled up on the couch in no time," he promised, and put her into the front of his rental vehicle.

The living room lights were on when they arrived at her place. Beckett met them at the door. "Do you need anything?" he asked.

"No," she answered, squeezing his hand. She was so lucky to have such amazing, caring friends. "But thanks. Oh, but maybe tell Sierra I won't be in tomorrow."

He grunted. "She told me to tell you to stay home tomorrow, and to take off as many days as you need after that."

Finn was waiting for her on the couch when she walked into the living room. She sat beside him, took his hand. "You okay?" she asked, searching his face. Worrying about what kind of emotional and psychological impact this would have on him.

"Yeah. What about you?"

"I think so," she answered honestly. "Still can't believe it happened."

"Tell me about it."

She nudged him with her elbow. "Aren't you glad I insisted on that family locator app?"

He flashed a grin. "Yeah."

"Me too."

He looked at Ryder, who had come in behind her and was standing near the entrance to the room. "And I'm glad you moved in next door."

The ghost of a smile touched Ryder's mouth. "Me too."

Finn sighed and rubbed the back of his neck. "Well. I'm going to bed." Then he paused, glanced at her, and leaned over to embrace her. "Love you, Mom."

Her throat tightened as she hugged him back, tears scalding the backs of her eyes. "Love you too, buddy."

She watched him leave the room, fidgeting with her fingers. "Do you think he's really okay?" she asked Ryder. "That he's going to be okay?"

"Yes," he answered, coming down beside her to draw her into his lap. She sighed and snuggled close, resting her head on the top of his shoulder. "He's resilient, and willing to talk to a therapist. He'll be okay." He rubbed a soothing hand up and down her back. "What about you?"

"I'll…deal with it," she answered. "Just like I've dealt with everything else. I'm resilient too."

"Yes, you are," he agreed, the pride in his voice warming her. His lips brushed the crown of her head. Her temple. Her cheek. "Ready for bed? Or do you want to stay up for a while longer?"

"Shower. Then bed." She wasn't even hungry anymore. At least, not for food. At the moment the only thing she was hungry for was the man holding her.

"I'm filthy," she said in disgust. Her jeans and sweater were caked with mud and stained with Josh's blood. She'd cleaned her hands as best she could at the police station, but she wanted a good scrub down.

"Same."

"Let's save water and split a shower. I'll wash your back if you wash mine."

"Deal."

TWENTY-SEVEN

In the en suite of her room, Danae turned the shower on hot and began stripping, not the least bit self-conscious that every imperfection on her perimenopausal mom body was revealed in the lights. She felt secure with Ryder, and all she cared about right now was getting clean.

She got in and immediately began scrubbing her hands and arms, digging under her fingernails and cuticles to get the last traces of rust-colored blood off, then lathered up her hair. She was getting ready to rinse it when Ryder stepped in behind her, and sighed when his strong hands began massaging her scalp.

"Keep going," she moaned when he paused.

He gave a low chuckle and dropped a kiss on the top of her shoulder, his fingers rubbing with steady, firm pressure over her scalp. He helped her rinse her hair clean, then she moved aside so he could get under the spray and returned the favor, ending with a leisurely exploration of his sculpted body with her vanilla-sandalwood soap.

By the time she was done he was rock hard, his erection standing up against his lower belly. Before she could do more than stroke him a few times, he pulled her hand free with a warning growl and wrapped her up in a bath towel.

Once they were dry, he led her to her bed and crawled in beside her, turning her onto her back and coming down on top of her. She sighed and wound her calves around his, running her palms over the breadth of his back.

"How's your jaw?" she whispered, touching it with gentle fingertips. She'd seen him working it earlier. He must have taken a punch there while he was fighting Kyle.

"It's okay."

"You sure?" She raised her head to kiss the spot, cupping his head in her hands to trail more kisses across his jaw and chin.

"Yeah."

"You know… No one's ever saved me before." The emotional bond she felt with him because of it was way more intense than she'd bargained for. "It's pretty romantic."

He drew back slightly to stare down at her. "I'd do it all again in a heartbeat."

Her chest hitched, her throat thickening. He hadn't risked his life for her tonight just because he was a bodyguard. He'd risked his life to save her because he cared. And he was still here with her now, to protect and comfort her.

Sliding a hand into her damp hair, he captured her lips with his. Danae gave herself over to it completely. She didn't want to think about what had happened—what had almost happened—or about the inevitable end of their time together in a few days' time.

Warmth and arousal slid through her with every stroke of his lips and tongue, every caress of his hands. She arched into him, clinging tight, allowing herself to be carried away on the tide of sensation he created. Floating, anchored by his weight and the sure grip of his hands while his tongue teased her swollen clit, slow and patient, until she was almost there.

She snagged a condom from her bedside drawer, her fingers busy where his tongue had just been, keeping her body at a simmer. He came back down over her, kissed her deep, then bent to capture a tight nipple as he eased the thick head of his erection into her.

The combined sensation was so good. She stifled a whimper, mindful of Finn just down the hall, and locked her legs around his hips, demanding more. Ryder groaned around her captive nipple and began a gentle, surging rhythm, angling his hips to give her fingers room where she needed them.

Pleasure drenched her, coating her in a thick, syrupy tide until it dragged her under. She fought to stay quiet as the orgasm punched through her, the pulses fading into ripples.

She came back to herself in time to fully enjoy Ryder, pulling his head up so she could fuse their mouths together. A deep groan rumbled from his chest as she rocked with him, squeezing and clenching around him to add more friction.

He plunged a hand into her hair, gripped it tight as he drew in a sharp breath and drove deep, locking there while his big body shuddered, eyes squeezed shut and sharp lines of ecstasy etched into his face.

Lying wrapped up in his powerful arms after, the stillness of the quiet house settling around them, a painful, crushing pressure began to take hold inside her ribs.

She'd never expected to feel this way about him, or so soon. When he left, it would punch another giant hole in her life.

FINN PAUSED outside his mom's bedroom door, hesitating. She was always up before him, but now it was almost nine and she hadn't come out yet. Ryder was still in there too, he was pretty sure.

He knocked softly. "Mom?"

"Yeah, what's up, buddy?" she answered, her voice sleepy.

Ryder opened the door a moment later, wearing just jeans. Finn looked past him, feeling awkward. "Sorry. It's just that I need to be at work in like, ten minutes."

"Oh, shit, sorry," his mom said, sitting up with the sheets gathered to her.

"I'll take you," Ryder said, turning around to grab his shirt from the floor and tug it over his head. "Take your time," he said to her, then shut the door. "You ready now?" he asked Finn.

"Yeah."

They didn't speak until they were coming down the hill toward the end of Front Street.

"How's my mom doing?" he finally asked. It was kinda weird to know she and Ryder had slept together, but he just wanted her to be happy. Ryder was a good guy and had risked his life yesterday to save her, and he'd been taking care of her a lot this past week.

"She's tougher than she looks. She's gonna be fine. What about you?"

"I'm good. Mom says I have to see a counselor though." He wasn't looking forward to that. While he wouldn't mind talking about all the bad things that had happened recently, it reminded him of the appointments he'd been forced to go to after his dad died. He'd hated them. Hopefully, the new therapist would be better.

"That's smart. You have anybody to talk to about things?

A friend back in Seattle maybe?"

"Yeah. I told a couple of them." Not Paul though. Finn was done with him and that whole crew forever.

"How you feeling about starting school again now?"

He shrugged. "It's fine, I guess." Not like he had any choice. He had to go. But he was dreading seeing Paul and Grant again. Rumors were already flying all over the place about what had happened. About Grant and his stepdad. About Finn and his mom.

He would do everything possible to avoid both of them from now on. "What about you, when do you leave?"

"Sunday."

Three days. And Finn went back to school that week. He looked at Ryder, noticed the tension in the man's jaw. "Are you…coming back?"

"I hope so."

Finn's stomach sank. That didn't sound too positive. He liked Ryder. A lot. Didn't want to lose him for good on top of everything else that had happened.

He faced forward, staring out the windshield at the heart of Crimson Point, and kept his tone and expression impassive to mask the ache inside. "Me too."

∼

TWO DAYS HAD PASSED since Ryder had raced to save Danae and knocked that bastard unconscious in the woods.

Less than six hours from this moment, he would be leaving her and Crimson Point behind. Less than eleven hours from now, he would be on a plane back to L.A.

His mind rebelled against it. His heart railed at him to do something. To fix this.

But there was no way to fix it, at least not anytime soon.

He'd thought of everything. He was locked into a contract. Becca was depending on him.

But how in hell was he supposed to walk away from Danae after all she'd been through? When she needed him, and he wanted to be here for her?

Holding her close in the darkness, listening to her even breathing, sleep was impossible.

"You need to sleep," she murmured, sliding a hand sleepily over his bare back. He'd stayed over the past couple nights, spending them in her bed, making sure he was out of her room by oh-eight-hundred in case Finn got up earlier than usual.

Not that he or Danae thought Finn didn't realize what was going on. It just didn't feel right to wave it in his face when there was no guarantee of any kind of future for them.

"Can't," he answered. "Don't want to miss out on this for even a second." He hugged her tight, savoring her warmth and softness.

"Me either," she whispered, pressing closer.

His chest constricted until it hurt to breathe. They hadn't talked about what would happen once he left, both of them holding off. He wanted to know what she needed and clear that up now, to avoid any unnecessary messiness and hurt.

"How do you want this to go?" he asked, bracing himself.

No matter what she said, he would honor it. If saying goodbye and cutting all ties for a clean break was what she needed to minimize the pain, then he'd do it. But fuck, at this point he wasn't sure which would hurt worse—having to let her go, or trying to make a long distance relationship work surrounded by so much uncertainty.

"How do *you* want this to go?" she countered, easing back to stare at him in the dimness, her face barely visible on the pillow in the faint moonlight filtering through the edges of the blinds.

He shook his head, hating this. Torn on every level, the protective part of him wondering if it would be kinder for her in the long run if he insisted on a clean cut and let her go.

Even if it would rip his heart out.

"I'll be in Australia for at least the next three to four months. Maybe more, depending on how the filming goes. After that…I have no idea what'll happen, or where I'll wind up." It was a lot to ask of her, to deal with that, waiting to see what would happen after four months of being apart.

Her fingers stroked over his bare hip. "You must get breaks from time to time though, right? A week off here and there?"

That felt like asking her to live off the crumbs he could give her. He wanted to make this work. But he didn't want her to make sacrifices she wasn't ready for. Namely, being committed to someone who was going to be away for long periods during the foreseeable future.

"Not necessarily," he said. "And even if I did, things could change last minute if Becca took on another project at the last second."

She made a frustrated sound and shifted her hand around to his chest, her fingers tracing the ridges of his pecs. "And I can't come to you, even if I could figure out how to make that happen, because you'll be on location and on the clock pretty much the whole time."

"Yeah."

"I guess you just can't quit, huh?" she said, her tone teasing.

"No. My current contract has another six months on it."

But it wasn't just time and distance they were fighting against. He also had his own shit to work through still. If he wanted a serious relationship with her, he owed it to both of them to conquer his demons, or at least start working toward that.

"I don't want to lose you completely," she said, her voice husky. "I couldn't stand that after everything that's happened."

He drew her close again and kissed the top of her head, aching inside. Holy fuck, it hurt to think of leaving her and Finn behind. Against his better judgment he'd allowed himself to dream about what might be, a possible future for them.

Of making a life with her here in Crimson Point. Living with her. Waking up to her in the morning and falling asleep next to her at night. Of being here for Finn, not as a father figure, but a man he could trust to have his back and talk to about things he didn't want Danae to know. School. Girls. Life. Whatever.

A terrible, yawning emptiness filled him to know it might never happen.

He'd gone over everything in his mind so many times over the past three days. If he'd had a different job, a different career trajectory, it would have been so much easier. He'd even thought about trying to find something in the same field that would allow him to move here, at least part time.

He kept trying to come up with a way out of this, but he couldn't up and abandon Becca and Chase right now, and it wasn't just because of the contract he'd signed. He cared about her, and Chase.

He was Becca's personal bodyguard, and given her status she definitely needed professional protection. He wouldn't let them down, and if he quit now after only being on the job a few months, his professional rep would take a hard hit.

He had to leave Crimson Point. There was no way around it.

"Can we... Can we just give it a try and see how things go?"

Her tentative question simultaneously broke his heart and mended it at the same time. He wanted the chance she was offering. Wanted it more than anything.

"Are you sure you're up for that?" He needed her to think it through. When she did, he wouldn't blame her for changing her mind. The last thing he wanted was to keep her waiting for him and make her miserable in the process.

Her fingers stilled on his chest. "Yes. I'm sure." She resumed the light stroke of her fingertips on his skin.

"You'd really be okay with just phone calls and video chats for that long?" Because that's all they would have while he was so far away.

"For the time being, as long as I know you're coming back eventually."

Eventually. The uncertainty behind that word was depressing as shit.

He closed his eyes, afraid to trust the fragile sense of hope welling in his chest. Long-distance relationships rarely worked out and were hard on both people involved. He'd seen enough of that when he was in the military. And they'd only known each other two weeks. Would she still feel this strongly about him once things had settled down and he was working overseas for the next four months?

"What about Finn?" he asked, wanting to think everything through.

"I think he'd be really hurt if you just cut ties and disappeared completely after everything we've all been through together."

It would hurt him too. Badly.

"Hopefully it'll only be six months max, but... God, I'm still really going to miss you," Danae whispered, the catch in her voice making his heart clench.

He closed his eyes, pain ripping at him. "Gonna miss you like hell too, sweetheart."

He had to be strong now. Had to be careful not to blurt out his feelings, just in case things didn't work out. She and Finn had already suffered too much loss and uncertainty in their lives. Him being gone for long stretches would add more of it to their burden.

Damn. He had dedicated his life to protecting others. But he couldn't protect her from this new hurt and didn't know when they would see each other again.

He couldn't stay. No matter how much leaving would make him bleed inside.

TWENTY-EIGHT

The bell went off, signaling the end of the first period that had seemed to drag on for three hours instead of one. Finn shut his math textbook, grabbed his binder and filed out of the room with his classmates, his mind on anything but school.

He felt the stares on him as he walked to his history class. Saw people whispering as he passed.

Everyone was curious about what had happened to him over Christmas break. A few people had even been ballsy enough to ask him straight to his face. He hadn't said much. He was more concerned with protecting his mom, and not earning himself any more enemies by saying the wrong thing to the wrong person.

He'd been nervous all morning and on the bus ride here. So far, he hadn't seen Paul, and he didn't have to worry about Grant, since he'd been sent to a juvenile detention center near Portland. Grant's mom had apparently packed up and moved away from the area when Victor's involvement in the kidnappings and murders had come to light.

Finn ignored the looks and whispers, hurrying to his next

classroom. He didn't have any friends here now. He was back at square one again. The new kid in town. Only this time, there were rumors flying about him. High school sucked worse than ever.

Everyone stopped talking when he walked into history class. His face heated on the way to his seat in the back, hating the murmurs and whispers. Maybe he could convince his mom to let him do online school for the rest of the year and start back in class in September. Maybe by then the rumors would have died down and he wouldn't feel like such a freak anymore.

"Hey," a friendly voice said beside him.

He looked up, startled to find Carly standing there, pushing her long, golden-blond hair over her shoulder as she smiled at him. Not a coy, calculating smile that meant she wanted to be seen with him to get attention from their classmates.

It was kind. Warm, even. "Hey," he said in surprise. She was super popular, ran with a popular crowd.

She glanced at the empty desk on his right. "Mind if I sit here?"

She'd never talked to him much at school before. "Not at all," he blurted, hastily moving the sleeve of his puffy coat aside to give her more room.

Holy shit, Carly had singled him out in front of everyone and come to sit beside him.

The quiet way she did it gave him the sense that she was almost doing it in a protective way. Like she was trying to tell everyone that he was cool, and to leave him alone.

More whispers. He barely noticed them now, too preoccupied by the girl next to him. Carly shot someone a hard, warning look, and it got quiet again.

Yeah, she was definitely protecting him. He fought back a grin.

"Have a good Christmas?" she asked while they waited for the teacher to arrive.

He flushed, assuming she was trying to get him to talk about his experience in front of everyone. "Not really."

"Me either. I actually don't even like Christmas much anymore. It hasn't been the same since my dad died."

He blinked, startled. He'd never known that about her. "Same. I mean, my dad died a while back too, so I know what you mean."

She gave him a soft smile, so full of empathy and understanding it made his chest feel tight. "Get anything good at least?"

Besides some harrowing experiences? "Not really. Except…" He thought of Ryder. "I made a friend." He hoped Ryder considered him to be one too. He'd only been gone a day, but the house had felt weirdly empty since last night, and a few times Finn could tell by his mom's puffy eyes that she'd been crying.

Carly's smile widened, showing a glimmer of even, white teeth. "Well, we can definitely all use another friend. Right?"

He smiled back, unable to stop himself. She was so pretty, and nice. He couldn't believe she was looking out for him like this. "Yeah. How did you like the Becca Sandoza movie, by the way?" He was dying to tell her he'd "met" the star but kept it to himself. Maybe he'd tell her later.

"It was awesome," she said excitedly. "Have you seen it yet?"

"No, there was kind of a lot going on over the break."

"Oh, yeah. Well, maybe we could see it together sometime."

It took everything he had to keep from grinning like an idiot. "Yeah, sounds good."

The teacher came in and started class, preventing either of them from saying anything else. But during the lesson, the couple of times he glanced over at Carly, they shared a little smile.

Suddenly high school didn't suck quite as much anymore.

~

"WHY IS it they're always setting you on fire? They trying to tell you something?" Ryder asked Chase as he perused the list of stunts his buddy was scheduled to perform for this movie. They'd just flown into Melbourne from Sydney last night, where the next scenes in this period drama were going to be shot.

Across the kitchen table in the rental house where he was staying with Chase and Becca, his best friend smirked at him. "It's because I'm so hot."

Ryder cracked a grin. "Easy with that ego, brother. You're not that hot. Trust me."

Chase's smile was unrepentant. "Becca says I am. She tells me all the time."

"I'm sure she does." She was currently in another room going over the script with the director. "What day do you start?"

"Thursday."

Two days from now. He perused more of the schedule. "Looks like we'll be on location with you for a bit next Tuesday."

On set his job was pretty low-key. He stayed in the background and kept eyes on Becca as much as possible, but things were more relaxed there because of all the other security around. Here at their home base, he did regular patrols and kept watch on the security cameras.

But when she left the safety of this gated property, or was traveling, or making a public appearance, that's when he had to be at his sharpest. She'd been kidnapped and nearly killed by an obsessed fan last fall. He was here to make sure no one ever threatened her again.

The company was sending someone else to back him up later this week so he wouldn't have to work 24/7 over the next four months. Ryder would train him to act as his replacement while they worked together, but he preferred to stay busy anyway. Gave him less time to pine over Danae and wonder what she was doing. Whether she was really okay.

They'd texted and talked a lot initially after he left Crimson Point, but she'd definitely been pulling away lately, and the remaining time he had here Down Under was going by way too slowly. He missed Finn too.

"You ready for that workout now, or what?" Chase asked, standing and stretching his arms over his head.

"Yeah, I'm down. Just let me change quick."

He jogged upstairs, put on workout clothes and joined Chase outside in the backyard. It was weird being in a place where January was the height of summer. Right now, the average temp hovered in the upper eighties, and it was even more humid than back home in North Carolina during the summer. Everything was green and lush, from the lawns to the gardens and other vegetation.

"So what are we doing today?" he asked. Chase had a specific workout regimen from his trainer he needed to do each week.

"Three-mile warm-up run, then we get to the good part. Lots of different kinds of pushups, pull ups, burpees, and some weights. You're gonna love it."

"Can't wait." He'd been keeping his twice-weekly appointments with his therapist, and now had a sobriety sponsor he had to check in with regularly. He still needed to burn off some of this restless energy, however. Not having touched a drink since Christmas Eve and missing Danae, he needed a different outlet for his worries and frustrations.

At the main gate he put in his earbuds and pulled out his phone. He stopped walking, staring at the screen as his insides tightened. Sometime in the past hour, Danae had sent him a playlist and a quick message.

These all make me think of you.

"Problem?" Chase asked.

Pure morbid curiosity demanded he listen to the songs. "Nope." He hit play, tucked the phone into the pocket on his running shorts, and broke into a jog next to Chase.

He recognized the first song instantly. "I Will Remember You" by Sarah McLachlan. He'd heard it plenty of times before, but never really paid attention to the lyrics before.

This time, the words hit him hard as his shoes slapped against the hot pavement. Pierced him, the constant pressure he'd been living with in his chest suddenly turning sharp and acute. Not only because he missed her like hell. But because being on the other side of the world from her made it all worse. And because the words confirmed what he'd already feared.

She was trying to let him go.

He let the other songs play, but that first one stuck with him, repeating in his head over and over on the return to the house. By the time they got back they were both dripping with sweat, and Ryder wished he'd never listened to the playlist.

Thankfully, the workout was punishing, and just what he needed. He craved the burn in his muscles, needed to push himself, using the time to channel all his emotion into putting his body through its paces.

"Damn, son. That was hard core." Chase eyed him as he finished up a series of burpees and pushups. "You okay?"

"I'm fine." Frustrated and sick to his stomach about Danae, but otherwise fine. Not that he was going to bitch to Chase about it when he was here on a job. That complicated things.

His phone buzzed with another text. He whipped it out, saw a new message from Danae, and quickly tucked it back in his pocket without reading it. He'd look at it later when he was alone.

Because he was suddenly afraid it would say something like, *We need to talk*. Or worse, *I can't do this anymore*.

"You don't need to do that."

"Do what?" he asked, feigning ignorance.

"Shove your phone away when she texts, like you feel guilty for looking at them around us."

"I'm working," he muttered.

"Not right now, you're not." Chase leaned back against the trunk of a palm tree and folded his arms across his chest, giving Ryder a level look. "Damn, Ry. You're my best friend and you're not being honest with me."

Ryder shot him an offended look. "What's that supposed to mean?"

"It means, I can tell when you're trying to hide something. And you definitely are." Knowing hazel eyes studied him. "You miss her."

He shrugged. Of course he fucking missed her. It felt like missing her was all he did anymore.

"Yeah, and I think it goes way deeper than that. Am I right?"

"Let it go, man." He picked up his water bottle and took a

drink. He was trying to make the best of this, get through it and maintain his professionalism along with his friendships with both Chase and Becca.

"Can't. You know what a nosy bastard I am. You're not on the clock right now, and it's just us out here, so spill."

"Nothing to spill. We met, went through some intense shit together, then I had to leave. Her life is in Crimson Point, and mine's here for now." And just like he'd feared, the distance was proving too hard for her.

Chase watched him for a long moment, his scrutiny annoying. "Ry, come on. You've been fucking miserable since you got back from Oregon."

"No, I haven't." It came out automatically and sounded hella defensive even to him.

"Yeah, you have. Maybe it's not obvious to everyone else, but I see it."

Ryder set his jaw. Getting into an argument with Chase about this would only make him feel shittier. "Don't worry about where my head's at. I'm focused on the job, and Becca's safety."

Chase rolled his eyes, frustration stamped all over his face. "You idiot. I'm not worried about you not doing your job. I'm worried about *you*, asshole."

What did Chase want him to say? Yeah, he missed Danae. Missed her so fucking much it hurt to breathe sometimes. Whenever they talked, it was both the highlight of his day and also the most painful part of it.

Since leaving Crimson Point, he'd put a lot of thought into how to make it work with her long term. He'd even floated an idea he'd come up with to his boss, but it was a long shot that required major funding and a shitload of trust, and he'd only been with the company for a few months. No surprise, it had been rejected.

Now Danae was pulling away. And he didn't know how to stop it.

"Doesn't matter," he snapped, his temper flaring. "Okay? It's done. I'm here, I'm doing my job."

"Yeah. But what about the rest?"

Blood rushed to his face as Chase's meaning hit. "I haven't touched a drink since Christmas Eve." While he'd thought about it a few times, usually at night when he was alone and the loneliness got hold of him. But he'd made a vow to himself not to drink anymore, and he never would have done it while on the clock anyhow.

Chase nodded, watching him in that unnerving way that said he saw right through him. "That's good, man. It's just… you're dealing with a lot of shit all at once, and that has to be hard."

His PTSD issues, Chase meant, on top of being separated from Danae.

"I'm handling it, all right?" He turned away. "I'm gonna hit the shower." Done with the inquisition, he stalked for the doorway.

"Ry." Chase's low voice stopped him.

He tensed, refused to turn around. "What?"

"What the hell happened over there?"

He didn't mean Crimson Point.

The concern in his best friend's voice sucked all the aggression out of him. Chase had asked him so many times before, tried to get him to open up, but he'd refused to tell him. Now Ryder realized he'd let this go on too long.

Releasing a deep breath, he turned around and met Chase's stare. He'd already told Danae and his therapist, and Jase. He wasn't sure what had held him back from telling Chase until now, a man he trusted with his life. Shame, maybe. Fear of losing Chase's respect.

Or worse, Chase condemning him for what had happened.

Ryder glanced around, debating whether to tell him. They were alone out here in the private back yard. No one could overhear them. It was time he came clean. "You sure you wanna know?" he asked.

"Yes."

So Ryder told him. All of it. In more detail than he'd shared with anyone. "Learning to live with the guilt is the hardest part," he finished. "But I'm working on it."

"Jesus, I knew it had to be bad, but…" Chase shook his head, staring at him. "It wasn't your fault, Ry. You know it wasn't."

"Still feels like it was." He was working on that too. Two steps forward, one step back. But eventually, he'd get there.

"Does Danae know?"

"Yeah. I told her when I was there." Dammit, how could she give up on them so soon?

Chase looked both surprised and impressed. "That's huge, man."

Ryder shrugged, uncomfortable, and left out the part about him being dead-ass drunk when she'd come to the door. But yeah, it had been a huge thing for him to spill his guts to her like that when he'd barely known her. Even at that point, he'd sensed he could trust her.

But what if it's too late now? His heart clenched at the thought.

Ryder didn't move as Chase came over to clap him on the shoulder on the way past. Once he was alone upstairs in his room, he read the message Danae had sent.

A picture of her and Finn, faces close together, both of them grinning at the camera. *Just thinking about you. Hope you're okay.*

A surge of relief hit him hard. All right, maybe she wasn't ready to call it off then.

She'd been seeing a counselor too. Molly sent him her own periodic updates on Danae. According to her Danae seemed fine. She'd jumped right back into work and her regular life as soon as he'd left. Moving on like the practical, responsible woman she was. Without him.

But he wasn't fooled. There was no way anyone could go through a trauma like that and not be affected by it. It made him crazy that he couldn't be there for her in person.

He also received updates on the investigation from Jase. The Feds were still working on cracking the larger crime ring, but Kyle Vanderhoff was still in prison awaiting trial. Danae would have to testify as a key witness whenever the court date rolled around. He might be called to testify as well.

Standing under the stinging spray of the shower, he kept thinking about her. About her strength in the face of adversities that would have crippled most people. The too brief but intense time they'd spent together. The songs she'd just sent him.

About Finn, Crimson Point, and the people Ryder had met there. People he felt comfortable around—fellow combat vets and their partners. People who accepted him and the issues he faced.

He had to get back there. Soon. Couldn't wait for his contract to be finished.

He needed to talk to Becca about his plans. Today.

When he checked his phone again, he found a message from his boss. *Call me. I want to talk about the proposal you sent again.*

Ryder frowned. The company had rejected his idea outright when he'd first sent it in. Why did they want to talk to him about it again now?

He'd just changed into work clothes and reviewed the route he would take when he drove Becca to a press conference in a little while, when a soft knock came at the door.

"Hey," he said when Becca poked her head in, all done up and wearing a flowy, turquoise dress.

"You look like you're almost ready to go. I can be downstairs in ten minutes if you want to leave early."

"Actually, there's something I need to talk to you about, if you can spare a few minutes before we go."

At his serious tone, she stepped inside, her expression curious. "I'm intrigued. Shoot."

"You know the company's sending someone as a backup for me?"

"Yes, they confirmed it with me last week."

It was standard, and the company always sent a client files on any potential backups for their approval beforehand. "He arrives in a few days. I'll train him on our protocols and procedures, and he'll shadow me for the first week or two to get a feel for your routine and preferences, but I want you to know up front that it's going to be more than just for backup."

"Okay." She raised her eyebrows. "And…?"

"I want you to get to know him as well, make sure you're comfortable with him, because I want to train him as my potential replacement."

She blinked. "Oh. Why, is something wrong?"

"No. It's a personal situation for me."

"Danae," she guessed, the expression in her light brown eyes kind.

He nodded, hoping he didn't seem unprofessional as fuck by telling her this. He owed her the truth. "I don't know what's going to happen yet. I'm not saying I'm going to leave before filming wraps up, and I wouldn't go unless you're totally comfortable with it and my replacement. I just want to have everything in order, in case."

A smile curved her mouth. "So you love her?"

He'd wondered before, not trusting it because everything had been so intense and happened so fast. Now he knew for sure. "Yeah." He was pretty sure he had fallen for Danae before he'd left Crimson Point.

"Just so you know, I'm totally on board with helping you get back to her. Although you're hands down the best security person I've ever had."

"You've had like, two of us in total," he pointed out with a half-grin.

"Yeah, and you're still the best one. By *far*," she insisted.

She was adorable. "I'm happy you think so. I want you to feel safe. And I don't want this to affect my relationship with either you or Chase."

"I do. And it never could, so don't worry about that."

An invisible weight lifted from his chest, making it suddenly easier to breathe. "Good. See you downstairs in ten?"

"Sure. And hey, Chase and I love you. We want you to be happy."

"Thank you. I appreciate it."

She paused at the door to give him a little smile. "Life isn't a dress rehearsal, and we only get one take."

Yeah. Dead on.

Ryder called his boss back, thinking about Danae and how to fix things between them. As well as the opportunity Becca's agreement would give him.

No matter how this worked out, he needed to make some major changes and break free of the past once and for all. Only then could he forge a new path and move forward with no regrets.

TWENTY-NINE

Boyd stepped out onto the front porch of his cabin as the sheriff's vehicle pulled to a stop on the gravel driveway. "Sheriff," he said as Noah climbed out in uniform, the steady rain pounding on the roof and dripping from the eaves all around the deep verandah.

"Boyd. Can I have a word?"

"Sure." He waved Noah inside. "Want me to put on some coffee or anything?"

"No, I just came from the café." He stopped inside on the mat in the entry and came no farther.

Boyd faced him. "What can I do for you?"

"Just wanted to stop by and tell you the latest in person."

He nodded. "Feds capture the other shooters yet?"

"No, but they've narrowed the field down to a list of names, and let's just say none of them are guys you'd want living within a hundred miles of you, much less next door."

He'd figured. A mass killing like that, it had to involve some kind of organized crime ring. Drugs, weapons, sex trafficking. "What about the survivor?" The media hadn't published her name or picture, for her safety. For once, they seemed to be doing the right thing.

"She's been offered a spot in WITSEC. I don't know whether she's taken it, and if she does, none of us will ever find out. What I do know is that she's safe, and still cooperating fully with authorities. Anyway, I just wanted to come by and tell you things haven't been resolved yet, and that you need to stay vigilant. If the killers suspect you might have seen something, you could be a target."

"I appreciate the concern."

Noah nodded. "My department has officially ended our involvement with the investigation, as well as the incidents involving Danae Sutherland. From here on out, it's the FBI's show."

"Understood." He always kept an eye out anyway. It was hard-wired into him. But he'd be extra vigilant for the time being.

He let Noah out, then paused at the door. He was vigilant by nature. A man didn't spend his entire adult life training for and conducting high-risk, covert operations for his country, and then turn soft. People in town whispered that he was a recluse. That he was paranoid.

He couldn't argue the recluse part so much since he was comfortable being on his own. But he wasn't paranoid. He was alert and noticed things most people didn't. It's partly what had kept him alive during all those years of military service.

Strapping a holstered pistol on his left hip, he covered it with a heavy sheepskin jacket, slid a small pair of high-res NODs onto his head, then put on his boots and headed out the door. The rain fell steadily as he hiked his way down the slope to the hiking trail that bordered the bottom of his property, the optics of the NODs lighting the scenery.

He followed it for a few hundred yards, scanning the quiet forest. A narrow trail cut off the main one down through the woods to the dunes.

He knew every inch of this area, could read the signs of recent human disturbance in the broken underbrush and faint footprints. The Feds had been out here by the dozen as little as a week ago, combing the area for physical evidence.

The human trail wound down to the edge of the woods, where the trees and underbrush gradually began to give way to sandy loam. Here the roar of the ocean was no longer muted, taking over the steady fall of the rain.

More tracks scattered in various directions onto the low, narrow strip of dunes standing between him and the water. Some human, some dog or maybe coyote. A few deer, and what looked like a cougar.

There was no one else out here. He turned right and headed north, toward the site of the murders. Cresting the rise of another dune, he stopped and crouched down.

Someone was standing at the edge of the sandy pit where the bodies had been dumped. A woman. He squinted as his NODS intensified the light source in her hand.

A candle.

He rose to his feet, watching as she stared into the pit for a long moment, then bent and stuck the end of the candle into the sand.

She turned suddenly, as if sensing his presence, and froze when she spotted him.

The hair on the back of his neck stood up as recognition hit, but before he could retreat to show he meant her no harm, she darted to the right and disappeared into the screen of trees like a fleeing doe.

But he never forgot a face.

She was the woman with the hiking group who had

spilled coffee all over him at Whale's Tale just days before the massacre.

She was the sole survivor.

~

"ARE you *sure* you don't want to come hang out at my place tonight?" Sierra asked her, placing the last of the files for the day on the table in the back.

"Thanks, but I'm not really in the mood to socialize tonight," Danae said. Most nights these days, actually. Depression was riding her hard right now.

"Aww." Sierra came around from behind the table and pulled her into a hug. "I hate seeing you so sad."

"I'll be okay. Just need to lick my wounds for a while, you know?" Being separated from Ryder while trying to deal with everything in the aftermath of what happened was way harder than she'd feared.

"I totally know." Sierra eased back, searched her eyes. "So I'm guessing this means you haven't heard from him?"

"No, we talk and text pretty much every day." But the depression was hard, and knowing she was going to be without him for at least the next four months made it so much worse.

Most days it was all she could do to drag herself out of bed in the morning, and when she got home, all she wanted to do was sleep. The counseling only helped so much. Looked like she might have to start contemplating some meds soon and see if that helped.

"It's hard being so far apart," Sierra said, her voice full of empathy.

"Yeah." She waved a hand, brushing those thoughts away before it pushed her to tears again.

She was sick of crying, hadn't felt this alone and abandoned since Terry died. It was like Ryder's leaving had triggered a weird sort of PTSD she couldn't pull out of. "Anyway, I'm gonna go home, take a bath, have a big piece of chocolate cake Finn brought back from the café for me yesterday, and put my feet up."

"All right. But if you change your mind and decide you want company, just come on over." Sierra gave her an encouraging smile.

"Thanks." She wouldn't though.

When she stepped outside the clinic later, the weather matched her mood perfectly. January had to be the most disappointing and depressing month of the entire year.

The Christmas season was done, taking any joy she'd felt with it. All the decorations were gone, and the weather was gray and miserable more often than not. Today a steady rain had settled in just after lunch and was still falling when she locked up the clinic. The streetlamps reflected off the wet, glistening sidewalks, the patter of the rain dimming the sound of the waves in the background.

Sliding into Professor Plum, she drove up the length of Front Street and climbed the hill. The days were getting longer now, but it was almost dark already. When she pulled into her driveway the kitchen light was on in the background.

She stripped her wet coat off outside on the top step, shook it, and walked in. It was quiet. "Finn?" she called, hanging up her coat on the hallstand inside the side door.

"Yeah?" He poked his head out from the kitchen, and her mood lifted a little. Since Ryder left, Finn had made more of an effort to be sociable with her.

"Hey, you hungry? I can make us some chicken and salad or something."

"Nah, I'm good. Going out to meet a friend."

She couldn't help the tightening in her gut. "Oh, who?"

"You don't need to worry," he said with a smirk.

"I wasn't worried," she lied. She trusted Finn. But since everything that had happened, his circle of friends was a concern for her. He was mostly online with his buddies back in Seattle and hadn't brought anyone new around.

Thankfully, both Grant and his stepdad had now been arrested and charged with drug and weapons offenses. Noah's department had matched the casings from the Christmas Eve shooting to a pistol they'd found at Grant's home, and it had his prints on it.

Grant was currently in juvie, but since he hadn't yet turned eighteen, he couldn't be tried as an adult. Though if evidence connected either him or his stepfather to the kidnapping, murders and trafficking, more charges would be forthcoming.

As for Kyle, he was locked up and likely to stay there. Turned out the receipt he'd wanted from her had information on it about payment and an upcoming shipment of trafficked women. The Feds had cracked it not long after taking him into custody.

She hoped they rounded up everyone involved and nailed their asses to the wall. Most of all, she just hoped Grant and his stepdad stayed the hell away from her son if and when they ever got out of prison.

"So, who is it?" she asked, curious.

A slight smile tugged at Finn's mouth as he walked up to grab his hoodie from the hallstand. "Her name's Carly."

"Oh." *Ohhhh.* "And is she... I mean, is—"

"She's just a friend. For now," he added with a secretive smile that hinted he'd like it to be more.

Aww. "Want me to drive you? We can pick her up on the way."

"Nice try, Mom. I'm taking the bus. We're going to see the new Becca Sandoza movie, and then to the mall for a bit after."

Her baby, going on his first, sort-of, kind-of date. "Okay. It's good, by the way." She'd gone to see it with Molly last week, solely because Ryder was in it—even though his face had been hidden beneath his helmet—and come home feeling lonelier than ever.

She opened her mouth to add more, but Finn beat her to it. "Yes, I'll have my phone on me, and yes, I'll be back by eleven."

"Ten."

"Ten-thirty."

She hid a smile. "Have a good time." She lifted up on her toes to kiss his cheek.

It was baby smooth, devoid of all the messy stubble he usually missed. And he smelled good for once. Like he'd used a bit of body spray or something. He'd obviously taken extra care when getting ready this time. Carly must really be something.

She closed and locked the door behind him. Silence settled around her, then the rhythmic drumming of the rain on the roof registered. She eyed the lock on the door, rubbed her hands over her arms and chastised herself for the tingle of unease in her gut.

Everyone who had put them in danger was in jail. She was safe here on her own again.

On the heels of that thought, memories flooded back of the night she'd been kidnapped. Of Ryder risking his life to save her.

Loneliness settled in her chest, heavy and oppressive. Determined not to give into it, she ran herself a hot bubble bath, soaked for a while with her current book, then bundled up in her fuzzy robe and slippers and climbed into bed to continue reading.

An assertive rap on the side door startled her. She sat up, hesitating.

Whoever it was knocked again.

A little apprehensive, she got up and started down the hall. Seeing the unfamiliar vehicle parked in the driveway through the front window, her pulse picked up as she approached the door. Beckett had installed a peephole in it for her. "Who is it?"

A male voice answered, muffled by the door and the rain.

When she looked through the peephole, her heart nearly jumped out of her chest. She told herself she was seeing things.

But nope, she pulled the door open and Ryder was standing there, close-shorn hair damp from the rain.

"Ryder," she said in surprise. "What are you doing here? Is something wrong?"

He stepped in, grabbed her and crushed her to him in a fierce hug that lifted her onto her toes. "Not anymore."

She clung just as tightly, her mind reeling. He had months and months left on his contract. He should still be in Australia. He'd still been down there yesterday when he'd texted. "What's happened? I don't understand."

He kicked the door shut with his foot and eased his hold to set his hand on the side of her face, his other arm banded around her waist. "I missed you. Missed you so damn much I could barely breathe, and it was worse being across the ocean from you. And Finn."

She stared at him, a lump forming in her throat and her heart thudding hard. She was afraid to believe this. Afraid to hope after how much she'd been hurting without him.

His dark brown eyes delved into hers. "I couldn't stop

thinking about you. Wishing I was here with you." His thumb glided over her cheekbone. "Lately you haven't been answering or returning my calls as much, like you were trying to avoid me. I could feel you pulling away, and it was making me crazy."

Tears flooded her eyes. She blinked furiously, trying to force them back. This was everything she'd wanted to hear. Maybe she was dreaming. "It's been so hard," she choked out, unable to hide it anymore. "I've been so down."

He nodded. "Sweetheart, I'm so sorry. I knew something was wrong."

"I d-didn't want to tell you. D-didn't want to make things harder." Or seem weak or clingy or all the other annoying things that would have surely pushed him away. And maybe a part of her had wanted to be the one to pull away, to save herself from more hurt when things ended. Until now, she'd been convinced there was no way forward for them.

"Hey." He wiped her tears away, his expression tender. "I don't want you to feel like you ever have to hide anything from me. You can tell me anything, good or bad."

She nodded, struggling to contain her tears. He was here. But for how long?

He cupped her face in his hands. "When I left, I didn't just leave you behind. I left my heart here too."

Her chest hitched, more tears rushing to the surface. "You did?"

"Yes. I love you, lady."

A hot rush of tears blurred her eyes. *Oh my god...*

"So I came back, because I need to be with you."

She flung her arms around his neck, pressing her face into his sturdy shoulder as the tears spilled over. "I love you too." The old her would have been horrified that she was saying that aloud after only knowing him a few weeks. Would have cringed at how weak and needy that sounded.

But she was far wiser now and trusted her gut. She knew what she felt and refused to second-guess it. She loved and needed this man and wasn't afraid to admit it.

He groaned and squeezed her tight, his spicy, masculine scent surrounding her.

"What about your job, though?" she asked when she'd gotten herself under control again, lifting her head to peer at him. That was the main obstacle that had pulled them apart in the first place. "You didn't quit because of me, did you?" Oh, shit, his professional reputation would be shot if he had. "You still had months left in your contract, and then—"

"You let me worry about all that." Wiping the tears from her cheeks with his fingers, the hint of a smile played on his lips. "I just need to know if you want me to be part of your and Finn's life?"

"Yes, of course I do," she said without hesitation.

He breathed out what seemed like a sigh of relief and crushed her to him again. "Then the rest of it doesn't matter. I'm willing to move here to make it happen. I've also floated the idea of starting a satellite office in Portland to my boss. And I've already talked to Noah about potentially working with him as a detective after I do the training if need be. If none of that works out, I'll find something else."

It sounded like he'd been thinking about this for a while. "Wait, what do you mean about a satellite office? Doing more bodyguard work?"

"No, I'd be responsible for managing the company, organizing and recruiting people to work under me. Mostly for protective details on movie sets in the Pacific Northwest, including B.C. There'd be some travel involved, and I'd have to work out of Portland pretty regularly, but the schedule and hours would be nothing like it is for me now."

Her heart squeezed. "You came up with that idea and pitched it to your boss?"

"Yep. Upper management is meeting about it tomorrow to discuss the details. They're going to let me know one way or the other in the next few days, but they seemed pretty interested in the idea." He kissed the tip of her nose, shook his head once. "I had to find a way to be with you. Whatever it takes, I'll do it."

"Ryder," she whispered unsteadily, overcome. All this time she'd thought their relationship was doomed to a slow death. That she would lose him forever and that she would spend the rest of her life alone, pining for him. "I'm so glad you're here."

"Me too. I know I'm not perfect by any means. I was drinking too much when we first met, but I'm still seeing a therapist and I have a sponsor now too, to keep me accountable. I haven't touched a drop of booze since Christmas Eve, and I'm going to keep working on myself no matter what."

"That's so great." She smiled up at him through her tears, proud of him, then grew serious. "But it's not just you and me in this scenario. There's Finn too."

His tender smile turned her inside out. "I wouldn't have it any other way."

"I'm glad you see it that way, but I can't uproot him again and move to Portland. Not when he's finally happy here."

"I wouldn't ask you to. If I get the green light on that, I'll commute back and forth on the days I absolutely have to be at the office."

Just then the door opened behind them. They both turned as Finn walked in and stopped dead, staring at Ryder.

"Oh, hey," Finn said to him in surprise, looking back and

forth between them with an unspoken question in his eyes. "So you're back?"

"Yeah," Ryder said to him, "and I'm planning to stay this time. You cool with that?"

Finn grinned. "Yeah, I'm totally cool with that. Can't stay, I just came back because I forgot my bus pass." With that he rushed past them to his room.

Danae chuckled and faced Ryder again, hardly able to believe this was happening. "And there's a ringing teenage endorsement," she teased, even though she could tell Finn was secretly thrilled.

Ryder tightened his hold and kissed her. "I'll take it," he murmured against her lips.

Danae melted into him, reveling in the moment, the solid feel of him. Her world had been so dark and gray since he left.

The worst was now behind them, but even if the future held more challenges and uncertainty, she would have Ryder to stand with her as they faced it together.

THIRTY

"Good job," Ryder said to Finn as the teen finished emptying the Glock's magazine at the target at the end of the firing lane.

It was almost the end of February already. He'd moved in with Finn and Danae almost exactly a month ago. It had been the best month of his life.

Finn checked the chamber to ensure it was empty as Ryder had taught him and set the weapon down on the counter. "Almost all center mass," he said proudly, pushing off his protective headphones.

"You're getting better every time you shoot. Had enough for tonight? Or you wanna go again?"

"I'm starving. You promised pizza."

Danae was hanging out with the girls tonight, so he and Finn were having a guy's night together. Danae said he should be honored that Finn wanted to hang out with him instead of his girlfriend, Carly. They'd been dating officially for a couple weeks now, since right after Ryder had moved in.

"You're always hungry," he said with a laugh. "You're like a human garbage disposal."

On the way home they stopped in Crimson Point at the pizza joint on Front Street, next door to the Sea Hag bar, and shared a large pepperoni with pineapple and chopped tomatoes. He listened as Finn talked about the latest video game he had mastered and compared it to his experience firing live rounds so far.

The whole time, nerves bubbled in the pit of his stomach. He bounced his knee, waiting for Finn to stop and take a breath so he could interject and change the subject to something far more important.

Finn finally stopped and gave him a funny look. "You all right? You look nervous as hell."

He was a combat vet Marine, and a trained bodyguard. "I'm not nervous."

He was totally nervous.

When Finn raised his eyebrows and bit into another piece of pizza—he'd polished off three-quarters of it so far and showed no signs of slowing down—Ryder cleared his throat. "Need to talk to you about something."

His expression turned wary. "If this has *anything* to do with *stuff* just because I'm seeing Carly now, you can just not. My mom already covered all that a long time ago, and besides, we've only been dating a few weeks." His face flushed and he scowled, shoving more pizza into his face.

"No, it's not that. But just so you know, you can talk to me about any of that stuff if you want to later. Anyway," he hurried on when Finn stared at him in horror, "not sure if your mom told you yet, but I got the green light from my boss, so I'm going to be starting the process of setting up a satellite office for the company in Portland. I'll be working from home as much as I can at first, then I'll need to find a location and hire staff. I'll still have to travel some, but not as much or for as long as I would as a bodyguard."

Finn nodded and kept eating, only paying partial attention to him now that the threat of The Talk was past.

"You know I love your mom, right?"

Blue eyes almost identical to Danae's lifted to find his. "Yeah..." He drew the word out, his tone a little guarded.

"Okay, well... This is a bit different, and you're the most important man in her life anyway, so..."

Finn gulped down his bite of pizza, his eyes widening. Then he broke out into a laugh. "Wait. Are you asking me if it's okay to propose to my mom?"

Holy shit, who would ever have believed he'd be nervous of a teenager? "Yeah. I just wanted to make sure you're okay with it first."

He had the ring in his pocket. Had been carrying it around for a week now, waiting for the right time and planning everything out. Danae wouldn't want anything fancy in terms of a proposal, but it would mean the world to her that he'd asked Finn for her hand.

Finn lowered his pizza, a wide grin splitting his face. "Yeah, you can ask her. I'm okay with it."

He smiled back, his heart swelling. Having kids wasn't something he'd ever wanted, but it was cool that he was going to be part of Finn's life from now on. "Then I will."

Warm, amber light filled the front window when they pulled up in front of the house later. "Don't say anything to her, okay?"

Finn made a disparaging sound. "Please. Of course I'm not gonna say anything. That's on you. Wait, are you gonna do it tonight?"

"Yeah."

Finn clapped him on the shoulder. "Well, good luck with that." With those parting words, he opened the door, climbed out, and headed for the house.

Danae met Ryder at the door. "Hey, you." She wound her arms around him and leaned up for a kiss.

He kissed her cheeks and nose for good measure too. "Hey. Have a good time?"

"Great time. You?"

"It was awesome. Love you."

"Love you back. And guess what? Poppy's pregnant."

"For real?"

"Yep. She's wanted this for so long, and she's just *ecstatic*. It's so cute. She's due in early September."

Tiana in May, and Poppy in the fall. Things were about to get even busier in Crimson Point. "Well, that's awesome. Good for them." He set his hands on the sides of her waist, tugging her close. "Feel like taking a walk down to the lighthouse? It's kind of our spot."

She quirked an eyebrow at him in surprise, then flashed a smile. "Sure. Let me grab my shoes."

Hand in hand they retraced the route they'd walked together for the first time on Christmas night. The closer they got, the harder his heart pounded. But not because he was nervous. No, he was pumped, and standing on the brink of a new chapter that would mark the start of the rest of his life.

"This view never gets old," Danae said, raising her voice to be heard over the wind. It blew her dark waves around her face and whipped pink into her cheeks.

The sun had set a while ago, leaving the sky streaked with turquoise and purple at the horizon, fading slowly into indigo where the stars winked overhead. An almost full moon painted everything in a silvery glow, mixing with the amber pool of light cast by the lighthouse.

Ryder drew her to stand between the lighthouse and the edge of the cliff, standing in front of her with his back to the water in an effort to block the worst of the wind for her. "Finn and I had an important chat tonight," he began.

She lifted an eyebrow. "Did you? Do I get to know what about?"

"Yes." Holding her right hand, he reached into his pocket for the diamond solitaire and went down on one knee in front of her.

She went completely still, shock rippling across her features. He held up the ring, the diamond sparkling in the combined amber and silvery light. "He said yes, and I'm hoping you will too," he told her.

But he could already read her answer to the question he was about to ask in the tears shimmering in her beautiful eyes, and the tremulous smile that made her lips quiver. He was going to marry this incredible woman and spend the rest of his life with her at his side.

—The End—

*Read Boyd and Ember's story in **Dangerous Survivor**! Coming January 2022*

Dear reader,

Thank you for reading ***Deadly Valor***. If you'd like to stay in touch with me and be the first to learn about new releases you can:

Join my newsletter at:
http://kayleacross.com/v2/newsletter/
Find me on Facebook:
https://www.facebook.com/KayleaCrossAuthor/
Follow me on Twitter:
https://twitter.com/kayleacross
Follow me on Instagram:
https://www.instagram.com/kaylea_cross_author/

Also, please consider leaving a review at your favorite online book retailer. It helps other readers discover new books.

Happy reading,

Kaylea

TAKING VENGEANCE

Vengeance Series
By Kaylea Cross
Copyright © 2021 Kaylea Cross

Her instincts had served her well over the years. In fact, they were the main reason she was still alive today. And right now, they were screaming at her that this might signal more danger was on the way.

Amber leaned back in her office chair, tapping her fingers on the armrests as she stared at her custom laptop. Lady Ada was so much more to her than just a computer.

She was a part of her. A near perfect creation that Amber had nurtured and kept improving on from the moment she'd received the individual components and begun the building process from scratch several years ago.

Lady Ada was never wrong. And right now she was telling Amber they had a serious problem brewing.

Amber shoved the rolling chair back on the rug, stood and strode from her highly secure office into the downstairs hallway of the two-story house she shared with her husband.

Large picture windows at the back of the house overlooked the lush green lawn and the acres of pastureland beyond it, anchored in the distance by the majestic, jagged peaks of the Rockies.

Beneath her bare feet, the rhythmic thump of bass and drums vibrated up through the floor long before she reached the door to the basement. The dark, gritty beat of an old Depeche Mode song hit her when she pulled it open and jogged down the staircase into what they'd made into their home gym.

At the bottom, she paused. Jesse stood in the middle of the mat-covered floor, facing away from her as he went to town on the heavy bag suspended from the ceiling.

Sweat glistened on his golden-toned skin and dampened his short, dark brown hair, highlighting every bunch and ripple of muscle across his back and shoulders with each punch he threw. Watching him now was a reminder that he was deadly, like her. That he had been trained to kill with his bare hands in addition to a variety of weapons, and that until recently he'd made a living as a hired killer.

Now those same skilled, deadly hands protected her. Made her tingle and shiver all over when they caressed her.

He was her partner. Her lover. The only man who had won her respect, trust and heart.

A wave of desire rolled over her as she watched him deliver a rapid combo of powerful blows to the bag, the sheer, masculine power of him momentarily taking her breath away.

He knew she was watching. Would have known the moment she opened the door at the top of the stairs, or maybe even before that, even with the music up loud enough to vibrate the floor. Because Jesse's awareness was as finely honed as hers.

Reminding herself why she'd come down here, she

pushed those thoughts firmly away and stepped forward. He met her gaze in the mirrors on the opposite wall and stopped, wiping a forearm across his sweaty forehead as he turned to face her, his pecs and abs flexing with each rapid breath.

She hit a button on the wall to kill the music, and suddenly Jesse's elevated breathing was the only sound in the silent room. "Need you to come look at something."

He held her stare as he removed his boxing gloves. Assessing her. "Something wrong?"

"Maybe."

Unwrapping his hands and wrists, he snagged a towel from a bench and prowled toward her, all sexy male grace and power. If she hadn't been so worried about the current situation, she would have dragged him off to the shower in the next room to enjoy running her soapy hands all over that chiseled body, and then following with her mouth.

Instead, she turned and jogged back up to the main floor and headed straight into her office. Lady Ada was continuing her latest scan as Amber sat back down in the chair to review what was showing on screen.

Jesse moved in behind her, quiet as a stalking panther and splayed a big, tanned hand on the desk to the left of her keyboard. He leaned in over her shoulder with the towel now draped around his neck, filling her nose with a mix of spice, sweat, and something all him that made her want to rub her face against his neck.

"What am I looking at?" he asked in that deep, dark voice that could easily distract her if she let it.

"It's something I've been monitoring for a while now." She'd always kept tabs on her remaining Valkyrie sisters, and still did in case of this exact development, to ensure they all stayed safe. God knew they'd all been through more than enough shit already.

"It started shortly after Kiyomi and Marcus's wedding," she added. This past Christmas Eve, to be exact. Already seven months ago now. "Lady Ada picked up the first hint of trouble on one of her routine scans and there've been a few other hints since then, but I've noticed a marked uptick in unusual activity over the past few weeks."

She closed one screen and brought up another, turning her head to watch Jesse's reaction.

His dark eyebrows pulled together instantly as he scanned the intel, his expression hardening. "All your names are listed."

"I know." All eight Valkyries identified by name—or at least the names they'd been known by while they were in the Program. That was worrisome in itself. No one should have access to that information anymore.

"Someone's been watching all of us," she continued. "Possibly trying to locate us, I'm still not sure. And I can't say for sure yet whether whoever is behind this poses a real threat or not. But as you can see from the number of hits Lady Ada has come back with, this person seems to be most interested in one of us in particular."

Staring at the data listed beside the other Valkyrie's name, Jesse raised his free hand and absently rubbed at his chin, the scar on the right side visible through the dark stubble. "Yeah, shit. Any idea why?"

"No. And before you ask, no, I haven't alerted the others, because I don't want to cause undue concern while everyone is trying to move on and find their footing." Trying to forge actual lives for themselves after decades of being government pawns and having to constantly look over their shoulders every time they left the refuge of their homes.

They'd earned that right. All of them had. Just as they'd all earned the money they'd taken back.

Now she was worried that this new development might threaten all of that. Everything they'd fought for—their futures. Their freedom.

She expelled a long breath and looked up at Jesse. Initially he'd been sent to hunt her down. Now he would protect and defend her with his last breath.

She would never take that for granted. Or his insight. She valued his opinion on security matters. "What do you think?" She was wired to be paranoid. Had been trained to be suspicious of everything and everyone, and to notice the smallest detail, no matter how insignificant it seemed.

More than that, aside even from her computer and skills as an assassin, first and foremost she'd been trained not to trust anyone. Ever. To never let anyone in. As a result, she'd been alone most of her life, with no one to turn to or rely on.

Her sister and Jesse had changed all of that forever, along with her other Valkyrie sisters. Now she couldn't imagine her life without them. That was why she was determined to stay on top of this emerging evidence, and head off any threat before it surfaced.

Jesse straightened, face somber as their eyes met. "Better call her and let her know what's up."

∼

FRIENDS FOREVER. No matter what happens.

Kiyomi pulled away from the memory and surfaced slowly in the present, that long ago silenced voice startlingly clear in her mind as she allowed herself to return to her surroundings. But even with all her training, she couldn't stop the inevitable barrage of images that followed.

Horror. Darkness. Blood. A face she'd loved that had

been savagely beaten until the features were almost unrecognizable. Except by her.

Kiyomi would always have recognized that face.

She released a deep breath and focused on her body even as the sharp talons of grief dug into her. Using all five senses to ground herself as she'd been practicing. Shifting her awareness to the solid feel of the earth beneath her where she lay stretched out on her back on a patch of sun-warmed grass. The sweet scent of roses and lavender carried on the breeze. Soft, trilling birdsong mixing with the rustle of leaves. The distinctive *kak-kak* of a jackdaw nearby.

Sometimes it was easy to keep the ugly memories at bay. Sometimes they stayed put beneath her consciousness.

Today wasn't one of those days.

She fought the last of the ghostly images away through sheer force of will and consciously slowed her breathing and heart rate. *You're okay. That's all in the past, it can't hurt you anymore.*

Maybe someday that would be true.

Opening her eyes, she blinked up at the canopy of leaves arching above her. Golden afternoon sunshine filtered through the branches, the leaves having faded from the acid green of spring into the deeper green of English mid-summer. A warm breeze washed over her, rippling the ornamental grasses where she lay inside the walled garden, making the roses and daylilies nod.

She wiped her damp cheeks with the heels of her hands and released another long breath, glad for the privacy this place gave her. Giving into tears was still embarrassing and seemed pointless, but her therapist insisted it was a sign that she was healing. All part of the unthawing process after believing herself to be numb and impervious to emotion for most of her life.

The faint crunch of footsteps on the gravel path to the left drew her attention, beyond the far stone wall. She glanced over in time to see Marcus step through the ivy-smothered archway framing the doorway cut into the stone, his wooden cane in his left hand, and his loyal Anatolian shepherd Karas at his side.

She didn't move, just watched him come, conscious of a lightening in her soul as he approached in faded jeans that clung to his hips and thighs, and a snug T-shirt that molded to the powerful muscles in his chest and shoulders. In another couple months he would switch out the T-shirts for cable knit sweaters and sheepskin-lined jackets he favored when the weather turned cool. She couldn't decide which look was hotter.

He stopped next to her and sat down, failing to hide a flinch at the pain in his left hip. His injuries had healed as much as they ever would a long time ago, but the scar tissue, muscle and nerve damage were a permanent reminder of his horrific captivity in Syria.

Just as the scars on her back would always remind her of the same.

He stretched out beside her on his back, tucked one arm behind his head, and captured her hand in his. Karas lay between their lower bodies, muzzle resting on her paws. She was still a daddy's girl for certain, but sometimes followed Kiyomi around now instead of him.

Marcus ran his deep brown gaze over her face. "Penny for your thoughts, love?" he said in his deep, Yorkshire accent she adored.

This place suited him, though it was a different world from the one he'd grown up in. Born into a blue-collar family in Yorkshire, he'd only ever come here occasionally during his summer holidays as a child.

It hadn't been until he was medically discharged from the military that he'd suddenly inherited the massive property from a great uncle. The abrupt shift in lifestyle had been a huge adjustment for him, but he had accepted the responsibility and massive workload that came with preserving this piece of his ancestral legacy.

"Just practicing my meditation. And remembering a friend," she murmured.

"Good thoughts, I hope?"

Mostly. "Yes." Bittersweet ones.

"Who were you thinking of?"

"Julia."

Flashes of memory from the stolen times they had spent together during the second, intense phase of the program without their trainers knowing. Sharing food, forbidden outside of strictly scheduled mealtimes during their training. Talking about hopes and dreams they'd both known were impossible back then, even before they'd been permanently separated into different specialties.

Kiyomi had been fortunate to survive her career as a Valkyrie, and finally win her freedom. Julia had not. Instead, her best and only friend back then had suffered at the hands of monsters before being dumped in a Moscow alley to die.

"Ah." Marcus rubbed his thumb over the back of her hand, watching her, the dappled sunlight highlighting the puckered and pitted scarring on the left side of his face and neck.

He was still the handsomest man she'd ever known. His scars, the suffering he'd endured and the courage it had taken to overcome it all, had transformed him into the man he was. The only man who could have broken down her walls and captured her ice-encased heart.

She could smell the sweet, dusty scent of hay and horses

on him, indicating he'd just come from the barn. She'd been out here longer than she'd realized. "Just get back from the northeast pasture?"

"Aye. Karas took a shift guarding the neighbor's flock again."

"Always on duty. Good girl." She reached down to pet the dog's soft head and received a wet lick on the back of her hand in reply.

"This is three days in a row you've come out here," Marcus said, taking in the garden. "Seems a good spot for thinking."

She had found an old, leather-bound copy of The Secret Garden in Marcus's study a few months ago, and had been entranced by the story. This was her very own secret garden, a magical place where healing was possible.

Turning onto her side, she came up on one elbow, resting her head in her hand to gaze down at her husband. "It's peaceful here. And it reminds me of Eden." A Valkyrie trained as a saboteur, and an expert with poisons. She would know every plant here, every one of their toxic properties. Now she was back in the States with Zack, tending her own poison garden.

Marcus met her gaze again. "You miss them."

Yes. And it was a strange feeling for someone who had lived a solitary life as an intimate assassin. "Sometimes." She ran her fingertips down the side of his face, across the scars partially hidden by his thick, dark stubble. "But every day I still wake up and pinch myself to make sure this is still real." Him. The life they were making together in this beautiful, historic place his ancestors had owned for hundreds of years.

He caught her hand, kissed her fingers, and reached up to slide his hand into the back of her hair. "It's real, love," he said quietly, and drew her down for a slow, thorough kiss.

Kiyomi let her mind go blank and melted into him, opening up her senses until there was nothing but him and the rising tide of longing and arousal he created. He made her come alive. She'd been dead inside until him.

A ring tone went off, disturbing the quiet. Not hers. She never brought her phone during therapy homework.

"That's me." He leaned back to fish his phone out of his pocket, glanced at it. "It's Amber."

Her interest sharpened. Amber and Jesse had pulled her out of hell that day in Syria and saved her life. She would never forget it. "Go ahead."

"Amber. How are you?" He paused. "One second." He put the phone on speaker. "Go ahead."

"Hey, Kiyomi. Listen, something's come up, and I need to tell you about it."

At her friend's somber tone, she met Marcus's gaze. "What's wrong?"

"I'm not sure yet. But we're being monitored. All of us."

She sat up, instantly on alert, the peace of the garden forgotten. "Monitored how?"

"Right now it's a low threat level. Seeking behavior. But the problem is, we've all been identified somehow."

Marcus's jaw flexed, anger sparking in his eyes. "Can you tell where the leak came from?"

"Not yet. Whoever this is, they're clever, and good at hiding their tracks. So far I can't even pinpoint *where* they are."

Unease slid through her. Amber was one of the best hackers in the world. If someone was looking for them and she couldn't crack this, there was definitely cause for concern. "What do they want, any idea?"

"Not sure. There's been nothing specific so far, but I'm keeping on top of it. Also, you need to be aware that whoever this is, they seem to have a particular interest in you."

An invisible fist grabbed her stomach. "Meaning what?"

"There are almost four times as many searches for you than for any of the rest of us. I don't know why."

Marcus stilled, his expression taut. "Looking for her location?"

"Looking for anything on her at all. Though as far as I can tell, the person hasn't found anything to compromise your safety."

Yet. "What about our marriage certificate?" She'd used a different surname that she'd adopted for all her IDs, but kept Kiyomi because she refused to give that part of her up. But if someone had found that record and realized it was her, it would lead them straight here to Laidlaw Hall.

"I scrubbed it from public record as soon as it was issued," Amber replied. "The only way anyone could get it now is if they accessed the original through the parish—which they would have to do in person—and so far, no one has. So far there's no credible threat. I just wanted to alert you about what's going on."

"Thanks. We appreciate it. How are you and Megan?" Her sister.

After they ended the call a minute later, Marcus brought her hand to his lips and kissed the center of her palm. "She'll stay on top of it. If there's any danger, she'll let us know straight away and we'll go to ground somewhere."

Kiyomi nodded and tried to downplay it. She didn't want him worrying about her. "I'm not worried. Amber's watching, and I feel safe here with you."

But a frisson of unease wound through her anyway.

The danger should have ended with the Architect's death last fall. They'd all gone through so much. Too much, and she couldn't bear the thought of losing anyone from the family she'd only just found.

Reading the concern in her husband's eyes, she put on an easy smile and got to her feet. "Let's go inside," she said, holding out a hand.

He took it, allowed her to help him up and immediately braced his weight on his cane while Karas popped up beside him, tail wagging. They walked hand in hand up the gravel pathway toward the old Georgian manor house, its warm, golden Cotswold stone glowing in the sunlight.

Thoughts raced through her mind with each step. Trying to figure out who could be targeting them now. What thread they might have failed to tie up last fall. Anything they could have possibly missed last time.

She came up blank, and that was almost worse. Because against all odds, they were being hunted again.

End Excerpt

ABOUT THE AUTHOR

NY Times and USA Today Bestselling author Kaylea Cross writes edge-of-your-seat military romantic suspense. Her work has won many awards, including the Daphne du Maurier Award of Excellence, and has been nominated multiple times for the National Readers' Choice Awards. A Registered Massage Therapist by trade, Kaylea is also an avid gardener, artist, Civil War buff, Special Ops aficionado, belly dance enthusiast and former nationally-carded softball pitcher. She lives in Vancouver, BC with her husband and family.

You can visit Kaylea at www.kayleacross.com. If you would like to be notified of future releases, please join her newsletter:

http://kayleacross.com/v2/newsletter/

COMPLETE BOOKLIST

ROMANTIC SUSPENSE

Kill Devil Hills Series
Undercurrent
Submerged
Adrift

Rifle Creek Series
Lethal Edge
Lethal Temptation
Lethal Protector

Vengeance Series
Stealing Vengeance
Covert Vengeance
Explosive Vengeance
Toxic Vengeance
Beautiful Vengeance
Taking Vengeance

COMPLETE BOOKLIST

Crimson Point Series
Fractured Honor
Buried Lies
Shattered Vows
Rocky Ground
Broken Bonds
Deadly Valor
Dangerous Survivor

DEA FAST Series
Falling Fast
Fast Kill
Stand Fast
Strike Fast
Fast Fury
Fast Justice
Fast Vengeance

Colebrook Siblings Trilogy
Brody's Vow
Wyatt's Stand
Easton's Claim

Hostage Rescue Team Series
Marked
Targeted
Hunted
Disavowed
Avenged
Exposed
Seized
Wanted
Betrayed

COMPLETE BOOKLIST

Reclaimed
Shattered
Guarded

Titanium Security Series
Ignited
Singed
Burned
Extinguished
Rekindled
Blindsided: A Titanium Christmas novella

Bagram Special Ops Series
Deadly Descent
Tactical Strike
Lethal Pursuit
Danger Close
Collateral Damage
Never Surrender (a MacKenzie Family novella)

Suspense Series
Out of Her League
Cover of Darkness
No Turning Back
Relentless
Absolution
Silent Night, Deadly Night

PARANORMAL ROMANCE
Empowered Series
Darkest Caress

HISTORICAL ROMANCE

The Vacant Chair

EROTIC ROMANCE (writing as *Callie Croix*)

Deacon's Touch
Dillon's Claim
No Holds Barred
Touch Me
Let Me In
Covert Seduction

Lightning Source UK Ltd.
Milton Keynes UK
UKHW011002150522
403009UK00003B/480